PRAISE FOR TESSA BAILEY

"Tessa disarms you with a laugh, heats things up past boiling, and then puts a squeeze inside your heart. The tenderness, vulnerability, and heat I am always guaranteed with a Tessa Bailey book are the reasons she is one of my all-time favorite authors."

 —Sally Thorne, bestselling author of *The Hating Game*

"Her voice feels as fresh and contemporary as a Netflix rom-com...Bailey writes banter and rom-com scenarios with aplomb, but for those who like their romance on the spicier side, she's also the Michelangelo of dirty talk."

 —*Entertainment Weekly*

"Bailey crafts an entertainingly spicy tale, with humor and palpable sexual tension." —*Publishers Weekly*

"Tessa Bailey writes pure magic!"

 —Alexis Daria, bestselling author of *You Had Me at Hola*

"When you read a book by Bailey, there are two things you can always count on: sexy, rapid-fire dialogue and scorching love scenes..." —*BookPage*

"[A] singular talent for writing romantic chemistry that is both sparkling sweet and explosively sexy...one of the genre's very best."

 —Kate Clayborn, author of *Love at First*

TOO HOT TO HANDLE

TESSA BAILEY

FOREVER

NEW YORK   BOSTON

Copyright © 2016 by Tessa Bailey
Excerpt from *Too Wild to Tame* copyright © 2016 by Tessa Bailey

Cover design and illustration by Caitlin Sacks. Cover copyright © 2022 by Hachette Book Group, Inc.

Forever
Hachette Book Group
1290 Avenue of the Americas, New York, NY 10104
read-forever.com
twitter.com/readforeverpub

Originally published in mass market and ebook in 2016
First trade paperback edition: June 2022

Forever is an imprint of Grand Central Publishing. The Forever name and logo are trademarks of Hachette Book Group, Inc.

The publisher is not responsible for websites (or their content) that are not owned by the publisher.

The Hachette Speakers Bureau provides a wide range of authors for speaking events. To find out more, go to www.hachettespeakersbureau.com or call (866) 376-6591.

ISBNs: 9781538740866 (trade paperback), 9781455594122 (ebook)

Printed in the United States of America

LSC-C

Printing 1, 2022

For Violet

ACKNOWLEDGMENTS

Too Hot to Handle is a love story between Jasper and Rita, but it's also very much a love story among four siblings. Between a mother and her children. It's a common belief that we need to love ourselves before we can love another—and family can often bully, shove, and argue us into recognizing our true selves in the mirror, whether we like what we see or not. But sometimes all it takes is seeing *their* reflections, standing at our backs in that same mirror, to realize we're worthy. I hope you'll hitch a ride with the Clarksons as they move across the map toward New York, falling in love, changing lives, and resolving their shared history—which has *only begun* to reveal itself—along the way.

To my grandmother, Violet, for the stories you've told our family over the years, thank you. Your timeless grace and class will stay with me forever. I hope I did (and continue to do) the names Belmont, Peggy, and Rita proud, as they belonged to your siblings. Sorry I couldn't use Violet. I don't think Poppy would want you in a kissing book.

To my husband, Patrick, and daughter, Mackenzie, for being my foundation, my happiness, the loves of my life, thank you for celebrating my triumphs and comforting me in defeat. I'm sorry that sometimes you are talking directly at my face, I'm nodding, and nothing is going in.

To my editor, Madeleine Colavita at Forever Romance, for wanting this series and believing in this rather tricky concept of writing four complete love stories over the course of one road trip, thank you. I do not take your faith for granted! I can't wait to take the rest of this journey with you and the Clarksons.

To my agent, Laura Bradford, who never bats an eyelash, thank you for not only helping me make this concept more cohesive, but for helping me find an excellent home for the Clarksons. I'm still coming down from those phone calls.

To Eagle at Aquila Editing, thank you for beta reading this book and giving great notes, as always. Your insight means a lot to me.

To Rebecca Stauber, my high school journalism teacher, thank you for telling me I had *some* talent, but not enough to pat myself on the back. That was a great lesson, and I'm still holding on to it.

To Jillian Stein for always being the person who says, "Yes! I love this idea! You must write it!" Thank you. Everyone comes to you for encouragement for a reason. It's always constructive and never forced. You're truly one of a kind, and I value you so much as a friend.

TOO HOT TO HANDLE

PROLOGUE

Miriam Clarkson, January 1

If you're reading this, stop. Unless something bad has happened, in which case, screw it. I'm obviously not there anymore to stop you.

I hope I didn't make a big deal out of dying. Hope there were no last minute confessions or wistful wishes that I'd seen more sunrises. If I did succumb to those clichés and killed everyone's vibe, I'm sorry. If I didn't? Well, bully for me. But I'm succumbing now, in this book, because I've had too much bourbon.

Oh, come on. At least pretend to be scandalized.

So, here goes. I love my kids. I love that I didn't have to say it every day for them to know it. To be comfortable in it. But looking back—

hindsight is more like 40/40 when you're about to croak—I know I only fixed minuscule problems and ignored the mammoth ones. I never cooked family dinners, which is pretty damn ironic when you think about it. I am—or was—a culinary genius, after all.

People make dying wishes and their loved ones carry them out. That's how it works, right? Well, I don't wish to put that weight on my kids. But I have no such qualms with a cheap notebook I bought at Rite Aid. So here it is. My. Dying. Wish.

Please be patient and try to remember that I often have—or had, rather—a plan.

When I was eighteen, I spent a year in New York City. On New Year's Day in 1984, I jumped into the icy waters of the Atlantic with the Coney Island Polar Bear Club. I was a guest of a guest of a guest, as eighteen-year-olds trying to make their way in New York often are.

Now here's where shit gets corny—apologies to my daughter, Rita, who of my four children, will likely find and read this first. See? I paid attention sometimes.

As I was saying.

When I walked back up onto that Coney Island beach, dripping wet and exhilarated, I could see my future. It wasn't perfect, but I glimpsed it. It glimpsed me back. I could see where I was going. How I would get there. Who would be beside me.

My life changed that day. If I had one wish, it would be for my four children, Belmont, Rita, Aaron, and Peggy, to jump into that same ocean, on that same beach, on New Year's Day.

Together.

Knowing I'm right there with them.

And no, Rita, I'm not joking. How dare you question a dead woman.

CHAPTER ONE

The roof! The roof! The roof is … literally on fire.

Rita Clarkson stood across the street from Wayfare, the three-star Michelin restaurant her mother had made a culinary sensation, and watched it sizzle, pop, and whoosh into a smoking heap. A well-meaning citizen had wrapped a blanket around her shoulders at some point, which struck her as odd. Who needed warming up this close to a structural fire? The egg-coated whisk still clutched in her right hand prevented her from pulling the blanket closer, but she couldn't force herself to set aside the utensil. It was all that remained of Wayfare, four walls that had witnessed her professional triumphs.

Or failures, more like. There had been way more of those.

Tonight's dinner-service plans had been ambitious. After a three-week absence from the restaurant, during which she'd participated in the reality television cooking show *In the Heat of the Bite*—and been booted off—Rita had been determined to swing for the fences her first night back. An attempt to overcompensate? Sure. When you've flamed out in spectacular fashion in front of a national TV audience over a fucking cheese soufflé, redemption is a must.

She could still see her own rapturous expression reflecting back from the stainless steel as she'd carefully lowered the oven door, hot television camera lights making her neck perspire, the boom mic dangling above. It was the kind of soufflé a chef dreamed about, or admired in the glossy pages of *Bon Appétit* magazine. Puffed up, tantalizing. Edible sex. With only three contestants left in the competition, she'd secured her place in the finals. Weeks of "fast-fire challenges" and bunking with neurotic chefs who slept with knives—all worth it, just to be the owner of this soufflé. A veritable feat of culinary strength.

And then her bastard fellow contestant had hip-bumped her oven, causing the center of her divine, worthy-of-Jesus's-last-supper soufflé to sag into ruin.

What came next had gotten nine hundred forty-eight thousand views on YouTube. Last time she'd checked, at least.

So, yes. Pride in shambles, Rita had overcompensated a little with tonight's menu. Duo of lamb, accompanied by goat-cheese potato puree. Duck confit on a bed of vegetable risotto. Red snapper crudo with spicy chorizo strips. Nothing that had existed on the previous menu. The one created by French chef and flavor mastermind Miriam Clarkson. Had the fire been her mother's way of saying, *Nice try, kiddo*? No, that had never been Miriam's style. If customers had sent back food with complaints to *Miriam's* kitchen, she would have poured bourbon shots for the crew, shut down service, and said, *Fuck it... you can't win 'em all.*

For the first time since the fire started, Rita felt pressure behind her eyes. Twenty-eight years old and already a colossal failure. Not fit to compete on a reality show. Not fit to carry on her mother's legacy. Not fit, *period*.

In Rita's back pocket, Miriam's notebook burned hot, like a glowing coal. As if to say, *And what exactly are you going to do about me?*

A hose-toting fireman passed, sending Rita a harried but sympathetic look. Realizing an actual tear had escaped and was rolling down her cheek, she lifted the whisk-clutching hand to swipe away the offender, splattering literal egg on her face.

"Oh, come *on*."

Denial, fatigue, and humiliation ganged up on her, starting in the shoulder region and spreading to her wrist. Secure in the fact that no one could hear her strangled sob, she hauled back and hurled the whisk, watching it bounce along the cobblestones leading to Wayfare's entrance.

No more.

She felt Belmont before she saw him. It was always that way with her oldest brother. For all she knew, he'd been standing in the shadows, watching the flames for the past hour, but hadn't felt like making his presence known. Everything on his terms, his time, his pace. God, she envied that. Envied the solitary life he'd carved out for himself, the lucrative marine salvage business that allowed him to accept only jobs that interested him, spending the rest of his time hiding away on his boat. When Belmont sidled up beside her, she didn't look over. His level expression never changed and it wouldn't now. But she couldn't stand to see her own self-disgust reflected back in his steady eyes.

"They won't save it," came Belmont's rumble.

Her oldest brother never failed to state the obvious.

"I know."

He shifted closer, brushing their shoulders together. Accidental? Maybe. He wasn't exactly huge on showing affection. None of the Clarksons were, but at least she and Belmont had quiet understanding. "Would you want them to save it, if they could?"

They were silent for a full minute. "That's a million-dollar question," she answered.

"I don't have that much cash on me."

His deadpan statement surprised a laugh out of Rita. It felt good for two-point-eight seconds before her chest began to fill with lead, her legs starting to wobble. The laugh turned into big, gulping breaths. "Oh, motherfucking Christ, Belmont. I burned down Mom's restaurant."

"Yeah." Another brush of his burly shoulder steadied her, just a little. "What she doesn't know won't hurt her."

Exasperated, Rita shoved him, but he didn't budge. "And they call me the morbid one."

Belmont's sigh managed to drown out the sirens and emergency personnel shouts. "She might be dead. But her sense of humor isn't."

Rita once again thought of the journal in her jeans pocket. "You're right. She'd be roasting marshmallows over there. Starting a hot, new upscale s'more trend."

"You could start it yourself."

No, I can't, Rita thought, staring out at the orange, licking flames. She'd already started quite enough for one night.

* * *

Rita and Belmont were sitting silently on the sidewalk, staring at the decimated restaurant, when a sleek white Mercedes with the license plate VOTE4AC pulled up along the curb, eliciting a sigh from them both. Rita shoved a hand through her dyed black hair and straightened her weary spine. Preparing. Bolstering. While Belmont's modus operandi was to hang back, take a situation's measure, and then approach with caution, her younger brother, Aaron, liked to make a damn entrance, right down to the way he exited the driver's side. Like a Broadway actor entering from stage left into a dramatic scene, aware that eyes would swing in his direction. His gray suit boasted not a single wrinkle, black shoes polished to a shine. His golden-boy smile had made him a media sensation, but for once it was nowhere to be seen as he approached Rita and Belmont.

Aaron shoved his hands into his pants pockets. "Fuck. Right?"

"Yep," Rita said, swallowing hard.

Her politician brother did a scan of the dire scene, brain working overtime behind golden-brown eyes inherited by all the Clarksons. Except Belmont, whose eyes were a deep blue, on account of him having a different father. A fact that Rita forgot most of the time, since Belmont had been there—an unmovable presence—since the day she was born. Aaron had come later. *The second coming.*

"Are you all right?" Aaron asked her abruptly, a suspicious twinkle in his gaze. "You must have been in there a while with the smoke. The soot around your eyes—"

"Hilarious, dickhead." Her heavy black eye makeup and general *fuck off* appearance were a constant source of amusement for her clean-cut younger brother. "You have a funny way of showing concern."

"Thank you. What do I need to handle?" Aaron adjusted the starched white collar of his shirt. "Did you make a statement yet or anything?"

Rita allowed the steel to leach from her spine. "I've been kind of busy just sitting here."

"Right." Aaron feigned surprise at finding Belmont on the sidewalk with them. "Jesus. I thought you were a statue."

"Ha."

"You smell like the ocean."

"You smell like the blood of taxpayers," Belmont returned.

"Well." Rita finally found enough presence of mind to yank the smoky apron over her head, chucking it into the street. "I think I just remembered why we haven't hung out since Mom died."

Truthfully, even before that rainy afternoon, the time they'd spent together as a family had felt mandatory. Organized by their mother and fled from in almost comical haste.

"Oh. My. *God.*"

At the sound of their youngest sibling, Peggy's, voice, all three of them cursed beneath their breath. *Let the family reunion officially begin.* It wasn't that they didn't love their baby sister. And in many ways, Peggy, a personal shopper to San Diego's elite, was still a baby at twenty-five. Her big Coke-bottle curls and cheerleader appearance guaranteed that she got away with just about everything. Including neglecting to pay her cabdriver, if the irritated-looking man following her with a receipt clutched in his fist was any indication.

"How did this happen?" Peggy hiccupped, playing with the string of engagement rings dangling from her neck, as

Belmont wordlessly paid the cabdriver. "I just had dinner here two weeks ago. Everything seemed *fine*."

Rita battled the compulsion to lie down on the sidewalk in the fetal position. *Oh God.* Her mother had bequeathed her an award-winning restaurant and she'd burned it down. On Rita's *first day back.*

Aaron was busy scrolling through his phone, the screen's glow illuminating his perfectly tousled dark blond hair. "Look at the bright side, Rita. Now you can pursue your dream of being a Hot Topic register girl."

Rita barely had the strength to flip him the bird. "Jump up my ass."

When Peggy approached, Rita couldn't look her in the eye, so she focused on her younger sister's toes, which were peeking out of strappy silver sandals. "Hey. I'm glad you're okay."

Rita's throat went tight. "Thanks, Peggy."

"I'm sorry about the restaurant, too. I know how much you loved it. How much Mom loved it." Her youngest sibling nodded and cast a discreet glance over her shoulder, turning back with a charming half smile. A smile responsible for four marriage proposals over the past three years. "Mom probably would have wanted me to talk to those firefighters, though. Am I right?"

Rita groaned up at the sky.

Meet the fucking Clarksons.

Chapter Two

Unable to stand the undercurrent of blame radiating from her siblings any longer, Rita came to her feet and walked toward what remained of Wayfare. She hesitated for the barest of seconds when she reached the yellow tape, but shrugged and ducked beneath it. Her Doc Martens crunched in the charred debris, which had cooled overnight as they sat across the street, watching the smoke dissipate. Even demolished, she knew which rooms she walked through, exactly which table numbers the black metal legs belonged to. She toed aside a burned piece of wood and spied the wrought-iron *Bonjour!* sign Miriam had brought back from Paris on one of her many trips.

Rita turned at the sound of footsteps behind her. Her siblings were wading into the restaurant's remains with varying degrees of caution. Aaron followed behind Peggy, giving her a quick poke in the ribs then pretending he hadn't done it when she whelped. Where Rita and Belmont had quiet understanding, Aaron and Peggy—the two youngest—made merry when together. They weren't necessarily *close*, but they liked one another and had developed a way to show it without sliding into dreaded emotional territory. They made it look so effortless.

What must that be like?

Aaron's usually smirking mouth moved into a grim line. "It's safe to say rebuilding is off the table."

Belmont drew even with Rita, kicking aside some splintered wood to pick up the *Bonjour!* sign. "Just tell me what you want. I'll tell you if it's possible to save it."

"Right," Rita said quietly. "This is what you do, salvage man."

"Hmph."

"Remember when I got the job working for Senator Boggs? Mom threw that cocktail party and invited three of my ex-girlfriends, who quickly figured out there'd been some relationship overlap." Aaron crouched down and tugged a wedged picture of Miriam standing in the French countryside from beneath a charred produce crate. "She *laughed* as I ran out the door."

"We were *all* laughing," Rita corrected, moving toward the remains of Wayfare's former world-class kitchen.

"Thanks." Aaron's response was drier than dust as he set the photograph back down, his movements brisk. Dismissive. "She called me later that night and said, 'There's your first lesson in politics, son. Everyone you've fucked over shows up at the same party sooner or later.' She was right."

Rita stopped beside a stainless-steel oven range, kicking it with the toe of her boot. Barely having spoken to her siblings in the last year, opening up to them took a fair bit of effort. But something about the funeral-esque feel of the burned-down restaurant erased that no-contact year for just a moment, bringing them back to a time when conversation came more easily. When they were still uncomfortable with one another but at least they were accustomed to it. And since someone *else* arranged time together—namely Miriam—they were saved from appearing to have made an effort, because God forbid, right?

"I, um, I made my first osso buco on this big boy," she said, nodding at the oven range. "It came out like shoe leather. Mom ate the whole thing, chewing every bite while the crew watched. And then she said, 'Thank *God* that sucked. If you'd gotten osso buco right the very first time, I would've had to step down as head chef. And I like being the main bitch too much.' Then she took a shot of bourbon and rattled off that night's specials."

While I stood there like a naked teenager on the first day of school.

Never again.

"Ooh. My turn." Holding Aaron's shoulder for balance, Peggy stepped up onto an overturned steel refrigerator and spun in a pirouette. "After I broke my engagement to Peter, I didn't want to leave my apartment...didn't want to work. Nothing. But Mom picked me up and brought me to Way-fare." Another ballerina-like move that had Aaron reaching without looking to steady her. "She sat me down in the dining room—at the center table in front of *everyone*—and gave me a skillet full of cherry clafoutis with a lit candle stuck in the center. She said, 'There. Now it's a *real* pity party.' I went back to work the next day."

A wind blew through Wayfare's ruins, swirling ashes around Rita's boots. Despite the distance between them, having her brothers and sister there was providing actual comfort. But that comfort turned to thorns with Aaron's next question.

"What will you do, Rita?"

Her mother's journal had turned to stone in her back pocket, creating a heavy downward pull. The Clarksons were not a family of oversharers. In fact, they weren't even *sharers*, which is why she hadn't yet told them about the journal Miriam had left for her to find. Their individual problems—and they each had *plenty* to boast about—were their own. While Miriam had occasionally broken through those walls to make a point, she'd been just as comfortable with her children being solitary entities. Dysfunctional islands that occasionally passed in the night. Her illness had knocked them all on their collective asses, because it was *fact* that the Clarkson siblings loved the shit out of their mother, but they'd never talked about it. Never grieved as a unit. As far as Rita was concerned—and she suspected she wasn't alone—that suited her just fine.

But with the journal came responsibility. Her siblings deserved to know about Miriam's final wish. A wish Rita was now determined to see through. Perhaps she was grasping at any excuse to leave California and her numerous fuckups behind, but the promise of a new beginning sounded better than melting butter. No more cooking. No more *failing*. She could finally indulge that secret fantasy of going back to school for anything but working in a kitchen. If Miriam's journal gave her the excuse she needed, she would thank her mother and take it. With or without her siblings in tow.

"I'm going to New York. The way she wanted. You're welcome to come with me, but I won't fault you for saying no. Just…here." Rita slid the brown Moleskin book from her jeans and held it out to Belmont. "Bel, can I borrow the Suburban? Sort of…indefinitely?"

Rita waited for her older brother's stilted nod before she turned and left them with the journal. She sat in her car, pretending to organize a pile of old mix CDs, watching as her family took turns passing around Miriam's penned thoughts, reading the first entry she'd marked. Although she couldn't hear them, Rita could vibe Aaron's incredulity, Peggy's nervous follow-up questions, and Belmont's silent, tangible gravity, his unawareness that the other two watched and waited, hoping he would weigh in verbally. It took them only ten minutes to approach the car looking like some kind of mobile intervention.

Aaron rapped on the window until Rita rolled it down. "Look, it's just not happening. Next year is an election year and campaign season is critical. I don't have time to fly to New York and dive into the goddamn ocean."

Peggy chewed on her thumbnail. "They just promoted me at the store. I'm up for manager next and Christmas is our busiest season. They'd ax me for sure."

Belmont stayed quiet.

Rita was unsurprised by their reactions. If you'd asked her two days ago if a trip to New York was on the agenda, she might have sighed over the far-fetched fantasy of such a notion but scoffed nonetheless. Just then, however, looking out over the charred remains of her career, guilt a smoky cloud around her shoulders, she couldn't remember a time when taking off *wasn't* part of the plan. If it were feasible to begin driving that morning, she would have done it without wasting a second.

Rita gathered her hair on top of her head and let it drop,

addressing Aaron's statement first. "You know I don't fly. I'm driving."

Aaron cocked an eyebrow. "You're actually going. On this weirdly specific mission to catch hypothermia."

"Looks that way," Rita answered, cranking the car's air conditioner. Their scrutiny was making her hot, and San Diego's elevated climate in late November allowed her to get away with the nervous action. Her heart was thumping in her chest, her decision cementing itself. Pride wouldn't let her change her mind now that she'd said it out loud, in front of her brothers and sister.

Rita hid her inward flinch when Aaron and Peggy sailed off toward Aaron's Mercedes, muttering to one another, Peggy throwing him the occasional shove. Belmont stood in the middle of the street, head down, but clearly halfway to bailing. *Fine.* She'd been without them for a long time. She certainly didn't need them or their stupendous neuroses now. Add the dysfunctional Clarkson clan to the list of things she would gladly leave behind when she hit the road. *Done.*

Starting the car's engine, Rita was a second from throwing the car into reverse when she caught Aaron, Peggy, and Belmont closing back in, varying degrees of irritation etched into their familiar features. Without turning her head, Rita rolled down the driver's-side window and waited.

"All right, look." Aaron smoothed a hand down the front of his still-pristine dress shirt. "The front runner for the presidential nomination—Glen Pendleton—is going to be stumping at the Iowa primaries on December tenth. Senator Boggs already recommended me as a campaign adviser; I just need to make contact. If we can pause our little road trip long enough for me to meet with him and secure the position I want..." He pinched the bridge of his nose. "I can't believe I'm about to say this, but I'm in."

"I have a condition thingy, too," Peggy chimed in, unable to stop herself from bouncing. "We stop at U of C between Iowa and New York. There's an old friend I've been meaning to visit." Rita narrowed her eyes at Peggy's blush. As far as Rita knew, Peggy had mostly maintained contact with her cheer squad from the University of Cincinnati, but why would that turn her face red? "I'm only asking for one day," Peggy added. "Maybe two, depending on how things...progress."

Nothing with her family could ever be cut and dried, could it? She jerked her chin at Belmont. "What about you? Any special requests?"

Belmont's gaze was locked on his shoes, but he tipped his head down in Peggy's direction. "I need...I might need—"

"Sage," Peggy supplied, surprising Rita. "You want me to invite Sage." Belmont didn't answer, remaining eerily still, but Peggy only nodded. "I'll ask her if she can take the time off, big guy."

Sage—as in Peggy's wedding planner? Why would Belmont need his sister's best friend along for the ride? Rita traded a baffled look with Aaron, but neither of them commented. Prying never worked with Belmont. He would only clam up more.

But they were *actually* considering coming along. There was a spark of gratefulness—maybe even reluctant excitement—in Rita's chest, but she doused it. "Look, if you guys are doing this because you feel sorry for me and my burned-down pile of bricks, I don't need your pity."

"Does that sound like us?" Aaron asked.

"Not even a little bit," Rita admitted, hands twisting on the leather steering wheel. "So . . . fine. I need a week to handle the insurance company and tie up loose ends. Unless Peggy has another wedding scheduled I'm not aware of, we leave Tuesday. December first."

Aaron did a quick check of his phone and sighed. "Fine."

Peggy clapped her hands once. "I'll bring snacks."

Rita's three siblings left her feeling as if the earth had shifted beneath her feet. In a matter of twelve hours, everything had changed. *Everything.*

What else could she have expected after committing arson?

CHAPTER THREE

The Suburban's fan belt blew two hours after they crossed the Arizona–New Mexico border.

Looking back on the day of departure, calamity had been inevitable. Having spent two days meeting with insurance adjusters and calling in favors to get replacement jobs for her Wayfare employees, Rita had shown up half asleep in her pajamas, drawing exasperation from Aaron and an offer to borrow clothes from Peggy. Each of them still wary about the whole trip and what it symbolized, the siblings had ridden in relative silence throughout the first night and into the morning, Belmont a steady presence at the wheel. Despite Rita's negative predictions of squabbling and battle cries of *shotgun*, leaving San Diego had gone almost . . . smoothly.

She should have known Murphy's Law would take effect sooner or later.

After all, disaster was the Clarkson way.

When Rita was sixteen, Miriam had taken the four of

them camping. For their family, camping had roughly translated into a borrowed Winnebago parked beside Carlsbad Beach, mere feet from convenience stores and a busy highway. Not exactly braving the harsh conditions of nature. Although, after one night, they could have fooled the emergency room staff at Tri-City Medical Center into thinking they'd just spent a week in the swamp.

Peggy had sneaked off with the son of their neighboring campers, skinny-dipping in restricted waters, leading to a nasty jellyfish sting. Upon hearing his sister's distressed screams, Aaron had sprinted toward the beach and carried a towel-wrapped Peggy back to the Winnebago, stepping in a gopher hole on the way and spraining his ankle.

That was the Clarksons' first and last family vacation, but the misfortunes hadn't started or ended there. Belmont had fallen into a well on a class field trip in third grade and stayed missing for four days. Later, they'd found out he'd shouted himself hoarse on the first day, leaving him unable to call out to the search party that passed by. On the fourth day, when firemen had managed to extricate him from the obscured thirty-foot-deep well, the media attention had been intense, complete with cameras and flashes going off and questions being hurled at young, filthy, and starving Belmont. At the time Rita had been too young to process why Belmont had withdrawn into himself after that, but the television footage she'd found on the Internet as an adult explained a lot.

Rita's personal misfortunes had once occurred with less notoriety or incurred medical costs, but were no less imprinted on her psyche. Such as slugging a classmate for Photoshopping her head onto a porn star's body and circulating it online. *Hello, expulsion.*

Little did she know her claim to fame would also come once again via the Internet a decade later. And for the first time, irony didn't amuse her.

Now, at the unmistakable sounds of car engine trouble, Rita shot up in the far backseat and pushed her dark hair out of her face. "The hell happened?"

Belmont jerked the Suburban into park and sat perfectly still, white-knuckling the cracked steering wheel. Peggy sat up slowly from where she'd been sleeping in the middle row. She sent Rita a troubled glance over her shoulder, then returned her attention to Belmont. Rita's concern for her oldest brother laced through her alarm. Ever since Peggy had shown up without her friend, Sage Alexander, Belmont had been wound more tightly than usual. Rita had been able to glean only a fraction of the story from Peggy before they'd been locked up in the car and private conversation had become impossible.

Sage had been Peggy's wedding planner for all four failed wedding attempts, and they'd become close friends. *Best* friends. As the stand-in for their absent father who would walk Peggy down the aisle, apparently Belmont had developed some sort of attachment to Sage, too. Because his reaction when Peggy apologized and told him Sage couldn't make the trip had been nothing short of extraordinary.

Rita wasn't being insensitive in using that description. Belmont rarely showed a reaction to anything, let alone women, whom he barely gave the time of day. But something about being *without* this Sage girl had turned him to ice.

Aaron roused in the passenger seat, tugging the headphones from his ears. "Is there something wrong?" He looked out the windshield just in time to see smoke curl from under the hood. "Oh, for the love of God. Tell me you have Triple A."

"Nope," Belmont said, his voice sounding rusty. "I have a toolbox in back, but that isn't going to help if we need a new part."

"Let's just call a tow truck." Rita was already searching through her purse for her cell. "Anyone know where we are?"

"Hopefully near a bridge, so I can throw myself off of it," Aaron answered briskly before pushing open his door and climbing out. They all watched as he rolled up his tailored sleeves, mouth moving to form what were obviously curse words.

When Aaron popped the hood, Belmont shook his head. "He has no idea what to look for, but I'm going to give him a minute to try."

Peggy popped a stick of gum into her mouth. "Didn't he negotiate his way out of shop class in high school?"

"No, that was Ethics," Rita said. She held up her phone, trying to map their location, but was thwarted by the lack of a signal. "Kind of gives him plausible deniability as a politician."

Belmont sighed when Aaron started to pace, holding his cell phone up in the air much the way Rita was doing. He shoved open the door and went to join his brother outside the car, followed a moment later by Peggy and Rita. When the sun hit Rita, she cowered back into the Suburban's shade. Sunshine was not her thing. Really, being outside at all went against her entire life philosophy. *Inside good. Nature bad.* Trips to the farmers' market for cooking ingredients was the typical extent of her excursions, and even then she rushed through the process as if she had a sun allergy. Those trips to purchase vegetables were over now, though, weren't they? Experiencing a rush of buoyancy at the thought, Rita peeked around the lifted hood into the steaming engine, where Belmont was busy waving smoke aside to inspect the damage.

"What's the verdict?"

"Not good." In a familiar gesture, Belmont rubbed his thumb along the crease in his chin. "There was a town about three miles back. Small. But probably has a garage. I'll go."

Aaron walked up between them. "Remind me again why you don't fly, Rita?"

"Because of *crashes*. Don't turn this on me."

"I won't." Her younger brother held up both hands. "I won't point out that we could have been in New York in under six hours."

"You're acting extra dickish because that stupid video went viral, huh?" Rita said, kicking the front left tire of the Suburban and swearing she heard it groan. "So what...we should all have to live like Tibetan monks because you decided to become a politician?"

"You went after someone with a *knife* on national television." Aaron finally lost his closely cradled cool, raking frustrated hands through his styled dark blond hair. "Do you have any idea how much shit I had to eat over that at work?"

"Oh, stop. You eat shit for a living. It's your *job*." Rita stomped away, circled back. "And that cheese soufflé was perfect. You have *no* idea."

Peggy edged close to the group. "Aaron, don't do it."

Ignoring his sister, Aaron straightened his sleeve. "The soufflé looked decent, but it certainly wasn't knife-attack worthy."

"Decent?" Rita forced out the word through a throat that felt rubbed raw by a sandstorm. The blinding sunlight turned her vision white, her siblings winking in and out of sight. Anxiety that had been building up since her disgraced departure from *In the Heat of the Bite* exploded from her nerve endings, and she launched herself at Aaron. Belmont caught her at the last minute, throwing her over his shoulder with little effort and stomping toward the rear of the Suburban.

"You're letting him get to you," Belmont said, setting her down and nudging her into a sitting position on the bumper. "Don't."

"What were we thinking?" She let her head fall back against the rear gate. "We'll never make it to New York without a murder being committed."

"I heard that," Aaron called from the car's front. "Should we check your luggage for knives?"

"*Aaron*," Peggy whined. "Not cool."

Rita launched herself off the bumper, only to be wrangled by Belmont once again, who gave a weary sigh.

That's when the motorcycle pulled up.

* * *

Good Lord. I should probably just keep on my way.

But Jasper Ellis had been raised with better manners than to leave folks stranded by the roadside, so he slowed his Harley to a stop, parking across the two-lane highway from the motley crew just to be safe. He might be disinclined to leave four obvious city dwellers to their respective fates, but he also valued his hide. And the dark-haired girl glowering on the bumper—seemingly against her will—looked hell bent for leather. In his thirty-three years, he'd learned better than to provoke a female when her eyes said *Bring it on.*

Unless they were in bed. Then all bets were off.

Jasper removed his helmet and slung it over the left handlebar of his bike. "Y'all in need of some assistance?"

The two people at the busted Suburban's front end traded a look, as if he'd just spoken in a different language. Yup, these were city folk, sure as he was standing there. Dude was dressed for a Sunday sermon, even though it was a weekday morning. The girl at his shoulder was dressed for the opposite of church in ripped jean shorts and a crop top. She knew how to have a good time, that one. Jasper had a lot of experience with her type and could admire the displayed skin without feeling that spark of attraction he used to get in his belly. Now, the Jasper of Party Girls Past would have already gotten her number.

Instead, he found his gaze drawn to the midnight-haired she devil spitting fire from the car's significant shadow. He could barely make out her features, but the suspicion radiating from her gave Jasper the odd urge to inspire trust instead. A weird reaction, to be sure, since she appeared to be spoken for. The dark-haired man's hulking arm was thrown around her slim waist as if restraining her from attacking, and Jasper couldn't help but chuckle at the suspended animation of the scene. What the hell had he stumbled on here?

Finally, Sunday Sermon spoke up, the whiteness of his teeth noticeable from across the highway. "Yes, actually. It's our fan belt. We need to call a tow truck and there's no cell reception."

"Cell reception?" Jasper asked with a perplexed look, just to fuck with him. City people were too easy. "I don't follow."

Jasper swore the guy turned pale as cotton. "Is there a garage nearby?"

"Sure." He jerked a thumb over his shoulder. "Back the way I came. I can take one of you to bring back the tow truck." Hulk released She Devil and Jasper frowned over the unexpected loosening of his chest. "How about you? Want a ride?"

She Devil's mouth fell open and she scoffed, "I'd actually rather get back in the car with my brother. And that's saying something."

He liked her voice. Kind of scratchy, like she'd been holding in a scream too long. What kind of things set it loose? "Which one is your brother?"

She combed fingers through her midnight hair, leaving it askew in places, but damn if the wayward pieces weren't cute. "Why?"

For once, Jasper didn't have a ready answer. "You're the only one dressed for a bike except for the big guy, and I doubt he'd fit." His hearty laugh sounded amplified in the dusty quiet of the road. "Sorry, I was just picturing him on the back with his arms around my waist. Go on and think about that. It's quite a picture."

Party Girl giggled, but Jasper couldn't take his eyes off She Devil, wanting to watch her as she took his measure. *What are you seein', beautiful? Mind telling me when you see it?*

A nudge of discomfort had Jasper turning back for his bike. "Listen up, I'm late for an appointment. If I'm late, I'll catch hell." He slid his helmet on top of his head. "I'm going to need an answer pretty quick."

She Devil stepped into the sunlight with a wince, telling Jasper she wasn't the outdoorsy type, an opinion only heightened by her attire. The fitted black shirt had small openings in the sleeves where her thumbs poked out. Her jeans and boots were worn-in and comfortable, holes decorating both. If Jasper were forced to peg her, he would say She Devil was probably the type to sleep in on weekends. The kind who enjoyed rainstorms. Once upon a time, he would have speculated how she'd be in between the sheets before anything else about her registered, but he'd learned to keep that part of himself penned.

Then she came a step closer and he stopped speculating on her extracurricular activities or weather preferences. She was a looker beneath all that makeup. Big-eyed, pouty, and challenging. And then, his mind *did* slip between the sheets before he determinedly yanked it back out. But not before a rough-edged thought slipped through: *She'd like a man who knows how to be a little extra bad.*

"Who is your appointment with?"

Jasper tilted his head. "Why?" he asked with a smirk, throwing back her one-word response to his earlier question.

She rolled her lips inward, as though disinclined to commend him for paying attention. "If your appointment is with a barber, as opposed to a cult, I might be interested in that ride."

Behind her, Hulk shook his head. "Nope."

She Devil sent the big guy what Jasper assumed was a reassuring look before locking those golden-brown eyes on him once more. "Well?"

"If you have to know, I'm meeting with a woman."

Was it Jasper's imagination or did she look disappointed? "Well. We wouldn't want to keep you. If you could just give us the garage's name—"

"Now, hold on one second." Jasper slipped his cell out of his jacket pocket and started to dial, pressing the button to put the call on speakerphone. Sunday Sermon narrowed his eyes at him. The foursome watched him curiously as the call connected and a woman's voice drifted out through the speaker.

"Jasper Ellis. Lunch is on the table and your hide is nowhere to be seen."

He quirked an eyebrow at She Devil. "I'm going to be a little late today, Rosemary." Covering the phone with one hand, he leaned forward a touch and whispered "That's my grandmother," before straightening again and returning to his conversation. "I'm playing Good Samaritan to some lost city dwellers."

A burst of static. "You might as well bring them on over. I made enough sandwiches to feed an army."

"Now, that's a nice thought, isn't it? But I don't think they'll all fit on my bike."

"I hate that thing."

"I know you do. I'll be over when I can."

Jasper hung up before his grandmother could ask if one of the city dwellers was a nice single girl. He was still trying to figure that out for himself, although he still had no idea why it mattered. This morning when he'd woken up, finding a single girl had been about the farthest thing from his mind. Now, though, he found himself measuring She Devil's proximity to Hulk and attempting to discern their relationship.

"So. Have I been found suitable?" Jasper asked the group as a whole. "I can recite the presidents' names, first through forty-fourth, if it helps, but I'm not in the habit of pissing off the family matriarch. She's meaner than she sounds."

Hulk and She Devil exchanged a look. "We know his name now," said Hulk.

She Devil fussed with her hair again, messing it up more. "Maybe this is just how people act down here in—er, where are we?"

"Hurley, New Mexico. Just outside Silver City," Jasper supplied, his answer fading away as Sunday Sermon strode over to his bike and took a cell-phone shot of his license plate.

"I have some very powerful men listed in my contacts. Feel free to annoy my sister, but bring her back alive."

She Devil gave him a nice long once-over as her brother headed back to the Suburban. Jasper was well used to once-overs from the opposite sex, except hers wasn't overtly sexual, as most tended to be. It was shrewd and gave away none of the inner workings taking place behind her eyes. He liked that. A little too much to drive away. So he was relieved when she relented.

"It's just a quick ride."

She sauntered toward him, thighs flexing in her jeans, and Jasper swallowed a growl. Something told him this ride would be anything but quick, but he shoved the thought aside and distracted himself by removing his helmet and transferring it to her head. And hell if he didn't have a hard time mobilizing himself under her scrutiny. Like she wanted to see past whatever was visible. He couldn't remember the last time he'd been dissected by a woman—and it was welcome.

Damn, she smelled like the forest, cut with cooking spices. He tried not to be obvious about sucking in a good lungful. His reaction to this girl was goddamn strange, to say the least, but he had no choice but to go with it since she was about to mount his bike.

It had thrown her off a little, his gesture of passing over the helmet, but she recovered to grant him a speculative look. Mumbling under her breath, she threw a leg over his bike and gripped the back bar. "You might not recognize me, but I'm famous for what I can do with a knife."

Jasper joined her on the bike in one smooth movement, groaning inwardly when her thighs gripped his waist. Had her breath caught? "I hate to disappoint you, but this isn't the first time a woman's threatened me with a knife."

"Yeah, but it would be the last."

His laughter was lost in the roar of the bike's ignition, the Suburban growing smaller and smaller in his rearview mirror.

CHAPTER FOUR

There was a reason Rita had gravitated toward the kitchen. Recipes. They were precise. They had instructions. You either added the correct textures and flavors, or you didn't. There was no gray area in cooking. It was all right there before her, written on a glossy page. Even she couldn't fuck up step-by-step instructions.

Wrong.

It had become starkly apparent while working under Miriam that there was a definite knack. And she'd apparently gotten in the "sarcasm" line instead of the "knack" line the day God had been doling out talent. She'd found fail-safe recipes and stuck to them, perfecting them in the privacy of her one-bedroom apartment, praying something new wouldn't be thrown at her the following day. Learning on the fly had been a constant fear, day in and day out.

So join a nationally televised reality show, right?

Perhaps throwing herself to the sharks had been Rita's way of grieving, of trying to find a way to feel close to her mother again. Or trying to flame out hard enough—once and for all—that she'd be forced into quitting the job she never quite performed more than adequately. Whatever the reason, she'd applied for the show knowing they couldn't deny Miriam Clarkson's daughter a spot, while somehow also knowing things would *change* afterward. Things would finally shift. Either she'd prod some dormant talent into animation or she'd cut herself off at the knees and it would be blessedly over.

At the very least, she'd learned a thing or two about *people* through working with food. What they chose to order from the menu, more often than not, classified them. Had they lived abroad, were they adventurous, extravagant or cheap?

Jasper Ellis was a twenty-ounce hanger steak with a side of garlic mashed potatoes. Easy. He didn't require much effort or imagination. It had a lot to do with the way he wore his jeans. Like he'd picked up the first pair he'd stumbled across on the floor that morning and slung them up around his cowboy hips. And son of a bitch, look at that! They fit like a dream. She could even picture him saying it in the mirror as he splashed water on his hair—and damn! Didn't his rich brown locks—with a touch of auburn—just style themselves!

Appetizing, yet effortless. Hanger steak.

Weirdly, she couldn't seem to shake the memory of how he'd zeroed in on her, only looking away when addressed by someone else. This good ol' boy had barely spared Leggy Peggy a passing glance, making Rita vacillate between classifying Jasper as a hanger steak and a porterhouse. A cynical part of her had taken the ride just to see how fast he would become predictable. Typical. Because while she could swear there'd been a spark of interest in his sky-blue eyes, men like Jasper were the opposite of her type. Not that she necessarily had a type, since she tended to find dating rituals repellent. In her world, small talk was on par with Chinese water torture, so her infrequent dates were usually men who'd been within her orbit for a while, like fellow chefs or market employees who sold her ingredients. Even then, date two was a stretch.

So, yeah. If an online dating service had matched Rita up with a Jasper Ellis type, she would consider suing them for false advertising. To put it bluntly, he was walking, talking sex. Kind of like a younger, more realistic, twice-as-magnetic version of Matthew McConaughey. Rita was a little surprised that a mob of women wasn't sprinting after the motorcycle as they cruised back toward Hurley. None of those women would be a social maladroit without a pinch of color in her wardrobe. Most likely, they hadn't threatened him with knife violence, either.

Between her thighs, his hips shifted just a fraction and she almost laughed at the way her body reacted. Warmth trickled into her stomach on cue, and she fought the insane urge to rub her stiffening nipples against the sun-heated back of his leather jacket. Honestly, the man must have trouble just walking down the street without being propositioned. *She* hadn't been propositioned in—ever.

Definitely not each other's type.

They were almost to town when Jasper slowed the bike to a stop at a red light, the engine purring beneath them. Their eyes met in the circular rearview mirror. "You're thinking awfully hard back there."

Rita hid her surprise in a shrug. "I was wondering why there's a stoplight here when I can't see another car for miles."

He cast a glance in both directions as if the thought had never occurred to him. "You reckon I should go through the red light?" He revved the bike's engine. "Think about it hard, now. You and I would be fugitives from the law. The Bonnie and Clyde of New Mexico. It's a big decision."

This man was ridiculous. "Clyde was impotent."

"Was he?" Jasper twisted his upper body around, appearing genuinely perplexed. "How did he keep such a beautiful woman around without all his parts working?"

"I don't know. Charisma?" Rita stared with impatience at the still-red light. Leave it to her to broach the subject of erectile dysfunction within five minutes of meeting revamped McConaughey. "Are we almost there?"

"Another mile or so." His hips turned on the seat, scooting her thighs a little wider, making Rita all too aware of the intimacy of their position. "I'd like to know your name before we get there."

Rita ordered herself to stop comparing the color of his eyes to the sky outlining him. "Why is that?"

"So I can introduce you properly to Stan, our mechanic," he explained in a patient voice. "I'd like to say, 'Stan, meet so-and-so.' Instead of 'Stan, this is some nameless woman I picked up.' It doesn't have the same ring."

Rita sorely regretted taking this ride. Jasper Ellis was turning out to be anything but predictable or typical, and she didn't like having her theories disproved. It was like sprinkling nutmeg on eggnog, then taking a sip and finding out you'd used chili powder instead. Why should this man who could wink a woman into the sack also have a personality? "Rita."

"Rita," he repeated, although with his accent, it sounded more like *Ray-da*. "I like that. Rhymes with cheetah."

The light turned green and they starting moving before she could respond. There were two conflicting sides of her. One wanted this damn ride to be over, so she could send Jasper on his way and stop worrying about his refusal to be categorized. And the other side sorely regretted that the ride was coming to an end. The scent of his worn-in leather jacket teamed with the waft of diesel was pleasant. More than pleasant. The helmet strap beneath her chin was soft, like warm fingers encasing her jaw. Rita didn't do outdoor sports, but being on the back of a motorcycle hadn't filled her with terror as she might have expected. When she considered it might have something to do with the steady energy of the man holding the handlebars, she shook her head to clear the thought.

Hurley sneaked up on either side of them, small but efficient. A hardware store, a diner, a bakery. Green, leafy shrubs and ice plants gave the town a well-kept feel, the residents clearly taking pride in the community's appearance. Its vibe was so far removed from the dusty two-lane highway they'd just come from that Rita felt like she'd been transported into an alternate universe. There were two convenience stores on either side of the main street, which was *actually named* Main Street, both with signs outside boasting deals on produce, the prices so reasonable compared to San Diego that she almost fell off the bike.

Several people waved at Jasper as they traveled through town, sending Rita shrinking down into the seat to avoid scrutiny. Had any of them seen her online disgrace? Not for the first time, it occurred to her how hilarious she must look on the back of a certified-cool-guy's bike. They probably thought he'd lost a bet or something.

Rita felt Jasper watching her in the rearview and ducked her head, grateful the drone of the engine prevented conversation. Finally, at the edge of town, they pulled into a garage. A man in coveralls set aside his newspaper and rose to meet them as they parked. "Shouldn't you be sitting down to lunch with Rosemary?"

Jasper held out a hand to assist Rita off the bike, sighing when she climbed off without his help. "Indeed I should, Stan, and I expect to catch some serious grief over my tardiness. But I had reason." He gestured to her. "This here is my friend, Rita. The rest of her group is stranded out along Highway Sixty, just east a few miles. Would you mind giving them a tow in?"

"You betcha," Stan said, donning a baseball cap he tugged from his back pocket. The older man looked flat-out excited to have something on his agenda. "Pleasure to meet you, Rita. I'll have them back in a jiff."

Rita walked toward the shade provided by the garage, joined by Jasper a moment later. They watched Stan pull his tow truck onto Main Street without speaking, and then they were alone. Without the hum of the bike's engine, the silence made Rita jumpy. What, was she expected to carry on a *conversation* now? "Thank you for the ride. I don't need you to wait with me."

She could tell he'd been expecting her to say that. "That wouldn't be very gentlemanly of me."

"But your grandmother is waiting for you."

Jasper leaned up against the concrete building, crossing

one ankle over the other. "I'll admit I'm feeling pretty guilty about that. Feeling hungry, too. But I've weighed the pros and cons of the situation carefully, Rita. And I think a few more minutes talking to you is worth the added guilt and possible starvation."

"Who even...*are* you?"

CHAPTER FIVE

Jasper kept his smile in place, although that question—
Who even…are you?—hit a little too close to home. If
Rita knew how many times he'd asked himself that same
thing lately, she would also know he didn't have an answer.
He kind of appreciated her confusion, actually. At least
she hadn't written him off as the town manwhore everyone
knew him to be.

There was no rule saying she *had* to write him off,
either. What if—to Rita—he could be Jasper, the decent
soul and sparkling conversationalist? Standing right in front
of Jasper was a woman without any preconceived—or hell,
conceived—notions about him, and he couldn't recall the
last time that had happened. Maybe he could find something
out about Rita, before Rita found out the worst about him.
Lord, the possibility made him feel lighter than he had in
years.

She was hiding something—maybe a lot of somethings—

underneath her attempt at a bad-to-the-bone appearance, which she didn't pull off by any measure. *Couldn't* pull off when her gaze was so skittish, so—defenseless. It was compelling, really, to watch her try so hard to act indifferent to him when she was clearly anything but. She was daring him to give up and go away. A handful of years ago, he would have. He would've swaggered away and found the next, easy conquest. That's what had landed him in his current position of Hurley's resident tramp.

But Rita didn't know that. Which meant Jasper was in control of the impression she walked away with. A sharp thud inside him wouldn't allow him to pass up the chance. If only to prove he could manage such a thing.

"Now, see. I'd rather talk about you." He propped his right shoulder on the wall, refusing to capitalize when her gaze snagged on his mouth, difficult as it was. It would be so easy to crowd her a little, brush a thumb over her hipbone and increase the awareness between them. That subtle dance that let a woman know he'd take care of her in bed, and then some. Thanks to her thighs hugging him on the ride into town, her breaths ghosting over his neck, his belt buckle was still feeling the pressure of his hard-on. Old habits were hard to kick. He was more than a good time, though. Probably. He was still working on finding out—and maybe Rita could help him do that. "Where are you traveling from?"

He could see her debating how much information to divulge. "San Diego."

"Hmm. I would have guessed a bigger city. Los Angeles, maybe."

"Why?"

"Your knee-jerk suspicion of someone offering help

might have tipped me off." Jasper rubbed at the stubble on his jaw and winced, realizing he'd forgotten to shave—two days in a row—which probably did little in the way of making him appear trustworthy. "I might as well have offered you a live hand grenade."

Those full lips of hers twitched, and he wrenched his gaze off them before they could inspire his wood to make another appearance. God, she was pretty. If he didn't think she would take his head off, he would ask to see what she looked like without the heavy makeup.

His voice dropped low, without his permission. "Were both of those men your brothers?"

Rita took a slow inhale and the distance between them seemed to shrink. "Yes. And my sister was there, too." She tugged on her shirtsleeves, wrapping her hands in the cuffs. "If one of them was my boyfriend, I doubt they would've let me ride off alone with you."

"Not if they had a lick of common sense." He adjusted his lean on the wall, trying not to be obvious in his relief that Hulk was a relation. "What do you do back in San Diego?"

Her expression took on a faraway quality. "Nothing anymore. I kind of...burned my bridges, so to speak. We're driving to New York and I'm going to stay there. Go back to school for graphic design. Never too late, right?" Seeming to think she'd said too much, she fidgeted, her movements jerky. "I don't know why I told you that. I haven't even said it to myself out loud yet."

Jasper leaned close, her cooking-spice scent teasing his nose. "Do you make a habit of talking to yourself?"

That earned him a glare. "You know what I mean."

"I suppose I do." Jasper estimated the tow truck was

about even with the Suburban by now, so he better work a little faster. Toward something he'd never thought possible, unless he changed his name and moved to Switzerland. "What's your idea of a good date, Rita? You seem like a coffeehouse type, but I don't like to assume anything."

His head might have been on backwards based on the look she gave him. "Wha—date? Why?"

"One question at a time. I'm working on an empty stomach."

She turned her attention to the road, like maybe she was thinking of throwing herself into oncoming traffic. "I don't date. It's a barbaric pastime created by mothers and narcissists. Does that about end this unprompted interrogation?"

"You're more of a movie-and-sushi girl, aren't you?" Her strangled growl made him want to laugh out loud, but he didn't think she'd appreciate it. "You're going to be in town for a bit—long enough for your Suburban to be repaired. And I hate to be the bearer of bad news, but Stan isn't as quick with a wrench as he is with a tow truck. You're here for the night." God*damn*, that mouth looked sweet. Holding himself in check was much harder than he'd anticipated. "This is me asking you out, beautiful, if my intentions were somehow unclear."

"Beautiful, huh?" She backed up a pace, and it took a concerted effort not to follow her. "You almost had me."

"Come again?" When she only gave an impatient head shake, Jasper pushed on. "Let me take you out, Rita."

She opened her mouth to answer but snapped it shut, considering him for long moments. "Is there a bar in town or something? So maybe it won't seem so..." She waved a hand around. "Date-y."

Damn. He could've sworn he almost had her sold on the

sushi. "Yeah, there's a bar." His inward sigh was so loud it echoed in his ears. "Although the Liquor Hole is more like a honky-tonk."

"Liquor. Hole." It took her no time at all to catch the double meaning. "As in, lick her—"

"Mmm." He wouldn't tell her he'd been twenty-one—and half in the bag—when he'd named the place. Yes, the trust fund bequeathed by his grandfather on Jasper's twenty-first birthday had been used to buy a sawdust-floored, neon-signed dive. Not for *college*, as the old man had intended. And thus began his decade of debauchery from which he'd surfaced two years ago only to realize that no one in his life took him seriously. He was everyone's good time. Not reliable or permanent to a single soul. So he'd set about changing it, starting with his livelihood. "That's the name of the bar. I'm opening a separate eatery in four days' time 'round back, though."

Rita did a double take. "You're the owner."

"Guilty." He blew out a breath that lifted the hair from her face. "Really, really guilty."

"I can see that," she murmured dryly, scrutinizing him. "Why don't you want to bring me there?"

Jasper saw his chances with Rita fading before his very eyes. "What did you do for a living back in San Diego?"

A small hesitation. "I worked in a restaurant."

"A restaurant." On cue, his stomach growled, making her eyes sparkle and Jasper almost lose his train of thought. "Okay, Rita. Would you take me on a first date to the place you worked? Let me pal around with the waiters and line cooks?"

Her eyes quit smiling. "Hell no."

"Why?"

She rolled a shoulder. "Because they've seen me at my worst."

"Bingo. Same goes for me and the bar." That revelation might have been too telling, because her demeanor turned polite, as though she might be considering that final brush-off. Jasper couldn't allow that. Not when he'd finally come across someone who seemed willing to—meet him. Talk to him without a pillow beneath their heads.

Just a little flirtation to ensure I see her again. Just enough to make sure he could pick up where he left off—with a clean slate. Hoping it was the right decision, Jasper slipped an arm around Rita's waist and tugged her up against him, barely stifling a groan. *Lord.* She might be buried under dark, shapeless clothes, but didn't she just curve in all the right places? Her gaze was glued on his throat, so he dipped down until they were nose to nose, saw the rush of thought going on behind her eyes. It was pretty damn breathtaking up close. "Mind cluing me in as to what's going on in there?"

"If—*if*—we need to stay overnight—"

"You will."

"—then I *might* see you at the bar." She wedged a hand between them and separated their bodies. "I'd rather see someone's worst than their best. Saves time."

Jasper heard the tow truck pulling into the garage parking lot and cursed. Not even remotely confident that his first attempt at polite conversation with an available woman had been successful, Jasper walked her backward until they were hidden behind a rusted pay phone. She'd broken away from his touch, so he was careful to respect that. He dropped his mouth to an inch above hers and said, low, "I didn't get near enough time with you, Rita. If you don't show up tonight, don't be surprised if I come looking." He laid his palms against the warm building, above her head, watched her gaze dip to his stomach. His lap. "And if I have to come looking, I'll be twice as determined to get that kiss."

Her head came up. "W-what kiss?"

Jasper lowered his mouth until their lips brushed. He listened to her breath accelerate, watched her wet her lips. "The one I want to give you right now." He allowed himself to linger another few seconds, then, with the effort of ten oxen, Jasper stepped back. "Tonight, beautiful."

On his way to his bike, Jasper tipped his hat at Rita's gaping siblings.

CHAPTER SIX

Ignoring her siblings and their huge personalities wasn't easy, but Rita had been practicing for quite a while, so she'd grown adept at one-word answers and avoidance. It hadn't occurred to her until recently that her methods had seeped into other aspects of her life, but that was neither here nor there. *There* being New York and here being *New Mexico*, where they were—as Jasper had foretold—holed up for the night in the Hurley Arms, a motel tucked into the center of town. They'd been assured by Stan, the mechanic, that the necessary part would be delivered by tomorrow, so the complaining had been minimal, at least for them.

Belmont and Aaron had taken one room, she and Peggy another. So when both brothers followed her and Peggy into their dim, stale-aired space, Rita turned around with a dark look, prepared for the worst. Apparently she hadn't escaped the inquisition that had started at the garage.

"Let me see if I have this straight." Aaron—of course—began the interrogation, big shit-eater grin on his face. "You won't fly on an airplane, but you'll basically dive onto the back of a stranger's motorcycle."

Rita threw her duffel bag onto the closest bed. "I'm not talking about this."

"You know, I kind of picked up on that on the death march over." Aaron carefully unbuttoned the sleeves of his dress shirt, rolling them to his elbows. "Thankfully, I can talk enough for the both of us. Probably all four parties present, if required."

"Oh, leave off, Aaron." Peggy jumped onto the bed Rita hadn't chosen, bouncing into a crossed-legged position. She lowered her voice to a whisper, passing a conspiratorial look over to Rita. "That man was wicked hot. I doubt many girls would pass up a chance for a ride."

Belmont and Aaron's expressions mirrored their disgust. "Your brothers are literally right here, in the room, Peggy."

"I meant a ride on his *bike*. Mostly." Peggy threw herself backwards on the bed with a monumental eye roll. "Either way, I'm twenty-five years old. I've been engaged to four different penises. Innuendoes will be launched at will."

Aaron looked as though he wanted to argue, but he visibly shook off the urge and refocused on Rita. "Far be it from me to give you a hard time—"

Peggy snort-laughed. "He said hard time. Right after I—"

"Please stop." Aaron held up both hands. "I just find it surprising that some y'all-in' *Dukes of Hazzard* look-alike would be Rita's type." He brushed dust off the ancient wooden dresser and sat, arms crossed. "He's nothing like Gerard."

Rita toed off her boot and kicked it in Aaron's direction. "You did *not* just bring up Gerard."

"I definitely just brought him up."

"Is this why you agreed to come along? To needle me until I'm carried off in a straitjacket?" Rita began shoveling through the items of her duffel bag with no idea what she was looking for. She just needed a distraction from the ball of heat spinning madly in her belly, the way it had been doing nonstop since—since *I'll be twice as determined to get that kiss*. Rita realized she was staring blankly at a bottle of shampoo and shoved it back into her bag. God, she needed a distraction. Or she might actually consider venturing out to a place called the Liquor Hole in pursuit of the town cool guy, who'd probably already forgotten her name. "Okay, talk about Gerard."

Peggy sat up. "He ate my hamster."

"That is hearsay and you know it." Peggy stared back at her blankly, forcing Rita to unearth the litany she'd been reciting in defense of her eighth-grade boyfriend since they'd gone their separate ways one night in their driveway. Just another middle-school romance pulled beneath the undertow of favorite-band disagreements and acne outbreaks. "He didn't have motive or opportunity to eat your hamster, Peggy."

"He *so* had motive," Aaron chimed in. "You broke up with him because he wasn't vampiric enough. That was your *Twilight* phase, remember?"

"I hate you."

"I liked Fluffy," Belmont said, drawing everyone's attention. "He was good company."

Peggy started to cry.

Aaron stood. "That's my cue to leave."

Belmont followed him out the door a moment later, casting a final backward glance of horror at his crying youngest sister. A look Rita understood well, because she'd never dealt well with Emotional Roller Coaster Peggy either. Rita herself hadn't cried in years. Even at Miriam's funeral she'd been too numb to do anything but stare straight ahead.

They'd *all* reacted differently that day. Peggy had sobbed. Belmont had watched the proceedings from the back row while Aaron acted as their mouthpiece, shaking hands and accepting condolences. There'd been a tangible resentment toward one another by the time it was over; whether it was in defense of their own way of grieving or disapproval of one another's methods had never been clear. She only recalled them driving away without saying good-bye.

Girding her loins at the prospect of comforting her younger sister, Rita turned—

And found Peggy smiling. "Got rid of them for you, didn't it?"

Rita failed to hide her surprise. "Wow. You've finally harnessed your powers for good. Or maybe that was evil." She rose and started to pace, her socks catching on the scratchy brown carpet. "Belmont looked trauma-tized."

"He always looks like that."

"True." It had been a joke, but Peggy's statement drew her up short. "Is he okay? This thing with Sage...What *is* this thing with Sage?"

"Complicated. That's what it is." Peggy twirled a curl around her finger. "I'd rather talk about you."

That was the second time someone had said those very

words to her in less than an hour. Which was a little discon-
certing since she could count on one hand the times in her
life someone had expressed a desire to talk about her. "If
this is about Jasper—"

"Oh, it is." Peggy's teeth sank into her bottom lip. "If
we'd pulled in a few minutes later, he would have been
pulling out."

"You really meant what you said about innuendo." Rita
noticed herself fidgeting and stopped. "There's nothing to
talk about. You know that kind of guy who flirts with who-
ever's available? That's all it was."

Peggy wasn't having it. "Rita, not that you aren't hot in
your own right, but he didn't even give me passing con-
sideration. And these shorts earned me my most recent
marriage proposal."

"Yeah, about that—"

"Eh. Nice try. Back to motorcycle dude."

Rita gave herself a sidelong look in the mirror. Nothing
out of the ordinary. For her, anyway. She hadn't switched
up her look in over a decade. Heavy eyeliner, thick bangs
ending even with her eyebrows. If she peered closely, she
could see the Clarkson good looks buried deep, but her siblings far outshone her in every category. If she were to don
Peggy's shorts, she'd look like a pasty chicken. The faded
black jeans currently covering her scrawny butt were Rita's
favorite because she'd once camped out on the sidewalk in
them for two days, hoping to score Megadeth tickets. There
was a tiny hole in the pocket where she'd gotten bored during the eleventh hour and tunneled through the material
with a ballpoint pen.

She attracted the hamster eaters of the world. Not
the smooth, charming, blue-eyed, aw-shucks-ing, lunch-

with-Grandma type. Was he one of those guys who liked his women grateful? Starstruck over the attention she—a loner who used her bangs as a hiding place—was receiving from such a certified catch? Rita was surprised to feel the stickiness of hurt over that possibility. How dare he make her hurt over anything after twenty minutes together?

Irritated with herself for wondering what Jasper had thought of her appearance, Rita tore her gaze from the mirror. "He owns a bar called the Liquor Hole." When that bit of news only made her sister giggle, Rita shook her head. "Look, the car will be repaired in the morning. Let's just order some shitty pizza and watch *Golden Girls* on your laptop."

Peggy's eyes went wide at the mention of the only pastime they'd had in common as kids. Something they discovered when they'd both contracted chicken pox and gotten quarantined in the same room. At first they'd simply been annoyed at the forced proximity, but somewhere around the third episode, they'd been hooked. "You still watch?"

"Rose was in the lead for a while, but Dorothy is back to being my favorite."

"I'm still a Blanche girl." Peggy's excitement drained away and she groaned. "No. We'll have plenty of time to watch *Golden Girls* on the trip. Tonight, we're going to the Liquor Hole."

Rita barked a laugh. "You're drunk. That's not happening."

"It's completely happening." Peggy leaned back on an elbow. "I'll be your wing-woman long enough to make sure Jasper's not a creepdog, then I'll leave you to your road booty."

"Road booty?"

"Hooking up on the road," Peggy explained with ex-aggerated patience. "Knowing Aaron—and myself—this won't be the last hookup perpetrated by a Clarkson before we reach New York. You should pride yourself on being the first."

"Forgive me for not cheering." Rita tugged on her plain, long-sleeved T-shirt. The urge to ask Peggy for something to borrow was strong, but she staunchly resisted. Going out for a beer and *possibly* running into a man was one thing; dressing up outside the black zone of safety was quite another. She wouldn't even allow for the chance of *road booty*. Taking her clothes off and getting sweaty with a stranger was something *other* people engaged in. Not that she judged those who went out looking for one-night stands, but she'd never understood casual sex. Being naked was about as vulnerable as one could get in Rita's book—nothing casual about it.

Unfortunately, as much as she wanted to decline Peggy's offer for wing-woman support, she could still feel Jasper's breath feathering against her mouth, the outline of his erection where it had brushed her belly. At the time, she'd told herself it was his belt buckle, but no. For some reason, he'd desired *her*. Some undiscovered part of her wanted to see that desire up close, just once more. Feel the gravitational pull she'd encountered outside the greasy garage, experience the earth tilting in a way that made her stumble blindly in Jasper's direction.

It was all too fast. Too risky to her self-esteem if some-thing went wrong, or someone else caught his eye instead. But she'd left San Diego for a reason. This was her new start. It was silly to officially begin that fresh start by putting herself into a situation where a random hookup might occur—not that she was allowing herself to hope—but maybe the mere act of *going* and *being available* was enough for now.

Rita pursed her lips at Peggy. "One drink."

CHAPTER SEVEN

It just *had* to be one of *those* nights, didn't it?

Every few weeks, the Liquor Hole regulars tended to get rowdier than usual. Drinking one whiskey shot over their usual limit, dancing more suggestively than they would if their mama was watching. There was no explaining or predicting when one of these witchy evenings would roll around. Jasper had even gotten out a calendar and tried matching up the occasions with the moon cycle, but no damn luck. He reckoned it was down to mob mentality of some sort. One regular acting up gave their friends the excuse to follow suit. The ugly cycle usually continued until either punches were thrown or make-out sessions got out of control at the bar, forcing the bartender to spray the couples down with water from the soda gun.

Wasn't it just his fortune in life that a full moon should be looming tonight, when he'd finally felt interest in a woman and expected her to walk through the entrance any moment? Hell, that was an exaggeration. He didn't expect a damn thing. That downright unmasculine tightness in his chest was *hope*, plain and simple. He *hoped* she'd walk through the entrance. Otherwise he'd have to go knocking on motel-room doors looking for her and that would just be awkward, especially if he located Rita's brothers first. Not to mention that leaving the Liquor Hole in the hands of his two bartenders—one of whom he suspected was one toke away from a coma—would be unwise.

If the gods were smiling down on him, Rita would show up. Then she'd let him take her out for some god-damn sushi. Jasper had a hunch that eventuality was about as likely as an indoor snowstorm in June, but the only weapon in his arsenal was optimism, so he would use it. Not that it was easy when witchy nights tended to make the female population of Hurley somewhat—twitchy. Up until two years ago, when his personal wake-up call had rung like a four-alarm fire, he would have been the go-to man in Hurley for a good lay. Now that he refused? Well, getting him back into the sack had become something of a challenge for some of his more amorous past conquests. On nights like these he'd taken to locking himself in the tiny back office, only coming out to restock beer or settle disputes.

If Rita actually showed, the local women who'd been trying to coax him *out* of the office and his self-imposed celibacy would only see his showing interest in Rita as a challenge to try harder.

You reap what you sow had never rung more true than it did tonight.

If Rita showed. And that was a mighty big *if*.

Hell, maybe this bone-deep necessity to have Rita see

him as something *other* than Hurley's orgasm machine was useless. Maybe he should have just *kissed* her that afternoon. Hesitation had never been part of his genetic makeup, but her big, wary golden-brown eyes had made any leftover game at his disposal seem like laughable bush-league bullshit. At least if he'd just let his mouth drop another inch this afternoon he would know how she tasted. Maybe he wouldn't have an incessant itch between his shoulder blades from wondering if she might actually leave town without him finding out. The reality was, she *would* leave town. Probably tomorrow. Which did nothing to decrease this edginess in his bones. A restlessness that made him think not seeing her before her Suburban vanished into the sunset would be a missed opportunity.

Jasper plowed a hand through his hair. "Nate, grab me a beer, would you?"

"Yeah, boss."

Nate dragged a Budweiser out of the ice, popped the top, and slid it down the bar, right into Jasper's waiting hand. "You feel the air in here, Nate? It's feeling real close, ain't it?"

"I don't feel anything."

Jasper made a sound of disgust and drew on his icy-cold beer. "Yeah, I reckon you don't." Wondering if he could find a hidden vantage point to watch for an unlikely Rita appearance, Jasper turned and surveyed the bar. Already Eleanor Nesbit was doing *that* dance. The one where she lifted her arms, closed her eyes real tight, and ground her hips on some imaginary pommel horse. Things like tempo or beat didn't matter to Eleanor—she just kept on keepin' on with that infamous move. Meanwhile, her friend Gina switched it up constantly. Just trying out a new move every four seconds or so, not committing to a single one. They made quite a pair.

"Hey, Jasper Ellis." Gina said his name the way most people say *cherry pie*. "You're thinking of joining us. I can tell."

Eleanor sent him a wink, breaking back into the same dance. Jasper had to admire her loyalty to the technique, but that was about as much admiration as he could muster. They were both attractive women, close to his age, and he felt exactly nothing but hollow when they spoke to him in that overdone cherry-pie manner. Beer bottle tipped to his lips, Jasper turned from the dance floor—

Just in time for Rita to walk into his bar. She brought a cool breeze in with her, a relaxing energy that thrilled at the same time. Her sister was in tow, for which Jasper was grateful. Hurley was safe enough, but he didn't like the idea of her walking to the Liquor Hole by herself in the dark.

Rita looked the same as this afternoon, hadn't gone and dressed herself up—thank God. She had, however, rid herself of all that makeup, and Jasper liked her unpainted face. The way it called Saturday mornings to mind, when the only stain on her lips would be from fresh strawberries. Her clothes might be plain, but they were form-fitting enough that he could see the taunting curve of her bottom. That's exactly what an ass like Rita's was. A taunt. It said, *Don't even try it, fucker.* But at the same time, her long-sleeved shirt, complete with thumbholes, made him think of long stretches on the living room floor while rain pelted the roof. The shirt would mess her hair up when it slid over her head, but they wouldn't give a shit on account of it being Saturday.

What the hell is in this beer?

Jasper gathered his far-fetched thoughts and rounded the bar in Rita's direction, remembering at the last minute to smile. Odd, since smiling typically came natural to him. *Intense* wasn't a description anyone in town would associate with him, but Rita seemed to coax it to his surface. The closer he came to their seats, the more anxious she appeared. As if she might jump out of her skin at the mere idea of talking to him. Laying that kiss he'd promised on her in lieu of hello was out of the question, because something told him he wouldn't stop, and he was determined to keep things slow and steady. Good thing slow and steady appeared to be what Rita needed, too.

"And here I was doubting you." Jasper made eye contact with Nate and nodded toward the ladies. "Buy them a drink on me, Nate. They're mourning a fan belt tonight, God rest its soul."

They gave their drink orders. An apple martini for the sister. Rita a pint of their IPA. Gorgeous, sharp-witted, and good taste in beer. Lord have mercy.

Jasper leaned against the bar beside a stiff Rita, but reached to shake the sister's hand. "I don't think we met properly today. I'm Jasper."

"Peggy." Her smile was warm and slightly giddy, her gaze darting back and forth between him and Rita. Did that mean Rita had been talking about him? He didn't have a chance to finesse the answer out of Peggy before she hopped off the stool. "You have a jukebox in this place?"

"I surely do. Please avoid Van Halen." He noticed the dance floor filling up, the couples moving closer to one another. "Tends to get 'em worked up."

"You got it."

Just like that, he was alone with Rita. Maybe the heavens were finally smiling on him. Now if he could only get her to *look* at him. She seemed more interested in the condensation on the pint glass Nate had set down on the bar. Before he could become entranced by the movements of her index finger, Jasper shook himself. "You talk to your sister about me?"

A flash of those eyes made his gut tighten. "It was kind of unavoidable."

"How's that?"

She sipped her beer so long he thought she might finish it. "That pay phone didn't hide much. They saw you..."

"They saw *us*."

"Well. But you—"

"Started it. Is that what you were going to say?" Jasper leaned closer, powerless to keep the grin off his face. "That's the oldest excuse in the book, but I'm going to let you use it. You know why?"

"Why?"

"Because I want to finish it, too." *Just the kiss. You can manage one healthy interaction, man.* "And you catch more bees with honey."

She turned until her legs were pointing at him and a blinking sign that said PROGRESS might as well have lit over his head. "Am I the bee in this scenario?"

"You surely are." Slowly, he swiped a thumb over her knee. "And I reckon you sting when provoked."

Rita exhaled in a rush of shaky laughter. "Wow. You are very good at this. Do you practice in the mirror?"

He'd already been halfway to irritated with himself before her question, but that brought it safely home. It had taken him exactly ten seconds to fall back into old patterns and habits. Behavior he thought he'd buried, but apparently his colossal attraction to Rita had dredged them right up. Jasper pitched to the side, supporting himself with an elbow planted on the bar. "Damn, can we start the conversation over? You don't have to walk back outside or anything. But pretend I just asked you whether or not you'd spoken to Peggy about me."

When she repeated her earlier response without a single hesitation, his desire to kiss her skyrocketed straight to the moon. "It was kind of unavoidable."

"I'm sorry I put you in that position, ma'am."

The edge of her mouth tugged. "No, you're not."

"No, I guess I'm not."

Rita laughed. If life had a rewind button, he would have hit it over and over again, the way he'd done with love scenes as a child watching his grandmother's taped episodes of *General Hospital*. Until he'd been caught and sentenced to a week of dish duty, anyway. Rita laughed with her eyes. They went a little glassy as her shoulders shook, but the actual sound was what crept over his skin like skimming fingertips, shooting him full of awareness. It was low and intimate, like a bass string being plucked in a smoky jazz club. He wanted the sound back as soon as it faded. Wanted to hear it vibrate against his belly. *Go easy, man.*

"So." He plunked his beer down on the bar. "Where were you four headed in that big, rusty Suburban before Hurley reeled you in?"

She looked pensive as her shit-stomping boots started to sway back and forth, bumping the wooden rungs of the stool. "We need to be in Coney Island by New Year's Day. So we can jump into the Atlantic Ocean."

"Why—what?" He dropped onto the stool beside her, his drink forgotten on the bar. "That's pretty high on the list of things I didn't expect."

"Oh, I know the feeling." A beat passed. "It was our mother's last wish."

"I'm sorry."

She nodded, brushing her hair back in a jerky motion, as if she were uncomfortable having someone's undivided attention. He'd never had cause to use the word *preposterous* before, but that was the only way he could describe her lack of confidence. Despite the inappropriate name, the Liquor Hole was his life's work, and, at the moment, it was nothing more than an unworthy backdrop for Rita. And, God, he was staring at her hands like an aggressive palm reader. "Most mothers want to avoid having their children turn into floating ice sculptures. What was her reason?"

"Good question." A hint of sadness winked in her eyes, and Jasper wished he'd let the subject drop. This was what happened when he avoided talking about sex. He stumbled right into deceased parents. And yet he wasn't sorry. Not even a little bit. He wanted to know everything. "I think...she meant it as some sort of symbolic bonding experiment. But I don't know. We're kind of unbondable."

"Got the feeling I interrupted a near-melee this afternoon."

"Aaron called my soufflé decent." A strand of dark hair caught on her lips when she shook her head. It took one hundred percent of his impulse control not to tug it away, but she beat him to it, anyhow. "It sounds silly now."

"Nah." Jasper couldn't help leaning in to get a whiff

of cooking spices. "He would have had it coming just for dressing like a preacher on a weekday."

Another one of those quiet, smoky laughs. "I guess there's a fine line between politician and preacher."

"Politician?" Jasper shivered, then recalled the threat Rita's brother had leveled at his head back on the highway. "Still, I can't help but like him for wanting you safe from a stranger. He can't be all that bad if he worries about you."

"Worried might be an exaggeration," Rita said.

When her golden-brown gaze lit on his mouth, Jasper realized he'd moved into her personal space without any conscious thought. One of her knees brushed the denim covering his hip and, God help him, if the bar were empty he would've been between her split thighs before she could call for Jesus. For someone who hadn't felt more than a passing appreciation for the opposite sex in years, his libido was sure trying to play catch-up tonight.

"What are you thinking about?"

Lie. He had to lie. *I want to strip you down and fuck you on this seat, but I'm trying my hand at being a gentleman,* was not an acceptable line. It was too aggressive when she seemed spooked merely from his close proximity. But she was leaving, leaving his town tomorrow, and the slow-game option had been ambitious for Jasper when he knew nothing about it. So he'd tell the truth while leaving out the oh-so-dirty reality in his pants. "I was thinking it would have been a goddamn shame if you'd broken down one town over." His voice was gravel, so he cleared it. "More than a shame. I'm kind of finding it hard to think about, if you want to know the truth."

For long moments, he couldn't hear a single sound in the loud bar. No music, no crunching ice or raucous laughter. And, somehow, he knew she couldn't hear the noise, either. It was there in the perplexity of her expression. He expected her to call bullshit or make a joke, but she didn't. She shocked him instead.

"I think I'll take that kiss now."

CHAPTER EIGHT

Holy hazelnut cannoli.

Rita would have smacked a hand over her mouth to prevent the words from escaping, but they were already out. She'd said them and they were immortalized in her cringe bank for all eternity, destined to pop up and mortify her all over again at inopportune moments. Did normal women who existed outside of sitcoms say things like *I think I'll take that kiss now*? Answer: no, they didn't. They—did something else. Right? They *flirted* and enticed the man closer until he made the move—right?

Only Jasper was coming closer anyway. Actually, closer was an understatement. His hips were inching her thighs apart on the stool, his attention so focused on her mouth that she held her breath so as not to break his concentration. He appeared to be wrestling with his hormones as much as she was, but what sense did that make? They were roughly the same age, which meant this wasn't their first rodeo, even if it really, honestly, felt like an inaugural bull ride.

He'd be a rougher ride than a bull.

He might as well have whispered that promise out loud because it surrounded him like an aura. Men like Jasper were supposed to be reserved for naughty Internet memes, but here he was. Her own private, moving GIF, only he didn't loop back to the beginning after three seconds. No, he just kept coming, like he might never stop kissing her once he started. Like he might do a shit ton more than just kiss with that mouth.

But he stopped. He stopped just a breath away, blue eyes lifting to slay her. "You're gorgeous sitting there, Rita. And I can see you squirming in that seat. God knows I can." His low growl was one of frustration. "But would you mind if we went somewhere and talked a while? Before we give each other that kiss?"

Confusion and chaos rippled in her bloodstream. He'd asked to *talk*? She shouldn't feel like her body had been dipped into warm oil, but there was no mistaking the wicked bottoming-out of her stomach. She'd heard of a thing called woman's intuition where men are concerned, but she'd never experienced it. Jasper definitely wanted to do more than talk, but he seemed to be holding back. Why?

Behind them, a chorus of voices hooted Jasper's name, and he flinched. And that flinch kept Rita from turning around. His gaze didn't stray from hers, either, gaining gravity instead.

Something akin to disappointment dinged in his expression when she hesitated over his offer to talk, and some of his leash appeared to unravel, right before her eyes. "Come with me, Rita. I want to be with you where no one's watching." The very tip of his tongue made contact with her lower lip and her brain nearly atrophied. If his echoing groan was any indication, he was just as affected. But that was impossible, wasn't it? This was *her* he was kissing. Rita Clarkson. The underachiever of the family, her career summed up in a thirty-second YouTube clip. Nary a romantic prospect to boast of.

"Come with you where?" she breathed.

"Just to my office." Obviously having interpreted her question for a *yesyesfuckinghurry*, his big, callused hand closed around her smaller one. "I promise not to keep you back there long enough for anyone to assume I'm taking advantage." His wink was raw sex with a sense of humor. "And I'll do my best to bring you back in one piece."

In somewhat of a daze, Rita allowed Jasper to tug her off her seat. She had the presence of mind to make eye contact with Peggy, who gave her an enthusiastic thumbs-up amidst the crowd of men who'd gathered around her. As she was tugged through throngs of bar patrons, Rita's attention snagged on the dance floor. And the rare sexual confidence she'd been experiencing thanks to Jasper plummeted with a vengeance. Women—*sexy* women, women in miniskirts—whispered behind their hands as they watched Jasper pull her through the crowd. It was a flashback to high school. To culinary school. To everyday life. She didn't belong with this charismatic man in this place. *God.* Had he just grown bored with the local flavor and wanted some strange?

Her feet dug into the saw-dusted floor, but when Jasper turned with obvious concern on his face, words refused to emerge. She couldn't very well admit out loud that she felt like a fish out of water. That she didn't understand what the hell he wanted or expected from her. It would make her twice as pathetic as she already felt.

Warm hands clasped the sides of her face, tilting it up. Jasper's hands, dragging her out of the rocky chasm she'd fallen into. "Sweet Lord. I've never had to ask someone what they're thinking so many times in one day."

"Why are you so interested?"

The question had fairly burst out of her, but Jasper didn't even flinch. "If I don't know your thoughts, how can I get inside them?"

She was being drawn back under his spell. But even her total awareness of the fog descending couldn't get her to pull away or heed the warning signs on the road to destruction. "You're there," she murmured. "Doesn't mean I don't want to kick you out."

"I can be stubborn when I have a mind to. You just wait and see," he responded, completely undeterred. "Are you coming back to my office so we can get to know each other better? Or do you want to be carried?"

Carry me. "Don't even try it."

His answering smile probably dropped panties from Hurley all the way back to California. "I'll ask you again later, when your knees are feeling weak."

She glanced down at their joined hands, noticing his tight grip for the first time, probably because she'd been ready to make a dash. His knuckles were white, the unbreakable hold so at odds with his casual demeanor. "We'll see if you can make them weak."

"Here's hoping I get the chance," Jasper muttered, turning once again to lead her through the masses. They'd only made it five steps when two dancing miniskirts sailed into their path. It was like that moment at the end of a concert when the lights go on and the atmosphere is obliterated. One second you're in a dark, magical place with musical notes painting the air, and the next? You're in a sweaty room with strangers and spilled beer on your shoes. Jasper visibly deflated with the women's arrival. And that reaction twisted Rita's stomach into a pretzel.

"*Jas*-per. Where you off to?"

"Excuse us, please, Gina," he responded, voice weary. "Just showing Rita the new eatery addition out back."

"Oh right, the *addition*." Miniskirt Number Two elbowed her friend. "You know, you can try and clean this place up, but it'll always be dirty. Just like you, isn't that right?"

"Mmmhmm. You come find us when you're done with this little *tour*," said Miniskirt Number One, putting air quotations around the word *tour*. "You'll still have enough energy for the both of us, if memory serves."

They started moving again—fast—but Rita's feet had transformed into sandbags. She wanted to pull her hand out of Jasper's grip but *didn't* want to be left standing like a loser in the middle of the bar, so she all but jogged along behind him. The few sips of beer she'd taken were like ball bearings in her stomach, rolling around and knocking together. She was used to being treated like she was invisible, but not in front of a man with whom she'd been making a sad attempt to flirt. Those women hadn't even spared her a passing glance, that was how nonthreatened they were by her. She just wanted to go back to the motel, crawl under the covers, and die a slow death.

"Let go of me."

"Can't."

"You *can*." Seeing what she assumed to be the office doorway up ahead, she attempted to free herself and failed.

They were inside the office with the door closed a moment later. With the music's volume muffled, their heavy breathing took precedence in the room. She waited for him to turn on a light, but he didn't, just paced in front of her, his frustrated profile highlighted by the street lamp just outside the window. "I need to get back to—"

"Why did you come here tonight?"

She threw up her hands. "You *asked* me to."

He stopped pacing, irritation clear in the lines of his hard body. "Rita, I've known you less than a day, and I know you don't just do things because someone *asked*."

Okay, fine. So what did he want to hear? She'd come because he fascinated her? Because she was attracted against her will? She'd rather draw and quarter herself with a carving knife after that scene with Miniskirts One and Two out in the bar. "My sister made me."

"Wrong again."

Rita ground her teeth together. A rebellion took place inside her, building and building in intensity. He wanted the truth, did he? What did she care? She'd already been humiliated, and tomorrow morning they would leave this nowhere town and never look back. Revealing her secret motivation might be embarrassing, but she'd survived worse. Internet notoriety. Her restaurant burning down. Life in general.

In fact, what if she went one step further with that line of reasoning? This man wanted her, whether it was a simple hankering for something new or genuine interest. What did she have to lose? At least it would feel good. At least she would feel *something* other than the failure and self-pity that had been dogging her lately.

Rita sucked in a breath. "I came here so you would fuck me."

CHAPTER NINE

There it was.

To be fair—although what the hell did *fair* even mean?—when he'd asked Rita why she'd come, he'd been flat-out begging for this answer. She'd come for the sex. Of course she'd come for the sex. What did he think lured her here? His dynamic personality? His oh-so-impressive career? Maybe he should ditch his new plan to be a decent human being and just take out an ad in the Sunday paper.

Come on down to the Liquor Hole. Tuesday is 10-cent wing night. Don't miss your chance for meaningless sex with the no-account owner.

There *might* have been a chance for Rita to see more. He'd vowed to himself they would stop at kissing. Just enough to fulfill the promise he'd made earlier outside the garage. Just enough that his every other thought wouldn't be *What does she taste like....What does she taste like. ...Oh, GOD, what does her mouth feel like?* Then his past had popped up and bitten him in the ass once again, the suspicions she clearly already had about him confirmed in the space of thirty seconds.

Well, *fine*.

Fine.

If that was the way fate wanted to play, *bring it on*. Common sense might be loitering in the back of his head, telling him his next move was a mistake, but he was too pissed off to heed the warning. And, yeah, he was ashamed. Probably even more than he was mad, actually. He'd been ashamed for a long time, though, and right now blocking it out seemed like a damn fine idea.

I came here so you would fuck me.

Didn't matter that Rita appeared desperate for the world to swallow her whole now, flames blooming in her cheeks. The words had been said, intentions made clear. "Jasper, I shouldn't have—"

"That *is* why you came, isn't it?" Talking dirty to a woman was just like riding a bike. Jasper rubbed a hand over his stubbled jaw and gave Rita a deliberate, head-to-toe once-over, watching her thighs flex under his notice. His cock gloried in the sight, hardening in his briefs. *Right, beautiful. I'll fit myself between them with enough force to show you who's taking the lead.* "You're an up-against-the-wall kind of girl, aren't you?"

"All girls are up-against-the-wall girls," she whispered, then look surprised at herself for having spoken. "I-I think."

Damn her for making him want to laugh when he needed to break something. "You have me there. Why do you think that is?"

Jasper propped one hand high above her head, tracing the waistband of her black jeans with the other, back and forth across her belly button. Slower. Lower. "Um…" Her stomach hollowed underneath his touch and shuddered back out. "There's nowhere to go?"

"That's right. You have nowhere. To go." He flicked open the button of her pants. "Maybe every girl does like it against the wall. But not every man can keep her up there long enough to call it fucking. It's only fucking when a man finishes the woman, in my book." He sucked his lower lip through his teeth. "That's why you're here, isn't it? You need a good, leg-shakin' finish and decided I'd be up for the job."

She opened her mouth to answer, but he eliminated whatever her response might have been by shoving a hand into her jeans and roughly cupping her pussy. Jasper groaned into the space above her head. *Fuck yes. She'd be a tight fit.* Rita almost collapsed, a sob wrenching from her throat, kicking up an ache in his chest. No hiding, no pretense in her pretty features. Just—pain. *Need.* Gorgeous, breathtaking need. It slapped the edge off his anger, brought him back to the present. Almost, anyway.

"How long has it been?"

When she flinched, he realized he'd barked the question. "I-I'm not answering that. It's none of your business."

He should have left it, but there was a driving need for knowledge about this woman that wouldn't be satisfied, despite her disinterest in anything apart from how he could get her off. So he went about getting information the best way he knew how.

Pressing his open mouth over her ear, he teased the edge of her underwear with his knuckle, letting it slip under just a touch. "You know you want to tell me. The longer it's been, the harder I'll set to work between these legs."

"Why do you want to know? So you can laugh at me like those women did? So you can write me off as a charity expense on your taxes?" Her breath puffed against his lips. "Screw you. I don't care what you think."

Everything inside Jasper seized. With denial, surprise, anger. All of them leapfrogging to be in the lead. "Whoa, now, Rita. Hey. You just wait one damn *second* there—"

She kissed him. It was such an unexpected move that his mind drained of anything but the soft curves of her lips interlocking with his. The subtle taste of original-flavored ChapStick. A pounding began, loud and dramatic, between his ears, growing louder when she opened her mouth to invite his tongue inside. There was a reason he should pull back—clarification of one pretty fucked-up misunderstanding was sure-as-shit necessary—but he couldn't fathom a way to stop. Not when she kind of fell into him like his mouth held the key to eternal happiness. For the first time in his life, he forgot he had his hand between a woman's legs because her mouth took precedent. Her breath, her scent, the way she sighed. If he could carve it with a chisel on his memory, he would've done it with gusto.

It took her fingers stroking down his forearm to cover the hand cradling her pussy for him to regain awareness of the intimate touch. Oh, and he remembered with a goddamn vengeance. She put pressure on his hand, moaning into his mouth with the universal language for *More, keep going.* With their tongues tangling together, lips slanting for frantic tastes, he had no choice. He yanked down her panties and slid his middle finger between her wet folds—so wet he tore his mouth away so he could curse.

"*God.* I would mouth-fuck this little sweetheart for days."

Rita moaned, her legs clamping around his hand. "Oh, you can't say things like that. Or this... will be over really fast."

Her honest reaction sent a delicious throb straight to the base of his cock, making it grow to the point of agony. So acute he felt liquid spill from the tip. Condom. Where were his condoms? Were they even in date? He had to get inside her and ride out the pleasure their bodies were begging for. *No.* There was a reason he couldn't be inside Rita, but he just needed longer to remember why. *Why?* His mind questioned while his mouth worked on its own. "You like hearing what I want?"

"*No.*" Her eyes were closed as he worried her clit. "*Yes.*"

His wrist was loose, his fingers working her in light circles, but he felt anything but loose and light. He felt like a dying man who would receive a free pass to heaven if he could relieve the pressure he felt inside Rita. Her hot body was whip-tight, her need obvious in a way he knew all too well mirrored his own. "I want to treat this tiny bud between your legs so special that she pays attention when I walk into a room. I want her to remember my tongue so well you have to excuse yourself when you see me coming because she needs a rubout."

Rita's eyes flew open at that—whether in shock or in the hopes of encouraging a more detailed explanation—and those glazed, golden-brown orbs slammed him back down to earth. He regained a slight handle on reality just in time for her to say, "I w-won't be here long enough for that."

"That's right, isn't it? You won't."

The ugliness from before began crawling out through the crack in his foundation, even though he wanted to stomp on it, keep it at bay.

Jasper took a pull from her offered mouth, drawing deeply of her healing balm, but that somehow only made it worse, as did the slickness coating his fingers. So delicious, so fucking *ripe*. But she wouldn't be here past tomorrow. Hell, she didn't *want* to be. Everyone thought of him as a fucking truck stop, but it was too much coming from this woman he'd been dying to convince otherwise. One shot, one failure. "You came here tonight for your turn with the town tramp," he said against her mouth, steel in his tone. "That's all this is. Good ol' Jasper, at your service. Just filling a need."

Her gaze cleared faster than a summer storm, parting for sunshine to break through. There was a dawning understanding in her eyes, tempered with denial. Alarm, even. He'd said too much. Way, way too much.

"No." She shook her head. "That's not right at all." Before he could process her apology or her devastated expression, she shoved his hand from between her legs and zipped her pants with shaking fingers. "I'm sorry I let you think that."

Then he remembered. Remembered why he shouldn't have allowed himself to be pulled under by her kiss. *Why do you want to know? So you can laugh at me?* His throat dried up at the memory of how she'd said it. Ah, Jesus. How was it possible they'd both gotten the wrong idea when his intention had been to finally behave *right* with a woman? Were they fighting different versions of the same demon?

When she plowed both hands through her dark hair, he reacted to the misery he sensed. "Hold on, now, beautiful Rita." Fuck, he was practically wheezing with the need for more of her taste. More of her skin beneath his hands. More, just *more*. "We got ahead of ourselves and that's my fault." Desperate for contact, he gripped her hips, positioning her back against the wall. "Let's just stand here a minute while my brain remembers how to operate—"

"No, I have to go."

She knocked his hands free and lunged for the door, but he beat her there. Her stricken face brought him up short. *What do I do here?* He'd never distressed a woman before, never felt like the ground might open up if he didn't coax a smile, make her happy. So he fell back on what he knew, even though he suspected he was damning himself in the process. "*Rita.* Two more strokes of that sweet clit and I'd of had you shaking in my palm. You walk out of here hurting because of me, I might die." He slid a hand over her pussy and rubbed. "Don't take this away from me, beautiful. It needs me." *And I fucking need you.*

When the door banged shut behind Rita a moment later, he slammed his head against it. Only a few seconds passed of him courting denial before he went after her. But she was gone. *No way that just happened.* No way in hell. Had he forgotten how to treat a woman in the last two years? Even as his mind posed the question, he knew the answer was moot. Rita wasn't just another woman. A reality he felt in the marrow of his bones, no matter how soon into their acquaintance. And she was leaving. Before he could correct his massive fuckup. God, he would no sooner laugh at her than he would go canoeing into an erupting volcano. He had to make sure she *knew.* Once he made it clear to her tonight had been about his own hang-ups, he would formulate his next move.

Ignoring the voices calling for him at the bar, Jasper turned on a heel and strode back to his office to make a phone call.

CHAPTER TEN

Rita could hear Peggy huffing along behind her, struggling to keep up, but her feet wouldn't slow down. At her behest, they were intent on getting inside their motel room as quickly as possible. Oh God, her cheeks had to be stained bright red. Mortified. She was completely mortified.

Honestly, where was her self-respect? On top of being laughed at by two strangers, Jasper had goaded her, all but forcing her to admit she was in the midst of a dick drought, and then—then he'd had the nerve to throw his own self-loathing in her face. Would he do something like that with a normal, socially well-adjusted girl? Nope. He hadn't even bothered with the charm once his hand was down her pants and she'd all but begged him for sex. Then she'd just been a convenient place to pour his issues.

One of the main reasons she didn't date was fear of rejection, fear of someone she actually liked seeing the worst in her. Or, worse, the *best* in her—and deeming it lacking.

The way her instructors in culinary school had done when the famous Miriam Clarkson's daughter's skill proved fair to middling, rather than extraordinary. She'd avoided the Internet message boards while competing on the reality show, but her fellow contestants hadn't hesitated to pass on the gist. She didn't measure up to the name. And tonight, she'd not only shown Jasper her insecurities, she'd somehow managed to point his out, with barely a conscious effort.

Don't look now, but here comes Rita, the keeper of mediocrity and shroud of doom. Avoid eye contact.

Might as well start hoarding, because a man wasn't in the cards. Hell, she didn't even have friends, unless you counted the kitchen staff she no longer worked with. At least they hung out after work and threw back a tequila shot or two. How had she repaid them? By burning down their place of work.

Really, everyone should just keep their distance.

"Come on, Rita," Peggy called, her voice carrying in the still evening. "It couldn't have been all that bad."

Rita snorted. "I think my definition of bad is worse than yours."

"Well." A beat passed. "I've never dated a hamster eater, but I've had my fair share of bad dates. *Horrible* dates. Mom's basement dates."

"It wasn't a date. It was like, the world's most confusing make-out session, and I'm not talking about it anymore because then it'll just keep being fresh."

"But this is *fun.*" Peggy seesawed a hand between them, finally having caught up. "Look at us. Talking about boys and whatnot. We're early-stages Thelma and Louise right now."

"Funny you should mention that, because I'm thinking

of driving off a ledge into a fucking canyon." When Peggy made a sympathetic noise Rita wanted to interpret it as genuine, but how could she? Peggy couldn't walk ten feet without someone offering her a white picket fence and two-point-five children. Interpersonal dysfunctions were not her territory. Rita had bought up every square foot of that particular real estate.

"I think you like him or you wouldn't be this upset."

"H'okay."

Peggy's nose wrinkled up like an adorable bunny's. "I guess it doesn't matter, since we're leaving in the morning anyway. But I had high hopes for Jasper." Rita hoped her sister would drop the conversation after that stomach-tightening statement, but no dice. "Oh, well. If I know one thing for sure, it's that you can't win them all. My senior year of college—"

Rita groaned up at the night sky. "Peggy, you can't be serious. Our experiences are not even remotely similar."

When hurt slashed across Peggy's features Rita started to apologize for her outburst, but Peggy held up a hand. "No, it's okay. You're right...our experiences are not similar." They stepped into the glow of the motel's sign and Rita saw an uncharacteristic weariness in Peggy's gaze. "For instance, I doubt you've been carrying a torch for someone so long you can't let another man—*four* good, honest men, actually—give you a happy life. Because being miserable for *him* is better than being semi-content with anyone else."

"Peggy." Rita couldn't swallow. "I had no idea....I didn't—"

All at once, her sister brightened, but her speech was stilted. "It's fine. I'm just blowing off steam." She jerked a thumb over her shoulder. "I'm going to head in."

Rita started toward the outside corridor that led to their room. "I'm coming with you."

"Actually," Peggy started, giving a subtle head tilt toward the parking lot, "I think Bel might need some company. And he appreciates my attempts at comfort about as much as you do. So…batter up."

Rita looked back over her shoulder to find Belmont sitting on the curb of the parking lot, still as a statue. The sight yanked her by the hair straight out of her pity party, but it didn't distract her from the guilt she was experiencing over Peggy. "Wait," she called to her sister, who was already heading toward the room. Peggy stopped at the sound of Rita's voice. "Thank you for trying to make me feel better. It worked. Even if you just annoyed me into feeling less like shit."

Peggy dipped, twisting her hips in a little boogie. "It's a start."

"See you inside," Rita said, even though Peggy had moved too far away to hear her. Wondering when her sister had developed a complex side—and how she'd missed it— Rita went to join Belmont on the curb. He didn't acknowledge her right away when she sat down, which wasn't a surprise. Her oldest brother spoke through silence. What worried her were the lines of strain around his eyes, the way he stared out at nothing in particular. Knowing he needed to be the one who broke the quiet, Rita took a moment to study her surroundings.

Hurley was a mighty contrast to San Diego. Even in winter, the air was dry and soundless as it filtered through the cars in the motel lot. While San Diego County was certainly spread out in a way that required a vehicle to go most places, New Mexico was actual desert. It stretched and stretched so the wind had nothing off of which to buffer. Rita didn't know if it was simply being out of her usual surroundings that made it easier to hear her own thoughts, to take a deep breath despite scaling Mortification Mountain tonight. She felt more at ease without work hanging over her head. Without pressure to maintain the restaurant's sterling reputation.

"Aaron snores."

Belmont's monosyllabic announcement startled a laugh out of her. "Is that what you're doing out here?"

He rolled his massive shoulders.

Rita folded and unfolded the hem of her shirt. "I think Peggy might have a broken heart and we never realized it."

Her brother's frown was ferocious, but he didn't comment.

"I mean, I don't know why we *would* know. We never see each other to find out these things. They just come out during an argument or on the Internet," she said. "I like knowing Aaron snores."

Belmont grunted, but she knew that meant: *Why?*

"It means he's flawed. I'm going to think about it next time he calls my soufflé decent." She picked at her shoelaces. "Just big old, window-shaking snores."

"It was a good soufflé."

That brought her head up. "You were watching?"

Another grunt.

Pleasure ran circles around her rib cage. "I probably shouldn't be happy you witnessed my almost knife attack," she said, rubbing the toes of her boots together. "But it's nice to know... someone was rooting for me."

Headlights illuminated the parking lot and Belmont's easy demeanor vanished. His hands clenched into tight fists, body tensing as if preparing for a fight. Before she could question herself, Rita reached over and laid a hand on her brother's shoulder—and he jerked like she'd burned him, dislodging her touch.

"I'm sorry," she blurted, alarm replacing the pride she'd felt a few seconds prior. Time moved very slowly as the car pulled into a parking spot about fifty yards away and an older gentleman got out, ambling toward the motel, a fast-food bag tucked into the crook of his arm. It seemed very important that they not move or be noticed, so relief washed over Rita when one of the motel doors opened and shut behind them.

Belmont didn't relax right away; it happened in degrees. His hands flexed and dropped to his knees, where they rested. His barrel chest rose as he drew in a deep breath and let it out. "Don't be sorry."

"Okay."

"I'm not out here because Aaron snores. The walls feel too close."

He looked irritated with himself for having revealed that. Rita could see him already beginning to clam up again and rushed to insert a wedge. "Is that why you live on the boat? No walls..."

Belmont stood abruptly. "If I'm not here when you wake up, I'm at the garage."

Rita came to her feet as well, although much more slowly. "Okay." Neither one of them moved. "Go ahead inside. I'm going to sit here a while."

Her brother shook his head no and pointed at the motel. "You go inside first."

The protectiveness was simultaneously annoying and—nice. Usually, all the macho brotherly instincts were reserved for Peggy, and while it felt odd to be on the receiving end, it wasn't so bad. She was pretty sure her eye roll wasn't very convincing as she passed him, clomping toward the motel. Her spirits dipped again, however, when she turned to wave good night to Belmont and saw that the faraway look was back in his eyes.

Had the road trip been a mistake? Her older brother was obviously suffering some sort of anxiety over being in unfamiliar surroundings. She'd pushed Peggy away—maybe even farther than before—when her sister had only been attempting to help. And Jasper—now that the worst of her embarrassment had cooled, she remembered the way his voice had vibrated with emotion when he'd called himself the town tramp. It hadn't been male ego talking or some kind of joke. It bothered him. Instead of being remembered fondly, she'd be the girl who stopped in Hurley long enough to prod his demons.

Shroud of doom strikes again.

A sigh left her. She couldn't do anything about Jasper now. They were leaving in the morning.

Rita ignored the discomfort in her chest and turned to find Belmont leaning up against the motel wall, arms crossed as if keeping guard. Maybe she couldn't do anything about repairing the rift between her and Jasper, but she could try to make the remainder of this road trip better for Belmont.

When she pushed open the door, Rita found Peggy applying night cream in the bathroom. Rita cleared her throat. "So…about Sage…"

CHAPTER ELEVEN

What do you mean it's the wrong part?"

Rita resisted the urge to whistle under her breath at Aaron's tone. She'd never heard him exhibit such leashed rage before. Usually it just came out in a well-articulated rant or he shook the issue off as unimportant. Now? In this part of the country, she believed they called it *fit to be tied*.

They were standing outside Stan's Auto Body with their luggage, morning sun clear and bright as it beat down on their heads. The Suburban was still tucked safely inside the garage, like a shy dragon hiding from its owners. For Stan's part, he appeared to be taking Aaron's anger in stride, sipping from a tiny carton of Tropicana while her brother paced.

"We can't be stuck here another day. How does this even happen?" Aaron visibly reined himself in, managing a twenty-dollar version of his million-dollar smile. "Not that Hurley isn't peachy as shit, but we're on a tight schedule."

Peggy flopped down onto Belmont's canvas bag. "Technically, one day isn't going to kill us. You don't need to be in Iowa for another week."

"Yes, but I was going to use that time to lay groundwork. I'm not the only one vying for the adviser position."

"So you're losing a day," Rita interjected, really trying hard not to think about how being in Hurley another day seriously upped her chances of running into a certain honky-tonk owner she'd never expected to see again. The fluttering in her belly was definitely anxiety—not excitement. Or relief. *Most* definitely not. "We'll figure out a way to make up for lost time."

Aaron massaged the center of his forehead. "What happens when another part blows or an axle bends or—"

Belmont interrupted his brother with a look that said, *Please, don't try and talk about cars.*

"Is there someone who can drive us to the closest used-car lot?" Aaron asked Stan. "By the time we reach New York we could very well have spent more repairing the Suburban than the damn thing is worth."

"Not leaving it," Belmont said.

Peggy stood, tugging down her jean skirt. "The Suburban was Mom's, Aaron. Remember when we used to ride along with her to catering events, holding everything steady in the backseats?"

The reminder of those early days—before Miriam Clarkson became a household name—shut Aaron down for a second, before he recovered. "When she wrote that journal entry, I'm pretty sure this isn't what she had in mind."

"How do you know?" Rita asked, without really thinking. "None of us knows what she was thinking because we didn't *ask*." All eyes snapped to hers, all housing identical wariness. She'd broken the Clarkson rule by bringing up an uncomfortable subject, which could quite possibly lead to undesirable answers and feelings and *yuck*. Well, over the last couple days, she'd spoken more to her siblings than she had in a year, and every passing moment made her wonder what the aim of Miriam's plan had really been. Maybe it didn't have shit to do with diving into a fucking ocean. But she'd gone about as far as she could with her siblings for now—it was right there in their posture, how quickly they were about to close themselves off.

Stan shifted in his boots, orange juice carton tapping against his thigh. "They said they could have the correct part driven in by tomorrow afternoon at the latest. I'll set to work on it right away."

"Thank you," Aaron enunciated before snatching up his duffel bag and storming back in the direction they'd come from. He was followed by Belmont and Peggy, who might as well have been escaping a tsunami—*her*. Rita. Weird how she'd gone her entire life without speaking up and now she couldn't seem to keep her trap shut.

Rita stared out across the open expanse of land behind the garage, kind of wishing she smoked so she'd have an excuse to loiter. So many of her fellow kitchen employees had bonded over smoke breaks throughout the years, but she'd always abstained, afraid it would affect her sense of taste. *Why am I thinking about this?*

Probably because she had an entire day to kill now and Jasper Ellis was within walking distance. She'd lain awake far too long last night replaying their encounter. Over and over, until she'd finally gotten up in the dark and shaved her legs, since smooth legs against cool sheets always made her sleep better. No dice, though. *I came here so you would fuck me.* She cringed just thinking about those words leaving her mouth, about the way he'd *expected* them. How would she feel if a man said the same thing to her?

Answer: not even remotely good.

It went against the introvert handbook to apologize, but she needed to make amends for her part of last night. Make amends and bail. Like ripping off a Band-Aid.

Now that they were in Hurley for another day, she didn't have a single excuse.

Weighed down by resolve, Rita turned from her view of the dusty, open land—and ran smack into Jasper.

"Hey." His smile was strained at both ends, his eyes running over her face as if trying to capture something elusive. "You're still here."

It took Rita a few breaths to get her bearings. Because there he was. Solid and soap-smelling. Big. Capable. A little rough around the edges, hair shaggy around his ears. Hollywood stylists probably toiled for hours to achieve his tumbled-in-bedsheets look. A man who woke up, stretched his flexing biceps over his head, scrubbed a hand down his abs, and grinned before getting up to drink coffee naked in his kitchen. Because why spend one unnecessary moment dressed? And speaking of clothes, the warmth coming off his tucked-in flannel shirt rivaled the sun. She would bet anything that if she sniffed the material curving around his shoulder it would remind her of snuggling into pajamas fresh from the dryer.

"Uh...yeah. Still here." *Stop shuffling your feet like a high school student.* "The wrong part arrived and my family is mere moments from a mutiny."

"Wow." His eyebrows lifted. "The wrong part, huh?"

"Yeah." She tucked both hands in her back pockets. "This is starting to feel like *Gilligan's Island.*"

Especially because her siblings were nowhere in sight—obviously having returned to the motel—leaving her to be captured by one of the natives.

Jasper seemed to deflate with relief, probably because she'd made a joke instead of sprinting out into the wild blue yonder. "Which character does that make you?"

A smile tugged at her lips. "Probably Gilligan, since he's the one always screwing up." She could no longer look at him. "I'm sorry about last n—"

"*No.* No, no, no." The toes of his boots met hers. Rita barely managed to contain a gasp at his sudden closeness, the excessive heat he threw off. "If you apologize I'm going to walk right out into that desert and dig a hole for myself."

She sounded obnoxiously breathless when she said, "That's pretty dramatic."

"I'm feeling more than a little dramatic over you, Rita." Those blue eyes were crystal-clear pools, but so much went on behind them. So much she couldn't read or understand. "And you're a Mary Ann, to be sure. She was always my favorite."

"I guess I should thank you for not saying Mrs. Howell." He was too *much* up close; she felt so much magnetism and energy she had to back up a few inches. "Does your local status make you one of the scary dudes with spears?"

"Nah, beautiful. I'm not the least bit scary." He bit his lip and eased closer, flat-out ignoring the distance she'd put between them, even though Rita sensed the same leash around his neck from last night. "Even if I did think about stealing you from your bed last night to apologize."

"Apologize." God, there was a *riot* taking place in her stomach. "I-is that what the kids are calling it nowadays?"

His laugh yanked her down, down like quicksand, but he sobered almost immediately. "I was a genuine asshole, Rita. Give me the day to make it up to you."

It was either the worst idea in history or the best. After one day of his acquaintance, she'd been certain no amount of time would dull him from her memory. Creating more of those mental images and moving pictures couldn't be wise. Common sense, however, did nothing to change the fact that spending the day with him sounded—incredible.

Even after the debacle last night, she couldn't deny that Jasper made her feel relevant. Not so awkward. Why would he have found her this morning otherwise? His apparent interest—God, it made her feel really good. She wanted to know more about the man who'd vacillated between supreme confidence and self-loathing. Wanted to know how such a thing were *possible*, and, crazily enough, she thought maybe there was a chance she could relate to him, this charming, sexual live wire of a man.

There was no denying that Jasper had started a bonfire of attraction below her belly button, and that heat was so new. She imagined him slipping through the darkness of her motel room to steal her from the bed, thought of him cupping a hand over her mouth and angling his heavy body over hers, muffling her moans as he gave her a preview of what was to come. A sharp thrust of rough denim over cotton panties— and the image caused warmth to spread between her thighs. Her neck was bright red; she could feel it. Knew the tinge of color was visible. She'd never been aroused in public before, and he'd barely done anything to warrant it besides standing there.

"I'm going to take that as a yes," Jasper said, voice scratching like the rough side of a sponge. "Being that I aim to take you to lunch at my grandmother's house, though, I think I should save the better half of my apology for later."

His perceptiveness over her condition turned Rita on even more. When had she turned so shameless? She'd seen the evidence last night of how women threw themselves at him. Apparently she was no different than any of them. Rita the Lemming. "I don't think that's necessary."

Jasper winked at her, then indicated his bike with a jerk of his chin. "We'll find out later, won't we?"

Rita sputtered a little, aware that she was being railroaded but also confused by the unwanted thrill of getting back on the bike. Behind Jasper. Feeling him between her thighs. But that meant meeting someone new, more opportunities for social faux pas. More cringe-bank deposits. "I-I... no way. I'm not having lunch with your grandmother."

He only smiled and crooked a finger.

Chapter Twelve

All right. Phase One achieved. She was on the bike.

Jasper wasn't proud of fibbing to a visibly wary Rita to achieve just that. Painting a picture of a little old granny pining away for company with three place settings arranged just so? The reality couldn't be farther from the truth, but with one phone call he'd started playing dirty pool last night and once the cue ball got rolling, it smacked into cushions and knocked other balls into new patterns. Nature of the beast, wasn't it?

He wouldn't dwell, however, and waste the extra day he'd carved out with Rita. Borrowed time was today's theme, and he best get down to figuring out a few pressing details. Why did he get the feeling she was running from something? And why was he determined to be a roadblock she couldn't get past? Someone she took seriously. More importantly, what if the impossible happened and Rita found him worthy of more than a roll in the hay? Tomorrow would bring her departure. It was one thing for a woman to enjoy an actual conversation with him, quite another for—what?

Jasper didn't know what was itching inside his belly where Rita was concerned, but if the universe had any regard for his sanity, an answer would be forthcoming by sunset. It had better be. Or he'd be setting up a different kind of roadblock. The kind that stopped the correct Suburban replacement part from entering Hurley.

"How did you know when to show up at the garage?" Rita asked in his ear.

Jasper kept his eyes on the road. "It's a close-knit place, Hurley. Four strangers hiking across the main road like a Beatles album cover tends to create buzz."

She was silent a while. "So...someone called you?"

"You're going to make me admit to being nosy, aren't you?" He took a right turn and Rita leaned along with him as he'd instructed before leaving the garage. "Men like to be described with words like *mysterious*. Or *devil-may-care*. If you could swap one of those for nosy, I'd appreciate it."

Her hum created a vibration along his spine. "You're both of those things, too. That's why I'm poking around."

"Well, good. I'd hate to be nosy by myself."

Laughter drifted over the back of his neck. "Thanks for the permission. I think." Her fingers flexed against his stomach. "Tell me about your eatery. Does it have a name?"

"Not just yet," he hedged, even though it felt good simply having someone ask. Not one person had since he'd begun the addition. "As you well know, I'm not much good at naming places. Kind of hoping it'll name itself."

Her laughter sent pleasure filtering into his stomach, like sand through a colander. "What's your game plan?"

"I get the feeling my game plan isn't going to meet your standards," he said. "Mostly since you used the words *game plan*."

"My standards have . . . shifted of late."

"Well. Shift them a little more, because I'm planning on setting the tables and opening the doors." He ran his tongue along his upper row of teeth. "Doesn't sound very sexy, does it?"

"Are you going for sexy?"

"I'm always going for sexy." Damn, he liked hearing her laugh. It was throaty, like she'd just gotten over a cold but hadn't quite regained her voice yet. And at the same time, it always contained a touch of surprise. She was surprised to be laughing. "See, my plan last night was to show you the addition. If you hadn't upended up my intentions with that kiss, I'd have done it."

The thighs around his hips flexed, forcing Jasper to talk his erection from the ledge. *Easy, buddy. We're going to Grandma's house. Come back toward the window.* "That is a pity," Rita mumbled.

"Now I definitely didn't say that." Jasper revved his engine when a friend passed by in a truck heading in the opposite direction. "Pity doesn't belong in the same breath as kissing Rita."

Her stomach shuddered at the small of his back. "Just . . . tell me about the restaurant addition."

"Stop trying to steer the conversation toward sex, would you?" She jabbed him in the ribs with a finger and he smiled. "I'd rather show you. Tonight, maybe."

She didn't respond until they pulled to a stop in front of his grandmother's house. "Maybe."

As was her custom, Rosemary Ellis made her appearance before he could switch off the bike, sweeping out onto the porch with arms spread wide, trying to give the whole world a hug. "Oh, you did it. You brought a girl." His grandmother tipped forward, slapping both hands onto her knees with a big expulsion of *huhhha*.

Jasper dismounted the bike and assisted Rita with the same, removing the helmet from her head when she made no move to do it herself. Kind of loving doing it for her, too. He'd never given much thought to a woman's hair before, but as he took off the helmet, Jasper found himself easing little strands free so they wouldn't pull in the process. What did she look like brushing it? Probably ripped through it, impatient to move on to something else.

Rita didn't notice his attentions, however, because she was transfixed by the petite ball of energy on the house porch. Rosemary, in her puff-painted sweatshirt—which appeared to depict a pug, but she couldn't be sure—was jogging in place, jazz hands aloft. His grandmother had a habit of listing everything in her sight lines. "Bike is parked. There's a girl. Black jeans. Okay, okay. Whose grandson is that, you ask? Well, it's mine. Okay, then."

"She calms down after a few minutes," Jasper murmured for Rita's ears alone. Then louder, "Now, don't go breaking out the childhood picture albums, Rosemary." He gave Rita's hip a squeeze to propel her toward the stairs. "Unless they're the ones where I'm naked. Even as a kid, I had a great ass."

Rosemary hooted, even though her cheeks went bright pink. "Get that manner of talk out of your system now. It won't be welcome at my lunch table." She zigzagged toward Rita, patting her on the shoulders like she was trying to subdue flames. "Helmet hair."

Oh, boy. "Rosemary, this is Rita. Rita, Rosemary."

His grandmother shook Rita's offered hand so rapidly it was a wonder it didn't tear clean off. "Nice to meet you. Good. Come on in."

Jasper gestured for the two women to precede him into the house, and Rosemary acknowledged the move with a gasp, a hand fluttering in the general area of her throat. "Such a gentleman," she cooed.

Now, he loved his grandmother. Far as he was concerned, the town's motto should be, "Hurley: Birthplace of Rosemary Ellis." But as a man, Jasper could look back and see—while he'd been growing up—she'd overcompensated for his parents' general lack of interest by going in the extreme opposite direction, praising his most minimal of efforts. He loved the hell out of her for it, too. Now, though, he often wondered if Rosemary's encouraging words had been authentic, or if his parents had had the right idea about him.

Not enough to stick around for.

Schooling his features into a casual expression, Jasper nodded toward the entrance. "Granddad joining us today?"

It was one of the rare times Rosemary stopped moving— whenever Jasper asked about his grandfather, who never bothered to leave the living room when Jasper paid a visit, while they kept to the kitchen and dining area. Occasionally on his birthday or Christmas, the old man gave him a scowl, but even that was a feat in itself. Weekday lunch would be pushing it.

Jasper didn't blame his grandfather for having a difficult time looking at his only grandson, a man who'd sunk hard-earned money into a shit heap. No, he didn't blame his grandfather for the hostility, but he wanted like hell to *change* it. Maybe not to approval—that would be a lot to ask for after twelve years—but something akin to forgiveness would be worth the time he'd put into the eatery.

As soon as they were inside the house Rosemary was off like a shot, parading back and forth between the kitchen and dining room with covered plates and condiments. Rita made the mistake of stepping into her path and the older woman nearly bulldozed her. "Um," Rita started, her back pressed against the wall. "Is there something I can help you with?"

"As it turns out, yes. There is a turkey warming in the oven, needs carving."

His grandmother paused long enough to address Rita. "I find these days that women don't know a teacup from a turnip. You know what you're doing in the kitchen?"

"I-I hope so," Rita seemed to force out. "Otherwise culinary school was a big waste of money."

Jasper stopped short of heading into the kitchen himself. "Culinary school." He pictured Rita in an apron and a hat, but couldn't make it fit. Not at first. Not until he thought of her hand holding a spoon, lifting the spoon to her mouth. Smiling to herself over what she tasted. Okay, yeah. He could see that. Liked it, too. "When you said you worked at a restaurant..."

"You thought I meant as a waitress?" She was pressed so far back against the wall that Jasper wondered if she were trying to fit through the wood grains. "You've known me one day and you can barely say that with a straight face."

"I'm smiling because I'm thinking of you tasting soup."

Her lips flinched. "Why would you smile about that?"

"Why wouldn't I?"

"Well, now." Rosemary's interested gaze darted between them, as if they were engaging in table tennis. "Is that a yes to the turkey carving?"

"Yes," Rita blurted, as if she'd also kind of forgotten they weren't alone. "Of course."

She bypassed Jasper on her way into the kitchen, and he followed. If a movie director had shouted, "Act smitten! Go completely over the top!" that was probably how he looked trailing after Rita, noting how at home she looked entering a kitchen. He stood by the door and watched as she took stock of the place in one booted-heel turn. Opening a drawer, she even found the carving knife on the first try. Was it crazy that he had the urge to see her move around his kitchen like that?

Deciding he'd better make himself useful, Jasper grabbed a pot holder and removed the turkey from the oven, nudging the door shut with his foot and setting the bird down on the counter. "Don't forget to take out the wishbone."

"I'm not a monster." Rita plugged the electric carving knife into the nearest outlet. "Does your grandmother usually cook Thanksgiving dinner for a casual lunch?"

"She's the reason for my gym membership."

Rita's answering chuckle was sliced in half by the whirring blade. Jasper watched in fascination as she held it over the turkey, the way a television surgeon holds a scalpel. Focused. Confident.

And then it all went away. The easy flow of a woman doing what she loved just dropped like a water balloon on the floor. With the juggering knife buzzing in her hand, she stared down at the turkey, but Jasper could tell she wasn't really seeing it. "Rita?"

Her answer was a great, gulping sob, and he felt it, dead center in his chest. Jasper reached out and grabbed the knife a split second before she dropped it.

CHAPTER THIRTEEN

Her hand was vibrating with the familiar buzz of the carving knife. And then it wasn't. But the gentle prying of the instrument from Rita's hand did nothing to cease the tectonic plates shifting underneath her skin. Half of her consciousness was still in the kitchen with Jasper—who was speaking too softly to be heard over her internal earthquake—but the other half was back at Wayfare. Not the night of the fire. Way before that. To a night when Miriam had stayed late in the hopes of perfecting Rita's soufflé technique.

* * *

"Wait for the ingredients to blend...let the eggs marry with the milk." Miriam winked at Rita. "They just met. You can't expect them to hop right into the sack without a little coaxing."

Rita rubbed bleary eyes, seeing double when she opened them again. "Is it okay to just admit you'll maybe never be good at one thing?" Her tone was as flat and characterless as her last five attempts at a soufflé. "I hear it all the time. Out...there. Outside the kitchen. People say, I can't walk in heels. Or, I can't draw for shit. But they're fine with it. Maybe I can just be fine with sucking at this one thing."

"Rita." Miriam said her name the way a hearth lights. Welcoming, glowing. "Your one sucky thing is already charades. You have no choice but to keep trying."

"If I was less exhausted, I would have seen the flaw in my analogy."

Miriam handed her a big silver ladle. "Take six."

* * *

"My soufflé still blows," Rita said, curling her fingers into the counter.

"What's that, beautiful?"

Rita almost hit the ceiling when Jasper's gruff voice broke into her reverie, coming very close to knocking the turkey to the floor. How long had she been standing there without saying a word? And why was Jasper holding the carving knife? More importantly, why would she rather go streaking through the fish market on a Monday then take the knife back from him? A weight was pushing down on her chest, making it hard to breathe. Her hands shook—or they did until Jasper set down the electric blade and grabbed them.

Jasper looked at her hands a moment, as if unsure how to proceed, then he placed them carefully on his wide, steady shoulders. Watching to gauge her reaction, he started to sway, side to side. Almost like they were dancing. It was ridiculous, yet it dulled the sharp edges of her panic. But panic over what? Carving a turkey? She'd performed the task a thousand times in her life. "I don't know what happened."

He pressed a thumb to the small of her back, moving it in a circle, and the remaining tension swirled down the drain. "You don't have to figure it out now."

"I think I might have to. Sooner rather than later." The dazed quality of Rita's voice made her sound as if she were speaking inside a closed shower stall. It could have been the cool blue of Jasper's eyes—the lack of judgment there—or the sudden lack of strain after her flashback. Maybe even the dancing. She didn't know. But words passed from her lips, quietly and without permission. "I don't think I can cook anymore." *Or try to be like her.* "I don't think I ever could, anyway."

His lips moved against her forehead. "Now, those seem like big decisions to make at a casual lunch."

The laugh fizzed up her sternum and broke free. "You probably wish you'd been a little less nosy, now. That'll teach you."

"Young people. Dancing in my kitchen." Clapping hands went off behind Rita. *Oh, God,* she'd actually forgotten they were at Jasper's grandmother's house. These people were virtual strangers to her. Tomorrow they would be a memory, and yet she'd totally just had a fucking panic attack in their happy, cactus-themed kitchen. They'd be talking about her for years to relatives and neighbors. *You're right, of course. We never should have handed her that blade. It could have been so much worse. A tragedy, to be sure. Please pass the salt.*

Rita pushed back from Jasper, who seemed oddly reluctant to let her go when he should literally be calling the local sanitarium. She held a hand to her forehead, searching for a way to make herself appear normal. "I, um—"

Jasper flipped the carving knife back on, lowering it to the turkey, which was probably cold by now. "What can I say, Rosemary? I must be some kind of secret chauvinist." He gave an exaggerated smirk. "I saw this little lady attempting to cut the meat and my ancestors wouldn't stand for it."

Obviously Jasper's grandmother was no stranger to his sense of humor, because she said, "Oh poo," while reaching past Rita to hit him in the back with a dishrag. "Be about your business, then. I have plans for the afternoon."

"I'm going, I'm going." He winked at Rita, his technique perfect as he operated the blade. *Of course* his technique was perfect. "Tell me about your plans, Rosemary. If you're seeing Mr. Wells for the third time this week, that counts as serious in my book and I'll be paying him a visit."

Rosemary nudged Rita's arm and threw a withering glance at the heavens. As if to say, *Can you believe this man?* And, no, Rita couldn't, exactly. Men usually found her strange or confusing. Sometimes she got *really* lucky and found a man who was turned on by strange, confusing women, but none of them cared enough to dance her out of a near panic attack. Or transitioned from calming her down to covering for her without missing a beat. Why was he donating so much energy to this temporary acquaintance? And why did she feel compelled to savor Jasper, too?

Realizing she'd been standing there too long without speaking—and paying way too much attention to the way Jasper's triceps flexed as he operated the carver—*gym mem-*

bership indeed—Rita opened a couple cabinets in search of a serving plate, wanting to give him a place to lay the slices of turkey. They sat down at the dining table five minutes later, passing around the kind of food usually reserved for once a year. Still feeling a little jumpy after the memory she'd collided with in the kitchen, Rita managed to eat only a few bites of mashed potatoes, cranberry sauce, stuffing, and turkey. Meanwhile, Jasper put away enough to feed a hungry construction crew, before asking for seconds.

"So, Miss Rita." Rosemary waved a dinner roll across the table as if it were a cell phone and she was searching for reception. "I don't know how much Jasper has talked about me—I'm assuming quite a lot. Did he mention my senior group?"

Rita swallowed the sip of Sprite she'd taken. "No, that might be the one thing he didn't mention." In her periphery she caught Jasper's grateful wink.

"Well. We meet once a week for an activity." She tossed her dinner roll back in the basket. "And it just so happens this is my week to choose what us birds get up to."

"Oh." She traded a look with Jasper, who'd paused mid-chew. "Did you come up with anything yet?"

"As it happens, something did fall into my lap." Rosemary leaned in. "Wouldn't it be a hit if you taught a cooking class? A big-time chef from—where are you from, exactly?"

"San Diego," Rita managed.

"San *Diego!*" Rosemary settled in with that fact for a while. "It would only be a few of us. We could do it at the new kitchen at Jasper's eatery. Maybe in the morning before the bar opens and all the scuttlebutt filter in."

Jasper was obviously thrilled over that description of

his customers. "There wouldn't only be a few, Rosemary. There's damn near thirty of you."

"Twenty-five," she muttered. "What do you say, Rita? Does this Saturday, the sixth, work for you?"

"I'm sorry, I won't be here that long." For some reason, Rita felt the need to avoid looking at Jasper. "My family and I are leaving as soon as our Suburban is repaired."

Why did Rosemary look skeptical? She did. One white eyebrow had lifted, along with the corner of her mouth. And, for a split second, the flightiness she'd exhibited since they'd pulled up fell away. "Sure you are."

CHAPTER FOURTEEN

Jasper pulled his bike into the parking lot of the motel, half wishing the place was another ten miles away just so Rita could cling to him a while longer. She'd been quiet since they'd left Rosemary's house. Then again, Jasper supposed he'd been quiet, too. When they'd set out this morning, time seemed like a relative thing, whereas now it was finite.

Well. He'd just have to set his mind to carving out more, wouldn't he?

Unfortunately, the more time he spent with Rita, the more he wanted to fuck her into an incoherent state. His missing ability to feel a significant, sweaty, down-low attraction seemed to be making up for lost time, directing itself now toward Rita like a high-wattage, phallic-shaped spotlight. God, he wanted her riding him. Wanted to do some no-holds-barred riding himself, her knees wedged up underneath his armpits. Male intuition honed from too many hours spent being bad told Jasper they would move well together. Better than well. *Explosively.* Because his attraction to Rita wasn't limited to physical need. Around her, his faults and decent qualities felt caked to his skin, everything hovering on the surface, wanting to—touch her.

The way she'd made him feel back in the kitchen, when she'd hit him with a sucker punch courtesy of two golden-brown eyes? He'd never experienced that kind of protectiveness before. Sure, he took his responsibility as an only grandson seriously, doing for those who'd done for him. But that buildup of steam in his chest while swaying back and forth with Rita—he wasn't letting the pressure seep out. He wanted to punch a few dials and see how much more steam he could handle. Those dials, however, were controlled by Rita.

He'd waged a heavy debate with himself back on the highway, confident that if he took the turnoff to his house, he could end up in bed with Rita. The *new* bed he'd purchased after burning the old one during a whiskey binge in his backyard. No one had been in the new bed save himself, but he could see Rita there. What he couldn't stand to see? Rita walking out the front door afterward, chalking him up to a satisfying fling on the road to something better.

So he'd gone right past the turnoff and kept driving toward the motel. Now, with their afternoon coming to an end, Jasper was feeling a mite anxious. Okay, more than a mite. In a different life, he might have banged Rita in his office last night and sent her a friendly wave this morning on her way out of town. He wouldn't have taken the time to roll around in her sense of humor or even *seen* the vulnerable girl in his grandmother's kitchen. And, hell, wasn't that just goddamn terrifying?

Without any actual communication between his brain

and his body, Jasper revved the engine of his bike and passed the motel entrance, circling around to the side, where no cars were parked. None of the individual room doors were located on this side of the motel, either, giving Jasper the privacy he needed.

"My room is back that way," Rita husked above his right shoulder.

"All right." Jasper pulled to a stop, turned off the ignition, and helped Rita climb down. He was in a do-or-die situation. Had spending the morning with him inspired a desire to spend more time in his company? Or less? He reckoned he'd know in a minute. "So I'll see you tonight, then?"

Her dark head came up, fingers working beneath her chin to unstrap the helmet. Not for the first time today, he wanted to wipe the makeup off her eyes, maybe count her eyelashes if she was in a mood to indulge him. "What?"

"For our date." He sent her a low wink. "You didn't forget, did you?"

Rita narrowed her gaze. "I can't always tell when you're joking, and that is very annoying." She hung the helmet from the handlebar of his bike. "But I *know* I never agreed to a date."

He acknowledged that with a nod. A step forward. "See, now, I was kind of anticipating you agreeing out of sympathy for a desperate man."

"Anticipating a yes? That's pretty cocky." She betrayed her intended put-down with flushed cheeks, a quick but telling glance at his mouth. "There might be a...small chance I could be persuaded."

Jasper disguised his groan with a cough into his fist. *Damn.* Celibacy was turning out to be a real asshole. Everything moved in slow motion as Rita ran a hand through her helmet hair, tightening the material of her T-shirt. Spiked nipples, *aroused* nipples, stood out against the front. If nipples could talk, Rita's would have been saying, *Too bad, so sad, your loss, hoss.*

"You just had to go and flirt with me...while looking like that, huh?" And shit, he'd said that out loud. There was a Rita-specific weightiness in his stomach, like a warm coating of lust slip-sliding down his insides. "Dammit, Rita. I'm trying here."

Her lips parted on a puff of air. "Trying to do what?"

No one had ever cared enough to listen to him once the bed springs stopped creaking, so putting thoughts she'd so thoroughly jumbled into words wasn't easy by any stretch. "If you could just agree to go out on a date with me tonight, without making me kiss the answer out of your mouth, I would sure appreciate it."

"But that sounds like so much fun."

"Fun for *you*." When she flinched, the slippery weight in Jasper's stomach turned to acid. It took two quick steps to bring him into Rita's personal space, tipping her chin up, even though she was trying her best to look at everything but him. "Wait. Just, wait. That came out ass backwards, beautiful. Look at me, sweating in this parking lot, trying to take you out for some damn sushi. You think I don't want to kiss you?"

"I...is that a rhetorical question?" The way he was holding her chin was smooshing her lips together, making her question emerge sounding like *Izata behoribal weston?*

"Jesus *God*, you're cute." He let go of her chin and planted a thumb in the corner of her mouth, before dragging it along her upper lip, feeling the slickness of original

ChapStick. When had she managed to reapply it? "Here's the thing. I swore off women. But then you came pedaling into town with this mouth, those eyes and the way they *see* everything...and *fuck yes*, I want to kiss you. I want to do all manner of things to you."

Her breath came out in little fits against his thumb while it raked back and forth. When had he pressed her ass up against the bike? Was he even in control of his actions around this woman? He needed to be. Needed to make this time between them count. Frown lines formed between Rita's eyebrows, so he moved his thumb up in that direction to smooth them out.

"Did you just say you swore off women?"

"I did."

"So why are you trying to take me out for some damn sushi?"

Jasper's mouth lost the battle with a smile, but seriousness descended almost immediately. *Important. This is important.* "Because I'm going to see you tonight. I don't want to think about *not* seeing you. And I need to put a table between us so I can find out what's going on in your head. Without that table, I'll—"

"What?"

He lifted her onto the bike seat, as if his hands were being operated by a remote control in someone else's possession. "Please don't ask me that," he growled. "I almost ruined everything last night."

Rita was staring at his mouth. "Who says sex has to ruin anything?"

"I guess..." Jasper stepped between her splayed thighs and yanked her close, swallowing hard when a shudder seemed to go through them both. *Fuck.* Was she having as hard a time breathing as he was? "I guess if I were a different man, it would be a subject for debate. But I'm this man. And I only know you won't want anything to do with me afterward. I'll have served my purpose."

Maybe he'd said too much. Or maybe he'd said just enough. Because Rita curled her hands in his shirt and pulled, pulled until he was wedged so firmly between her legs he could have rubbed her to orgasm with the ridge behind his fly, just by lifting up and down on his toes. "You said something like that last night." She glanced up from her perusal of his panting mouth. "I didn't really...like it then, either."

She'd actually listened to him last night. Heard his words without writing them off as bullshit coming from a bullshitter, the way everyone tended to regard anything that came out of his mouth. Not this woman. Not yet, anyway. And one day of keeping this interesting woman's attention was a miracle in Jasper's book. "I'm going to try and stop saying things you don't like, but I can't guarantee anything."

"If you just said a bunch of things I liked all the time," Rita breathed, "I wouldn't believe the good stuff when you say it."

Jasper's hand shot up and buried itself in her hair, as if propelled by Rita's words. An outsider would have no idea what they were talking about. And he loved that. Coveted it. He'd never had that with a single other person, for any space of time. "Believe this, Rita. I think you're gorgeous as sin and I need your mouth on mine."

Rita nodded, meshing their wet lips together in the process. "I want to believe that. You might have to help me."

"Thank Christ."

Their mouths slanted and somehow—somehow—that feast of lips and tongue and teeth was even more potent than the night before. His knee rammed into the bike— almost as if his leg had tried to buckle—shooting pain up his right thigh, but it vanished under the pleasure. Vanished into vapor. The stroking, hot, abandon of Rita. They were both breathing through their noses so as not to break the voracious mouth-fucking they were engaging in, and that shouldn't have been so all-out sexy. But it sure as shit was. They were attacking each other with seeking tongues and open lips, playing chicken to see who would give in first.

When her hands slipped under his shirt and pulled down on his belt buckle, putting pressure on Jasper's cock, he cursed into her mouth, securing his fist in her hair like a goddamn barbarian. And she liked it, too. Why else would she be tugging on his belt, encouraging him to rock into the notch of her pussy? *Too far.* This was going too far. Any farther and they'd end up somewhere naked.

She'd leave the encounter with no doubt of his experience, because, hell, Jasper knew every button to press, when to change rhythm, when to be forceful or pull back. Knew it all. But Rita wouldn't look at him the same way afterward. She'd see the local tramp, like everyone else.

She'd leave. And he'd have failed in his one attempt to be *more* to someone. To *Rita.*

Jasper tore his mouth free, releasing a gruff exhale into her neck. "You have me ready to bust in my jeans, beautiful. I was smoother than this in high school."

"That's a scary thought," she breathed out in a rush, her fists still curling in his shirt. "Was that the other half of your apology for last night? B-because I have to say, it was pretty effective."

"At the risk of sounding arrogant, Rita, I haven't even moved my hips yet. You've barely gotten a preview of how thoroughly I can...apologize."

"Don't leave me in suspense," she whispered, those golden-brown eyes going as big as salad plates.

Don't do it. You'll have a hard-on for a decade. "If you agree to go out with me tonight, I'll rub that wet, aching seam of yours with my own ache."

Rita's head fell back on a whimper. "Fine. Yes."

Victory moved through his veins like liquid gold. Drugging him, relieving him, propelling him. With an arm wrapped low around Rita's hips, he dragged her forward to the edge of the bike seat. Teeth gritted against her soft neck, he imagined her naked in his king-sized bed, imagined that first thrust into her tight body after about an hour of foreplay, give or take. "I really am sorry...about last night," he lifted his head and husked, mouth a mere centimeter away from hers. *Lord, don't kiss her while you dry hump her. You'll rip her jeans off right here in this parking lot.* Already groaning, Jasper rammed himself into the notch of her legs, pinning her ass against the bike, agonized by the outline of her pussy where it branded the fly of his jeans. "*I'm sorry.* You want the other half of my apology?" Another five rough, pounding pumps that made the bike creak and teeter beneath Rita. *Creak, creak, creak.* "I'm sorry."

When her head lolled to one side, his mouth latched on to the sensitive flesh of her neck and sucked. *Damn right I'll leave a mark. Any way I can.*

"*Again,*" she moaned. "Just a little more. I'm so—"

"Stop. Don't tell me." Jasper ground his forehead against her shoulder, in utter disbelief that he wasn't going to finish her. This woman who seemed to have his cock on a leash.

Risky move, man. You think you're good enough to earn the reward?

"I don't know," Jasper said out loud, taking a last inhale of her scent before stepping away, turning his back to calm himself. Which wouldn't happen if he kept looking at her.

"You don't know *what*?" Rita asked, sounding dazed.

When he heard her boots find the ground, he faced her. "Nothing, beautiful." His throat was raw. "I'm picking you up at seven, all right?"

"Okay. I'll wait here."

They both laughed, but the notes held more pain than humor. "Go ahead inside. I need to watch the door close behind you for my peace of mind."

Rita blinked at him for a few beats before ducking her head. Why did his concern seem to surprise her? She shuffled forward a few paces, then stopped, sending him a self-conscious look over her shoulder. "I accept your apology."

"Now that's something."

She stared out over the parking lot. "I don't like sushi so much."

His chest felt light. "Italian, then." When she nodded and walked toward the front entrance, leaving him behind, words just kind of left his mouth without warning. "Rita, how do you feel about going to dinner right now?"

She kept walking, but her shoulders were shaking. "See you at seven."

CHAPTER FIFTEEN

Rita was still staring at the closed motel room door when the commotion started outside. Commotion might have been too strong a word, but since she'd been sitting in silence for an unknown quantity of time, trying to piece together how some desert-dwelling player had wedged himself underneath her skin in a matter of twenty-four hours, any disturbance in the force qualified as a commotion.

Really, she should call off the date. And if her pride allowed her to go back on an agreement—even though it had been made in the heat of the moment—she might have done just that. What was stopping her from canceling? Why was she wasting her time? Funny enough, she'd asked herself the same questions before the sparse dates she'd been on in San Diego. Those men would never mean anything to her, or vice versa. They were looking for a Peggy. Or some other cool girl who cheered for a specific sports team and got invited to poker night. Jasper couldn't be so much different from those men she'd so easily disregarded, could he?

So why did calling off the date with Jasper feel like sacrilege?

You won't want anything to do with me afterward. I'll have served my purpose. She could still hear the conviction in his voice, the pain. And not deconstructing the recipe that was Jasper and finding the incorrectly added ingredient went against a grain she hadn't been aware of. Although, unlike the act of putting together a recipe, Jasper didn't make her feel anxious. Like she was on the cusp of failing. Just the opposite, actually. Around him, she couldn't seem to escape the optimism. Which made Rita wonder if trying to downplay the good had *always* been her default.

A car door slammed outside, followed by a squeal. Rita would have recognized that squeal as Peggy's in a stadium full of squealers, so she rose and padded to the window to investigate. On the other side of the foggy glass, Peggy stood with her arms around a slight girl. Or woman? It was hard to tell because the hug recipient was so short. She only reached Peggy's chin, but when the two broke apart and Rita got a good look at the new arrival's face, her identity was somehow obvious.

Sage Alexander.

Of course. She'd been so bamboozled by a certain honky-tonk owner she'd forgotten the plan she'd hatched with Peggy last night to fly Sage to Hurley. After agreeing that Belmont's behavior was growing increasingly worrisome, Peggy had called her best friend and wedding planner, explaining the situation without too many details. *She knew what I was saying without my having to spell it out,* Peggy had said after hanging up the phone. It was still a mystery at this point what kind of relationship Sage had with Belmont, but Peggy seemed confident that the wedding planner's arrival would be good for him.

Rita would have stayed inside the room watching the scene unfold through the glass if Peggy hadn't spotted her, waving Rita outside. *Damn.* She shoved her feet into the black boots she'd discarded by the door and trudged outside, hands in pockets, hovering to the side while the two women recapped every minuscule task they'd performed since the last time they'd spoken. Although, to be fair, the yammering was more on Peggy's end while Sage listened with an indulgent smile, her fondness for Peggy clear.

"*Anyway.*" Peggy heaved a breath before reaching out and curling a hand around Rita's bicep, pulling her forward. "I can't believe you've never met my sister. Sage, this is Rita. Rita, Sage."

Sage extended a professional hand. "Nice to meet you, Rita. We didn't quite reach the one rehearsal dinner I managed to get scheduled."

"Ah, yes. My first engagement." Peggy tilted her head as if searching for flavors in a fine wine. "That was a close call."

Rita shook Sage's hand. "Hi," she said, pretending she didn't feel the tremor in the other woman's hand. "Thanks for coming."

"I wanted to come." Sage picked up her suitcase and put it back down. Adjusted her round, clear-framed glasses. Her nerves were obvious, but she was clearly trying to put on a friendly face. Peggy launched into a description of Hurley's charms, listing dinner and entertainment options like the concierge of a five-star hotel and giving Rita the chance to study Sage. She appeared to be in her midtwenties, although with the freckles dotting her nose and cheeks, she could have passed for a college freshman, if necessary. Her light blue paisley dress was conservative—and that was putting it mildly. The neckline covered everything below her collarbone, the hem extending well past her knees, like some kind of throwback to the fifties. When Rita heard the words *wedding planner*, her mind conjured up a woman with sharp cheekbones and high heels that could double as a weapon. Sage couldn't be a stiletto assassin on her worst day, if Rita was judging her correctly.

Peggy's speech was cut off when one of the motel room doors opened behind Sage. Both sisters turned to find Belmont standing in the doorway of his room. Sage, however, didn't look. She stayed perfectly still, smoothing those shaking hands down the front of her dress, eradicating nonexistent wrinkles. After that, Rita couldn't stop gaping at her brother. Belmont was intense at his most relaxed, but she'd never seen him quite like this. Almost like he had the ability to freeze time and they were all caught up in the stillness until he decided activity could resume. Even Peggy, whose hands usually fluttered more than humming-bird wings, just watched, watched Belmont. As Belmont watched Sage.

The sisters had debated telling Belmont about Sage's impending arrival, but thank God they hadn't. If Rita hadn't seen his reaction, before that stoic mask moved back into place, she might never have known Belmont's world was made up of Sage Alexander. It called time travel to mind. A man going back and meeting his wife all over again, while still retaining the memories of their original lifetime together.

He emerged from the doorway after a good two minutes,

creating a wide berth around the three women, eyes never leaving Sage. For the wedding planner's part, she seemed to gain courage with each second that ticked past, her chin going up a notch here and there. But her fingers. They fussed over one of the pleats in her dress until Rita started to worry it might catch fire.

Sage still hadn't turned around when she broke the silence. "Hello, Belmont."

A gruff sound left him, his face turning away. "Thought you couldn't make it."

Wind whistled past in the ensuing pause. "December isn't very popular for weddings. I moved some things around."

"Why?"

"Why is December not popular for weddings?" Rita saw Sage's lips twitch after posing the question and thanked God the woman had a sense of humor. Didn't they all need to have one around this family? Honestly, here they stood in a strange town, outside of a ninety-percent-vacant motel, watching their brother prowl around someone who hadn't even bothered to *look* at him yet. And somehow it all seemed like par for the fucking course.

"Why did you move things around?" Belmont clarified, a hint of impatience in his tone, which sent Sage's fingers back into their attempt to start a blaze. Peggy started twirling her hair, too, which didn't escape Belmont's sharp attention, and it became obvious to Rita what her brother was trying to ascertain. If they'd asked Sage to come because of the way he'd been acting. Which they *had*, of course. But it had gone unspoken that he wouldn't appreciate that information.

Just as Rita was beginning to get desperate to fill the silence, Sage's entire body lifted with a deep inhale and she turned around. Belmont went back a step. And time seemed to freeze again. What in the hell?

"I needed a vacation," Sage murmured, chin lifting, then dipping again. "Is that allowed?"

With his eyes narrowed on the tiny wedding planner, the desert behind him and his jaw ticking, ticking, ticking, Rita thought her brother looked like an old Clint Eastwood movie poster. "You do something to your hair?" he asked Sage in a gravelly voice.

"I got bangs."

"Bangs," Belmont repeated, as if it were some awkward, foreign word. "I don't think I like them."

Peggy gasped. "Bel—"

"Any longer and they're going to hide your eyes," he pressed on, ignoring his sister. Ignoring everything—but Sage. "Could be any day now. Could be any day that they're hidden from me."

Sage shook her head. "No, I won't let them be."

Belmont was doing his best to stare Sage into the pavement, but he seemed to realize it and glanced back toward the parking lot. "Have you checked in yet?"

"No."

Without looking, he gestured toward the building. "This side is better lit than the other."

"Okay."

"Tell them to put you on this side."

After delivering the order and waiting to make sure Sage acknowledged it, Belmont seemed at a loss. He started to back toward the motel-room door he'd left open, but reversed his direction suddenly without telegraphing his intention. He circled Sage slowly, scrutinizing her hair, her neck, her clothing. And she let him, somehow maintaining her poise. Until he brushed their shoulders together and her eyes closed. Just for a second, before popping back open, wider than before.

None of them said anything until Belmont was back in his motel room with the door closed. At which point Peggy clapped her hands together, breaking the slow-motion spell. "So"—she interlocked her arm with Sage's—"was there a movie on the flight?"

CHAPTER SIXTEEN

Thirty-three years old and this is my first date.

That kind of made him a virgin in a way, didn't it?

Even Jasper had to laugh at that comparison. He pulled his truck into one of the numerous empty spaces at the Hurley Arms and ran a hand through his hair, not surprised to find himself feeling edgy. He'd be spending the next while in the company of an intelligent woman. An interesting woman. And he couldn't even remember the last time he'd jumped the small-talk hurdle with a member of the opposite sex. Twenty minutes from now, he could very well be asking Rita her favorite color, but he hoped like hell it didn't come to that.

On the way to pick up Rita, he'd stopped into the Liquor Hole to ask Nate what women like to talk about. After the bartender had finished laughing over Jasper asking *him* for advice on women, he'd mustered up a one-word answer: themselves. If that were true, Rita talking about herself suited Jasper right down to the ground. He just didn't find it realistic. In fact, he reckoned she'd probably turn his questions right back around on him, the stubborn woman. The stubborn—gorgeous woman.

His small talk might have been so underwhelming in the past that it had been the deciding factor in deeming Jasper good for one thing and one thing only. Rolling in the hay without delay. Hell, for all he knew, Rita felt that way, too. Although she didn't strike him as the type to suffer a man she didn't like, even if he was a good lay. He'd have to trust that gut instinct.

Okay, the longer he sat in the truck, staring at Rita's motel-room door in the rearview mirror, the more shitty scenarios his brain would conjure up. Time to move.

Jasper climbed out of the truck and traversed the parking lot, running a hand around the waistband of his jeans as he went, making sure everything was tucked in. Not for the first time since leaving his house, Jasper commended himself for rubbing one out in the shower. Because, Lord. He didn't even have Rita in his sights yet and the blood in his veins pumped faster. That full, deep beat played in his ears, muffling the traffic that passed behind him on the road.

"Man alive, you've got it bad," he muttered under his breath.

That sentiment became the understatement of the year when Rita answered his single knock. Yeah, he had it worse than bad. He was fucked up beyond all recognition. The first thing that hit him was the hanging scent of a shower. Not just any shower, though. A *woman's* shower. The scents of peaches, pears, and oatmeal soap floated out through the doorway and hooked him like a trout.

But that was before Jasper let his gaze drop from her parted—excited?—lips, to everything beneath. "You smell that good under those clothes?"

"What?"

Rita breathed the word, doing this little writhe move just inside the door. The tight, red denim skirt she wore shifted along with her hips, dipping low enough that Jasper could make out the indentation of her belly button beneath the black tank top. "Please tell me you're not alone in there. Tell me there's a brother or sister watching reruns of *Cheers* somewhere."

She shook her head and the streetlight illuminated whatever she'd used to gloss up her mouth. Definitely not ChapStick this time around. "No, my sister is helping her friend get settled."

Jasper braced a hand on the frame and leaned close to Rita, looking down at her body through the narrow separation between them. "Stop rubbing your thighs together," he growled.

Those pointed tits started to heave up and down in a hypnotic movement, a mere centimeter from his chest. "I'm not. I'm just not used to wearing skirts."

"I'm not used to you wearing skirts, either."

"You're not used to me wearing anything." She squeezed her eyes shut. "You know what I mean by—"

"I know I'm thinking about you naked now." Jasper backed Rita into the room, grimacing inwardly over the war raging between the ticker in his chest and the swelling below his belt. Had someone pressed his *default setting* button on the way across the parking lot? Or was he just so fucking into this woman he couldn't see straight? He didn't know. Didn't *know*. So he needed to slow the hell down. But it was difficult as all get out when she was wobbling her way back toward the bed like she wanted to be fucked on it as soon as possible.

She was horny. That was the main problem here. Although, if Jasper used that defense in a court of law, a jury would send him up the river for sure. Because a truly turned-on woman was one of life's treasures. Now, a turned-on *Rita*? She was the ninth wonder of the world. Her gravitational pull dragged him forward until the backs of her legs were against the mattress, until his hands were slipping up the outsides of her lithe thighs. So, yes, this was a problem. Because it went against Jasper's nature to allow Rita to remain in such a state. Leaving her in the parking lot after their dry humping session had damn near killed him, but they wouldn't make it through the evening if she kept looking at him like that.

"I was going to put you in my truck, start the engine, and go." Jasper ducked his head to sip at the hollow of her neck. "You weren't supposed to answer the door asking for it, beautiful. I can't fuck you before the date even starts."

Her hands lifted, rummaging through his hair, holding him in place as he licked a path from throat to ear. "I would respect that, too, if I thought your reason made sense," she all but gasped.

"It does make sense. You'll see." Frustration lanced his gut. Every instinct screamed to give Rita what she needed—what he needed—but his chest felt hollow when he envisioned what would come after. What *always* came after. "Where is your suitcase?"

Rita's head lifted. "Huh?"

Giving her neck one final, open-mouthed kiss, Jasper

stooped down and tugged a duffel bag from beneath the bed. Somehow he'd guessed the location of her luggage correctly, but where would she keep her—

"Are you looking for my—"

"Yeah." His hand closed around something smaller than he'd expected, but the shape left no question about its identity. "Found it, too."

When Jasper straightened, Rita sputtered, staring down at the object cradled in his palm. "You can't just...*present* my vibrator."

Jasper tested the weight of it. "Is this even considered a vibrator? In my experience, they're shaped like a cock."

"It's a...a butterfly...massager."

During Rita's explanation, he watched in amazement as a flush spread across her cheeks. "Oh, beautiful. You answer your empty-motel-room door in a tiny little skirt and now you're blushing at me? If I wasn't already planning on masturbating you, that blush would have sealed your fate."

She split a cautious, but curious, look between him and the vibrator. "Why?"

Jasper moved until their bodies were flush, yanking Rita up against him so he could suck her lower lip into his mouth. But just as she opened up for his tongue, Jasper nudged her backwards, forcing her down onto the bed. She went up on her elbows, surprise evident in her pretty features. Really? Surprise? It was almost like she'd never had a man desperate for—

And shit. Turns out, Jasper didn't enjoy thinking of Rita with anyone else. In fact, he liked the idea so goddamn little that he flipped Rita onto her stomach with more aggression than he'd intended. An apology might have been forthcoming—*might* have been—if she hadn't moaned into the comforter. If that red skirt hadn't slipped so high during the flip he could see her black, shoestring thong.

"*Fuck*, you hot, little piece." Jasper's vision doubled before meshing back together. He slipped his finger beneath the string, running it up and down, through the wetness of her pussy. Then he pulled the thong back a couple inches and snapped it against her warm flesh, savoring her muffled scream, before lunging on top of her body, pressing her down, down into the mattress. Because of their difference in size, he was careful not to lean his full weight on her smaller frame, just enough so she wouldn't be able to escape the pleasure he intended to inflict.

"What are you—*oh!*"

Jasper's teeth closing around the lobe of Rita's ear cut off her question, set her hips to jerking underneath him. "You buck that ass up into my lap again, I'll think that means you want me off. And I don't think you do." Without looking, Jasper slid the switch along the vibrator's side, getting a feel for the way it shuddered in his palm, groaning as he imagined Rita using it on herself. Not tonight, though. It was his orgasm to give.

Jasper pushed her legs wide with his knees, feeling her ass cheeks spread against his lap, picturing the way that black string stretched, hiding nothing. *Christ.* His mouth found its way into Rita's hair, her name freeing itself on a groan. He eased up the downward pressure of his body long enough to slide the vibrator beneath her hips, pushing lower until it met the juncture of her thighs. Right over her clit. And then Jasper dropped the weight of his hips down, pinning Rita between him and the massager. Pressing, *pressing*.

"*Oh my God*," she screamed, clawing at the comforter. "I can't...you can't. It's too much. I don't usually..."

"What?" It actually hurt to speak because he was exerting so much will to keep his hips still, keep himself from thrusting into the valley of her ass. Fuck, he could feel every inch of her through his jeans. The image of that little black shoestring wedged in between two tight cheeks blazed in his mind. "You don't usually *what*?"

"Do it that hard. Or that...*much*." She drew that last word out until it became a whimper of his name. "*Jasper*."

"Play offense," he demanded in her ear. "Push down into it. Fuck yourself up against it. I'll help you get where you need to go, beautiful. You answered the door begging for something bad from me. So that's what I'm giving you. You and this sweet, neglected pussy. Now *fuck* your vibrator."

For a split second, worry broke through Jasper's lust craze. Had he gone too far? He'd all but ambushed her since walking into the room. His needs—he'd been capable of holding them off until Rita. Rita, *Rita*. God, no one had ever felt this good, smelled this good, sounded this *good*. This *right*. Living without sex hadn't even been difficult until he'd seen her stranded on the road. Now there seemed to be no way to stem the flow of want. The goddamn pressure of it was so immense he couldn't stop putting marks all over the clean slate she'd given him.

"All for you," he chanted against the back of her neck. "*All* for you."

When he felt Rita's hips give a prolonged downward roll, they both expelled muffled curses into the dark room, where the only other sound competing with them was the noisy air conditioner. "Go on, Rita. Move. You have no choice, do you? Not with me holding you down, keeping your clit right up against that buzz." He slid his knees back, applying a touch more of his weight down onto her ass, and she curled her fists into the comforter with a cry. "Nowhere to go. No way to escape. Not until you rub your pussy on the offering in my hand and come like you're told." He breathed into her ear. "Go on, beautiful. I won't tell anyone."

Whether it was modesty that had been holding her back or fear of too much intensity, Jasper felt Rita's tether snap. And, *fuck*, did it ever snap. He'd never felt a woman move like Rita, so fluid, like water running over smooth stones. The movements started in her shoulders and rolled down, through her back and over her hips, not even stopping when it reached her thighs. Oh, no. They moved, too, pushing apart and back together with the use of her knees. Jasper's lower body caged her against the mattress, but she might as well have had him caged, too, because he wasn't going anywhere. Couldn't.

"*Jesus*, the way you move your ass," Jasper gritted out. "You might as well be giving me a hand job right now, Rita, with those pretty white cheeks moving up and down on either side of my cock."

"Oh—oh my God. I—*please*."

There was no help for him after that because Rita—seeming to be encouraged by his filthy talk—only started to move faster, simulating sex as they bore down on the pleasure device. Up until her hips started to pump in obvious desperation, up until her moans started to crack and shatter, Jasper had managed to remain stationary, merely providing the downward pressure. Now, though, their hips began to move in tandem, their breaths breaking free in violent bursts.

"We're fucking it together now, aren't we, beautiful?

Grinding down, making it feel so damn good." Jasper used his panting mouth to push her hair to one side, giving him access to lick up and down her neck, hips never ceasing their quickening thrusts. "Who're you going to think about every time you use this thing? Every time you're alone in your bed, lights off, panties down."

"Jasper," she cried.

"I'm going to know every time you use it," he husked against her neck. "I'll know what you're doing, I'll know what speed you have it on. I'll know you're thinking of me pumping against your bare ass."

God, the hand he held between her legs had grown so slippery. It would be so easy, so fucking easy, to unfasten his pants and finish her off from behind. She was the definition of ready. Begging for his thrusting cock. He might have broken down and followed through, too, if he hadn't felt Rita holding back. Just a little. Whether she was struggling against him or the pleasure, he didn't know. But it sure as hell wasn't working for him. He wanted *everything* from her. Wanted to overwhelm and satisfy her enough that she would need him *again*. And wasn't that root of it all?

Jasper moved the hand between her legs in a tight, circular pattern, making sure to keep the vibrations on her clit. She shuddered beneath him—hard—saying his name like a reproof. Her legs writhed, restless beside his own. *Almost have her. Come on, come on.* Jasper took a fistful of Rita's hair, hauling her head back until they locked fevered eyes. There was an electric connection there. Something unexplainable that had Jasper releasing Rita's hair and sliding his hand around her throat, exulting in the whimper that took shape against his palm.

"It's okay, Rita." The more pressure he applied, the more she started to shake, moan. "I like my fucking a little rough and a lot dirty, too." At the exact moment he squeezed Rita's throat, he bore down without mercy, grinding her lower body against the massager without any chance for escape, closing his eyes when she screamed. "My name is all over this orgasm, now I want it coming out of your mouth, too. Let me hear it."

"*J-Jasper.*"

Lord, when she climaxed beneath him it was like riding a bucking mare. Her back arched, legs kicking out, arms reaching out for purchase. There was an answering need in Jasper to give Rita that anchor, so as soon as the most brutal part of her orgasm passed, he turned her over. Suctioned their mouths together for a kiss that worked to stabilize not only Rita, but Jasper, too. Because, hell, he'd never been more linked to another human being before, reading her, feeling her pleasure. While he hadn't found his own release—and, yeah, there was a motherfucker of a case of blue balls headed his way—he felt...fulfilled, just having gotten Rita there.

Her fingers twined in his hair as they kissed, mouths moving in sensual rhythm, tongues easing in and out. Their heartbeats were audible everywhere. Between them, in his ears. The *boom boom, boom boom* made it impossible for Jasper to ignore the throbbing in his pants. If he didn't stop kissing her soon, they wouldn't be leaving the motel room tonight.

With ten gallons of reluctance, Jasper pulled away—and the absence of her mouth caused the first frisson of doubt to intrude since Rita had opened the door. "You still want to go to dinner with me, right?"

Rita sat up slowly and he did the same, both of them still breathing heavily. "Yeah. Yeah, of course I do, but..."

His heart dropped straight through the floor, probably even down into the basement. "But what?"

Her languid gaze slid over the fly of his jeans. "Don't you need me?"

As soon as Jasper's relief was done backhanding him in the face, the compulsion to reassure Rita took its place. When she said *Don't you need me*, he knew damn well she meant sexually—and there was no denying he did. *Badly.* But when he answered? Hell, Jasper didn't think he meant it the same way. "Yeah, beautiful. I do need you." When Rita went still, Jasper forced a smile. *Too much, asshole. Pull back.* "I *need* you to get dressed, because I'm starving."

Jasper climbed off the bed and went to wait at the door, pretending not to notice Rita staring after him, her pretty face flushed, maybe even a touch disappointed that he hadn't taken the offer. That disappointment twisted a knife in his gut, but it was better than the alternative. Climbing back on the bed and delivering the only thing he'd ever been good for, before finding out if maybe he could be good for more.

CHAPTER SEVENTEEN

There weren't many things that could throw Rita for a loop. Working in restaurants—kitchens, specifically—she'd been subjected to all manner of drama, arguments, human quirks, and that one customer *request* that she spit in his soup. Culinary school alone, with its sabotaging and opportunism, had been a miniature version of the stainless-steel world she'd lived in. Throw in television cameras—such as there'd been on *In the Heat of the Bite*—and that behavior was only amplified.

But Rita understood the mechanics of that world. Be the best or get demoted. Be original or get panned by critics. Be be be. Although she'd ultimately buckled under those pressures, she'd lived inside of them semicomfortably for a long time. They were familiar. As was her self-imposed solitude.

Unfamiliar was now. Tonight. This drop-dead-gorgeous motherfucker of a man pouring wine for her across the table. Why? What did he want from her? Not sex. *That* had been made abundantly clear. In fact, her feminine pride felt like a few holes had been poked in it. And she hadn't even known she *possessed* any feminine pride. The women available to Jasper probably owned stock in that shit, spritzed it on like perfume. Meanwhile, she'd sat there on the bed with her big mouth hanging open. Just the memory of him burning rubber toward the door made Rita want to face-plant in the bread basket.

Jasper was experienced. Which was an underexaggeration on par with "Gandhi was pretty chill." When her dates made it into the "might as well sleep together" zone—which was once in a blue moon—there was a lot of awkward bra fumbling and trying to avoid eye contact. Jasper operated with the kind of sexual confidence she'd never personally felt. Ever. She still couldn't quite get over what they'd done together in the motel room— full-contact masturbation?!—while Jasper's current easy, good-old-boy demeanor suggested he'd just come from yoga class.

Seriously? She couldn't even cross her legs without biting down on her lip to prevent a moan from flying out. Everything was sensitized after being given such forceful treatment. Was she even fit to be in public right now?

Jasper reached across the table and squeezed her arm, sending a rush of diamond-encrusted tingles all along the limb. "I'm going to order you a drink, Rita. You look like you could use one."

"Thanks." She wasn't even going to argue or pretend vodka didn't sound like manna from heaven. "So, um. So…this place looks fun."

When Jasper lifted an eyebrow, Rita wanted to dive under the table. Maybe make a tablecloth fort. "Fun." She could hear the rasp of his stubble as he stroked his chin, looking around the restaurant. "Sure. I guess you could say that."

She reached for her menu and flipped it open, seeing nothing, but grateful to have her hands occupied. "I'm sorry, I just don't know what to talk about after...that. You're supposed to go to sleep after something like...that, right?"

His amusement flourished. "Has that been your experience?"

"I have different experiences."

He tipped her menu down, probably so he could actually see her. "It seemed like you were enjoying yourself. Was I wrong about that?"

"You can't even ask me that with a straight face. That's how much you know you're *not* wrong about that."

Instead of his seeming satisfied by her answer, a touch of worry crept over his features. "And why is it bothering you now?"

"Can we change the subject?"

A few beats passed. "Yes." He appeared deep in thought a moment, a line forming between his eyes. "But only because I don't want to hear about how you *usually* start a date. Or end a date. Or anything even remotely in that neighborhood."

Warmth spread in Rita's belly. "Okay, then."

"Okay, then." With a shoulder roll, Jasper picked up his own menu. "I have to tell you, I'm kind of nervous taking a chef out for a meal. Are you obligated to storm the kitchen if you don't like the food?"

"Yes, it's part of the oath we take," she answered with

a straight face, but she couldn't quite hold it. "What is the best thing on the menu? I'm not in a storming mood tonight."

"Chicken milanese."

"Done."

Rita had to admit the restaurant had atmosphere. Slow, pumping mood music. Dim lighting, clusters of candles placed strategically around the seating area. The tables were spaced far apart, unlike in San Diego, where diners were usually crammed in due to high rents and limited space. Turnover had always been key at Wayfare. But not here, apparently. The waitstaff appeared just as relaxed as the customers, some of them even sneaking sips of red wine in the waiter station. Miriam would have appreciated the casual setting, although she never allowed alcohol until the final dish was sent out.

The reminder of her mother and the restaurant she'd loved broke Rita's smile, but she attempted to shake herself when Jasper reached across the table and ran his thumb down the side of her cheek. "I'd love to know what you're thinking about."

She stared to say *Nothing*, but saying that about her mother felt eminently wrong, so the truth tumbled out instead. "My mother. She ran a very different restaurant. I ran it, too, for a while." Her hands were itching for something to do again, so she traced the base of her wineglass. "Wayfare."

Jasper said the name silently to himself. "I like that name. Why aren't you running it now?"

"It burned down."

"Shit." His double take was comical. "I'm real sorry, Rita. When?"

Pressure built in her rib cage, memories of flames dancing and roaring up the walls. "Last week."

For a few seconds, Jasper showed no reaction to that news. It was clear he was stunned at how recently the incident had occurred, but something chaotic was playing out behind his blue eyes, making the muscle in his cheek tick. Rita wasn't sure she wanted to know what it was. Or maybe she wanted to know every detail. "Were you working when it happened?" When she nodded slowly, he cursed, falling back in his chair. "I'm feeling ill over that, beautiful."

Light pinged between the pulse points of her body. "Don't be. It's—I'm—fine."

Jasper looked her over as if deciding whether to believe her, his expression serious. "Is that why you don't want to cook anymore?"

"Who said I—" Then she remembered the flashback in Rosemary's kitchen. The way she'd frozen up, unable to perform even the simplest of tasks. Until now, she hadn't recalled saying those words to Jasper—that she didn't want to cook anymore. But she knew she'd meant them. Knew she didn't want to be less than extraordinary anymore. Less than Miriam.

"Hey." Jasper raked an impatient hand through his hair, appearing irritated with himself. "I didn't mean to pry like that. I'd just been wondering why someone talented enough to graduate culinary school and run a restaurant...wouldn't want to do what they love anymore."

Her throat beginning to feel singed, Rita sipped from her water glass. She wanted to let it all pour out. *Talent, ha! Questionable at best. I don't even know if I ever loved it.* But she held back, afraid if she let those secrets go, somehow, somewhere, her mother would hear them and weep.

The way she must have been inwardly weeping all those years when Rita couldn't rise to the occasion. "What about you, Jasper? What do you love?"

The debate between letting her change the subject and pressing for more took place on his handsome face, interspersed with flickering candlelight. But then her question seemed to sink in—and it sank low. "I love people. Family." He reached for his beer. "But I'm not sure I love any one thing. Nothing lasting like you had." A beat passed as he scrutinized Rita. "You love Wayfare even though it's gone. It's in the way you say it."

Had she really tried to write this man off as some no-account, revamped McConaughey? She would consider the possibility that he might be reading her thoughts—if her thoughts were clear enough to be legible. "You have to love something. What about the bar?"

His laughter was short. "Maybe at one time. Or maybe it was just a place for my friends to hang out. It's hard to remember what was going through my mind at twenty-one." He scrubbed a hand along his jaw. "I sure as hell didn't realize what a mockery I was making out of my grandfather's life's work. He probably thought I would do something meaningful with the money he'd set aside. Turns out he was wrong."

Rita gathered that he was referring to an inheritance of some kind. An inheritance he'd used to purchase the Liquor Hole. "Yeah, but you're doing something about it now, aren't you? Opening the eatery?"

"Yeah." He nodded once, shifting in his chair. "Yeah. I'm hoping it's not too late."

"It's not," Rita said, surprised by her own vehemence. She actually had to restrain herself from reaching across the table and—what? Grabbing his face or hair or something? It wasn't clear, but it felt imperative that she convince him he would succeed. The eatery would be a success, if he just focused all his energy on it.

But wouldn't that make her the ultimate hypocrite? Even before her catastrophic dinner service her first night back from the reality show, she'd been on a path to bludgeoning the restaurant's success to death. Success her mother had all but ensured. What business did she have trying to convince Jasper his outcome would be any different?

"If you're doing it out of guilt or...maybe you want to sleep better at night knowing your grandfather approves...it won't work." Despite her attempt to drown them with wine, the words climbed up her throat and dove out. "Open the eatery because you want to, not because you think it will make someone else happy."

Jasper rotated his beer bottle, those discerning blue eyes fastened on Rita. "You sound like you're speaking from experience."

"I am." Why was she telling him this? God, he would think her twice as pitiful, knowing how many advantages she'd gotten but still failed. "My mother was Miriam Clarkson."

And, *yup*, even honky-tonk owners from New Mexico recognized the name. "From the Food Channel all those years back? What was the program"—he snapped his fingers—"*Miriam's Main Dish*."

"Got it in one," Rita said, her lips lifting involuntarily. "She opened Wayfare when it went off the air. We were still mostly teenagers."

"Rosemary loved that show." His gaze strayed to the side as if trying to recall something. "She recorded the Christmas dinner special over my VHS of *The Goonies*. One of my youth's greatest tragedies."

"That is truly awful. I feel indirectly responsible."

"You *should* feel that way. You owe me a new copy on behalf of your mother."

They were laughing when the waitress approached to take their orders and refill Rita's wine. Jasper declined another beer because he was driving, ordering a glass of milk instead. Apparently the catchphrase was true. Milk *did* do a body good. Fucking great, actually, she amended, remembering the way his abdomen had flexed against her back on the hotel bed.

"What are you smiling about over there?" Jasper asked when the waitress retreated. "Looking real secretive-like."

God, it was like he already knew. Too bad she wasn't going to confirm any possible theories. "Nothing, really. It's just…usually, when I tell people about my mother, they ask a million questions. Did she cook amazing dinners every night of the week? Did she ever just drive us through McDonald's?" She waited. "You're not going to ask me any of that, I guess."

"Not unless it's going to tell me something about you."

Ohhh. And the crowd goes wild. Well, technically it was her loins going wild. Not because she was a sucker for sweet one-liners. But because his words felt genuine. *He* seemed genuine. "It won't," she murmured.

"Then let me ask you something different." She could almost see the wheels cranking in his head, letting off big puffs of steam. So much effort, just for her. "You say I should open the eatery for me, not the town who think I'll fail, or my grandfather." He paused awhile. "Who were you cooking for?"

"I'd rather talk about McDonald's," Rita said quickly, reaching for her full glass of wine, thankful for the path it burned on the way down. She wasn't completely blind to the textbook case she appeared to be on the surface. Mother sets high standard. Daughter can't reach said standard. All very tidy when spelled out, but it didn't leave room for the gray, patchy areas. So many gray areas. And she certainly wasn't used to having her issues presented on a silver platter, which accounted for the touch of bite in her voice when she said, "I didn't realize this date would be so therapeutic."

Jasper's head fell forward, briefly, then lifted. "Shit, Rita. I don't know what's wrong with me. It's like I'm trying to cram fifteen dates into one because you could leave any minute." He shoved a frustrated hand into his already haphazard hair. "That's not even really it, though. I just want to know something about you no one else knows. And if that isn't creepy for a first date, I don't know what is. We haven't even eaten chicken milanese yet."

The crowd had gone wild earlier, but it was roaring loud enough now to crumble the whole damn stadium. When was the last time anyone had been so honest with her? He looked so disgusted with himself, when it should have been the opposite. "When I was eight, I wanted to be a detective." She threw a small laugh up at the ceiling, unable to believe the nonsense she was sharing with him. "I wore sunglasses inside for a month and called myself Gumshoe."

"What's the part you never told anyone?"

"Gumshoe is still my e-mail password." She wet her lips, positive her face was on fire. "I guess I have to change it now."

"Nah, I won't snoop." A slow smile spread across his face. "Thank you."

When had she started fidgeting? She flattened her palms on the table to stop herself. God, the way he was looking at her. Like he'd just won some fabulous prize and it was sitting on top of her head. Crazily enough, Rita thought she might be looking at him the same way. And meaning it. "Also. When I'm nervous, I like to listen to people list the daily specials. Sometimes I just do it myself with old menus."

Jasper's head immediately turned, obviously seeking out something to read from, but Rita stopped him with a hand on his forearm. When he stared down at her hesitant touch, Rita resisted the urge to snatch her hand back. "If you know the new eatery menu by heart already...maybe you could tell me that?"

His gaze searched hers. "I do. I came up with it myself."

Rita felt like she was standing on the edge of a diving board, getting ready to jump. "Good. I guess, I...want to know something about you, too."

He bent down and placed his lips on her knuckles, dampening them with a slow, open-mouthed kiss she felt right in the pit of her stomach. "Will you let me show you?"

"Oh, yeah," she breathed.

Warm air puffed out on her hand when he laughed. "I meant the restaurant, beautiful. I want to show you my restaurant. Tonight."

"Those were some mixed signals you were sending."

Without warning, her chair was yanked closer by Jasper's hand, unseen under the table, bringing her right up against him. With her *whelp* still hanging in the air, Jasper stamped his mouth down on hers, stirring murmurs around them from the other patrons. "Does that unmix them for you?" he asked, his voice having dropped around ten octaves.

Rita nodded, bumping their noses together. Something spun in her chest like silk, sticky but smooth. It took her a moment to decipher the sensation. Relief. They still had *more*. Every time she saw Jasper, it was potentially the last. But they had the whole night now. She should be excited. So why did tonight suddenly seem like way less than she needed?

CHAPTER EIGHTEEN

Apart from the kitchen crew and waitstaff he'd spent the last few weeks hiring, Jasper hadn't shown the new eatery to anyone. After the months he'd spent framing the addition, insulating the walls, carefully installing Sheetrock, sanding and lacquering the floors, with only sporadic help from local contractors, the eatery had become something of a private relic. He'd kept it sealed off from the bar, behind the plastic sheet, distracting everyone from its existence with half-price beer. Now even a man with no food-service experience knew that was no way to create excitement. It was almost as though he were trying to lower everyone's expectations so if they were even remotely impressed he could call it a win.

By showing it to Rita, he was throwing in all his poker chips. Even before finding out she'd been raised by Miriam Clarkson—hell, *trained* by the woman—he'd been on the fence about giving Rita a tour of the modest fifteen-table addition. But she'd exposed parts of herself for him at dinner, and he wouldn't take without giving. In fact, there was gnawing impatience in his stomach that grew stronger as they pulled in behind the Liquor Hole. Probably due in part to him sticking his goddamn foot into his mouth several times over the course of the evening. Going into tonight, Jasper hadn't known the rules of dating, but he could now recite rule number one with conviction.

Don't attempt to figure out a woman's every insecurity, fear, and fault before the meal arrives. It was just plain bad manners.

As if that rule applied to anyone but Rita.

Jasper didn't have an explanation for the way he'd pried without much encouragement, only that she'd sat down across from him looking shell-shocked and puffy-lipped from kissing and being her closest confidant had become his life goal. That hadn't changed on the drive home. And it was starting to become pretty damn obvious that goal wouldn't evaporate with the morning sunrise.

Careful to shut the driver's-side door without alerting anyone inside the Liquor Hole to their presence, Jasper then crossed to Rita's side, grateful when she waited for his assistance in climbing out. He caught a peek of her panties beneath the stretched red skirt as she turned, and barely checked the instinct to slam the passenger door and shove her up against it. God. He'd known his blue balls tonight would be a motherfucker, but they were shaping up to feel like ten homicidal maniac motherfuckers out for vengeance. It certainly didn't help that Rita was definitely feeling the wine she'd drunk at dinner, making her loose-limbed and relaxed.

Lord save me.

Instead of attacking Rita's mouth the way his brain urged, Jasper took her hand, leading her through the back entrance. He caught the screen door before it slapped the splintered wood and removed his keys, smiling when Rita rubbed her hands together vigorously.

"You're excited."

"Yeah. *Yeah.*" She tried to peer in through the glass door. "No one has eaten here yet. No bad, good, or mediocre meals. No reviews. It's a clean slate."

Jasper turned the key and pushed open the door, but when Rita attempted to precede him, he grabbed her wrist. "Hold on, now. If we're doing a big reveal, we're going to do it right. Close your eyes."

She did as he asked, humming in her throat as Jasper led her through the small hostess section, into the dining room. It felt more natural than breathing to hook an arm around her middle, drawing her back against him, exhaling into the fragrant skin of her neck. "Okay, here goes."

Jasper flipped on the lights.

He hadn't put his lips against her pulse purposefully, but *hell.* Having them there, feeling her pulse kick up into overdrive as she scanned the dining room? Might have been the best moment of his life. Because someone paying homage to the four walls he'd built, what he'd done inside them, would have been nice. But having undeniable proof that he'd managed to accomplish something worth a damn— now that was priceless. The fact that it came from Rita made it all the sweeter.

When he'd decided to build the addition, he'd only been able to see shapes, colors. No real vision for what the place should look like. So he'd thought of Hurley. How its people were unique—sometimes uniquely *crazy*—but somehow meshed into a pattern. He'd tried to portray that with mismatched antique furniture, eclectic lighting, different-shaped tables tucked back into quiet corners. To describe it out loud, the dining room would sound like a straight-up disaster, but it somehow flowed together in person. He hadn't quite planned for every table to have a different theme, but that was the way it had worked out. And knowing he wasn't the only one who thought so was one hell of a relief.

"Jasper." She pulled out of his arms and took a few steps into the dining room, running her fingers over one of the chair backs. "Why did you let me think...you said you were just going to open the door and see what happened."

"That wasn't a lie. We open two days from now." He leaned back against the wall and crossed his arms. "After that, it's up to the town."

"That's always the case. In *every* restaurant." She looked up at the chandelier fashioned from faux deer antlers. "How much time have you spent putting this together?"

Time had never been a factor since he owned the building free and clear, so he hadn't kept count, but he wanted Rita to keep looking around, keep talking to him—would he ever get used to that?—so he thought back. "Including the time it took to build, I'd reckon it's been around eighteen months. I've been driving up to Santa Fe on the weekdays, bringing back pieces I liked, going to auctions." He nodded toward the back. "Kitchen is that way if you're interested."

Jasper could only see Rita in profile, but he caught the flare of curiosity in her eyes, even as her shoulders tensed up. "Yes. I am interested...in a minute." A loud round of laughter drifted through the wall, invading the eatery's intimacy, but Rita's lips only twitched. "Smart idea, putting separate entrances. Are you going to serve food at the Liquor Hole, too?"

"No. Just here."

Rita nodded and continued her slow turn around the room. "I can't believe this has just been sitting here, like...buried treasure."

An ache speared Jasper through the chest. "That's it. That's the name."

"What?"

"Buried Treasure." Trying the name out a few more times under his breath, he pushed off the wall. "All the knickknacks and antiques, you know? One man's trash..."

"...is another man's treasure. Wow. It fits." When they stared at each other too long, Rita ducked her head. "But you should name it. It's your place."

Or maybe it had been waiting for Rita to walk through the door, say a few words, and make it real. Make it a possibility instead of just a project. Maybe it wasn't *just* his place and that—*that*—was why he'd dragged his heels opening it. Something had been missing. It seemed obvious that Rita wasn't ready to hear any of that out loud, however. Apparently they were at the point where she would share intimate details about her life, but not the point where he could attempt to include himself among those details.

Rita broke his stare and headed for the kitchen, Jasper following a moment later. He found her testing the knobs on his oversized stainless-steel range. Nodding in approval over the utensils hanging above the workstation.

"Who's going to cook here?"

"The only local man with decent experience." He went to join Rita near the stove, but she'd already moved on to the storage area, the pantry, beyond. "He used to work at a hotel in Gallup and retired a few years back. He's going to get me up and running, training one of the other local guys to eventually take over."

Rita nodded, then she was on the move again.

Since flipping on the lights in the restaurant, he could swear they were performing some kind of dance. A dance that kept Rita just out of reach—and he didn't like it. Something about the restaurant seemed to have done it, though, rather than him. Needing to witness her reaction to every small thing, Jasper found Rita just as she exited the walk-in freezer and could only describe her expression as subdued excitement, with a hint of anxiety.

"You didn't cut any corners," Rita murmured. "Everything is where it should be, functionality wise. There's room to move, to breathe. Lots of ventilation. Anyone would be lucky to work in this kitchen."

"Glad to hear it."

Rita shook her head, laughing a little beneath her breath. "Jasper, why don't you see this place is extraordinary?"

He moved into her space, relieved when she didn't try to lunge away. "Why do you seem so sad about it?"

"Why would I be sad?" She wouldn't look at him. "I don't know. Maybe this is how I always am in a kitchen."

Ah, beautiful. "Talk to me about it."

"I'd rather not." The serene expression she slapped on was fake and they both knew it. "I'm fine."

Jasper reached up a hand, slipped it into Rita's hair, and used his grip to tug her body the remaining distance. "How about I kiss the fine right out of you?"

She exhaled in a big rush. "Okay. I could go for that."

It was a gamble, to be sure. Kissing Rita in a dark, enclosed space where they were guaranteed to have zero interruptions. His lips were only a breath away from hers and already he tasted wine. Woman. *Rita.* There was an audible catch in her throat when he leaned in, grazing their mouths together. Those hands of hers twisted in the waistband of his jeans, as if that slight touch alone could do her in. Which made it painfully hard to restrain himself, to kiss her slowly. He pressed his lips to hers, widening them enough to rest his tongue on her full lower lip. Just resting it, and yet, a shudder passed through Rita like a roll of thunder, quaking her against him.

Without warning, she sucked his tongue between her lips, one pull, two, before she began to kiss him in earnest. Jasper's answering moan was so loud he wondered if anyone could hear it above the music next door. *His cock.* His goddamn cock sagged under the rush of hot need, then hoisted like a rising anchor inside his pants. Rita had to feel it, because she whimpered into his mouth, her hands growing more insistent on the waistband of his pants. There was none of her usual hesitancy in the kiss. He could all but feel Rita trying to distract herself from whatever ghosts the kitchen had stirred back to life. "Rita, beautiful...let's stop and catch our breath here—"

"Please," she breathed, golden-brown eyes focused on his mouth as if it were her last meal. "Don't you need me back?"

"*Yes,*" he gritted. "That's why I'm trying to take it slow."

"Oh...Jesus. I can't take the riddles anymore. I'm not as experienced at playing...whatever game this is." When Rita slid out from under him, walking in a stilted manner toward the exit while smoothing her haywire hair, Jasper pounded his fists on the metal rack. *Fuck,* he wanted to give in. Wanted to drag her back out into the dining room and create his first lasting memory there. One neither of them would forget for the rest of their lives. If she hadn't shut down on him right before they'd kissed—if he hadn't felt right on the verge of knowing her, *really* knowing her tonight—maybe it would have been their time. Their *right* time.

But he would be selling them short. *I can push for more. I will create time for more, somehow, some way. Whatever it takes.*

"Wait up. I'll walk you back."

She disappeared around the kitchen wall, boots sounding on the dining room floor toward the restaurant's front. "That's really not necessary," she called.

Hell. That was definitely hurt in her tone. "*Rita*," he grated, jogging after her. Thankfully, he caught her just before she swung the entrance door open, yanking her back against him. "Don't leave like this. You might as well drive a stake through my chest, walking out of here with that wobble in your voice."

Her sharp laugh was devoid of humor. "What is this about for you? What do you want from me?"

Everything. This acquaintance with Rita was no longer some test of his worth. It was something bigger. He could *feel* it. "Time. I need more *time* with you, Rita."

"There is no time. There was *never* going to be any time." She tried to jerk away, but Jasper held tight until she settled with a heaved-out breath. "God, I know it's a double standard, but…it's kind of shitty, as a woman, to be turned down for sex like that. *Are* you playing a game with me?"

"No," he groaned into her shoulder, feeling as though his insides were being blowtorched. "God, no, beautiful. I wouldn't do that. You can feel how much I want to be inside you, right?"

"Thus confusing me more."

"Okay." Maybe in order for more time to be a possibility—for her to even want more time with him— Jasper needed to leap first. Could he do that without pushing Rita away? Making himself a laughingstock in her eyes, too? "Would you listen for a few minutes?"

There must have been gravity behind his question, because Rita's tension ebbed as she turned in his arms. She sidestepped him and nodded once, falling into one of the dining room chairs. He immediately memorized which one.

It took Jasper a few beats to collect his thoughts, being that he'd never spoken of the incident out loud. Now that it had come time to share with another person, sourness ran rampant in his stomach. "One night, a couple years back, I was on a bender. Nothing new for me—I was probably on a bender more often than I was off one." He glanced at the wall separating the eatery from the Liquor Hole. "Anyway, I fell asleep in my office. Woke up the next evening and headed out to the bar for a glass of water, but the space had been booked. Women were taking up most of the bar with these giant sub sandwiches and Norah Jones music. Back then, I didn't schedule events of that sort. Really, I just let the place run itself, so I figured one of the bartenders booked a party."

He checked to make sure Rita was still with him, found her listening with cautious interest. "It was a wedding shower, turned out. And they were . . . talking about me." He cleared the rust from his throat. "Comparing notes. Laughing about me always being available for a quick visit. But—

and I quote—it was obvious from my shit-hole of a bar that I wasn't good for much else."

"Jasper..."

"The bride-to-be asked if I was going to be the paid entertainment." Relating the story didn't even hurt anymore. More than anything, it was the icy-cold shock he remembered. He'd never been in a serious relationship with any of the women with whom he'd made time, but the revelation that they all thought of him as nothing more than a punch line had forced him to look back. To remember those blurry encounters and how he'd always woken up alone. Or how the experiences had always been hurried. *Hurry, before someone finds us. Faster, I have an appointment.*

"I stopped getting drunk after that. Kind of stepped back." Jasper ran a hand down his face. "My customers— hell, my own employees—couldn't have a serious conversation with me. I'd just become their good time. But they sure as shit didn't respect me." He focused on Rita a moment, thinking of the women approaching him on the dance floor. "You saw it last night. And that was an improvement."

Rita stood, running her palms down the sides of her skirt. She closed the distance to him halfway and stopped, appearing to weigh her words carefully. God, she was beautiful in the partial light, surrounded by his restaurant, shifting on the creaky floorboards. If he wasn't a semirational man, he might have tied her to the waitress station and forbade her ever to leave.

"Everyone does things they regret. Believe me, I know. You should Google me sometime." She blew out a breath. "Those women should regret not getting to know you. And you *will* get respect with this place. I know you will." A sad smile passed over her lips. "You had mine before you even unlocked the door."

Instead of a sense of completion at having earned Rita's admiration, a hole in his stomach yawned wide. "Why do I hear a 'but' in there?"

"Because we're at an impasse, Jasper. I'm leaving tomorrow." She shuffled backward a step and that one, simple movement almost sank him. "I understand that you need more from a woman now—"

"Wrong. *Wrong*, Rita. Just you."

"I can't offer what I can't *give*." She glanced toward the door. "This road trip is important to me and my family. I think maybe there's something at the end of it for us. My mother never did anything without a reason—that's why we had to respect the wish. Time is something I can't offer. There's . . . school and finding a new job. A *noncooking* job. I'm running from a restaurant and you're *opening* one." She blinked as if everything had come into startling focus. "So I think, maybe—"

"Don't say it," Jasper husked.

"This is good-bye."

Rita's smile was sad as she turned for the exit—

But she was brought up short when a crash sounded in the adjacent bar, accompanied by shouts. Raised voices Jasper didn't recognize, but apparently Rita did, because she wasted no time sprinting for the Liquor Hole, Jasper right on her heels.

CHAPTER NINETEEN

Rita's heart banged around in her chest like sneakers inside a washing machine. That was Belmont's pissed-off voice she'd heard, followed by Aaron's. *Christ on a cracker.* If pent-up sexual frustration, followed by a hefty swing into regret and sadness—courtesy of Jasper Ellis—didn't kill her, the shock of seeing her brothers brawling in the Liquor Hole just might.

Standing inside the entrance for a few breathless beats, Rita couldn't move. Since Belmont had gone missing for four days at age ten, Belmont and Aaron's relationship had been stilted. Belmont had shut down, especially regarding his younger brother, to whom he'd once been closest. But they'd never actively argued as adults, apart from the occasional sarcastic swipes at one another. Par for the course in the Clarkson family. The behavior they were exhibiting now was completely out of the ordinary—but after a quick scan of the bar, Rita had a theory as to what might have been the cause.

Peggy and Sage stood toward the back of the rapt crowd, which had formed in a thick, pushing semicircle around the dance floor. Sage wrung her hands while Peggy consoled her with absentminded shoulder pats, looking even more shell-shocked than Rita felt.

"The Devil Went Down to Georgia" was playing, making the fight seem like something out of a shitty cable television movie. Rita winced when Aaron landed a right hook, snapping Belmont's head to the side. Damn. She hadn't known Aaron was capable of delivering a blow like that. How the hell did her older brother remain standing? Belmont looked almost delighted when blood welled on his lower lip.

Jasper laid a hand on Rita's waist, planting a kiss on her neck. "Boys will be boys, huh?"

"No, this is nothing like them. I think, anyway." Her throat got tight. "I'm not sure I know either of them as well as I should. I *know* I don't."

Jasper's regard caressed the side of her face. "I'll take care of it."

"No, I'm responsible for them—"

"If you think I'd let you step in between two men with tunnel vision and flying fists, beautiful, you're crazy."

Before she could respond, Jasper weaved through the crowd, everyone collectively sagging in disappointment that the boss had arrived to end the fun. Did Jasper notice their reaction? Did he not see the proof that they'd already learned to respect his authority? "All right, gentlemen. This place is enough of a dive without you wrecking it any further. Break it up."

Belmont and Aaron continued their staring contest of death as if they'd never heard Jasper. It was obvious the brothers hadn't gotten the aggression out of their systems, and just before Jasper could muscle his way between them Belmont swung on Aaron, connecting with his jaw to a symphony of bone crunching. A white object flew through the air, the crowd parting to give it a place to land. Which it did, skittering to a stop at Rita's feet. A tooth. Not just any tooth, though. *Aaron's* tooth.

"You motherfucker." Aaron lunged for Belmont, but Jasper and the bartender managed to wrestle him off. Rita picked up the tooth—formerly a component of Aaron's golden-boy, rising-star politician's smile. She finally got her feet to move, joining Peggy and Sage across the bar and still cradling the tooth.

"What happened?" She half shouted because they'd just entered the goddamn fiddle solo of "The Devil Went Down to Georgia."

"It's my fault," Sage said. "I shouldn't have come."

Peggy shook her head, curls bouncing. "No, it is *not* your fault. And you *should* be here. Just as much as any of us." She sighed when Rita made an impatient motion for her to continue. "Aaron put his arm around Sage's shoulders and Bel didn't like it."

Rita waited for her sister to continue but was greeted only by silence. "That's it? That's why they're fighting?"

"Little things to other people are just…bigger to Belmont," Sage said, hitting Rita with serious hazel-green eyes before they landed back on Belmont. "I'll go talk to him."

"I don't think that's a good…" Rita's warning was left hanging in the air when Sage crossed the dance floor, planting herself right in front of Belmont. From Rita's vantage point, Sage looked like a lamb facing off with a giant. Belmont's big shoulders were still heaving up and down and his jaw was clenched, blood painting his right cheekbone. But he no longer paid any attention to Aaron, who was slowly being talked down by Jasper.

Over Aaron's shoulder, Rita and Jasper's gazes clashed, and she swore they were communicating without words. At the very least, Jasper's message came through loud and clear.

Don't you dare leave this bar.

Beside Rita, Peggy whistled through her teeth. "Lots of testosterone floating around this place. Let's go order a cosmopolitan before we start growing hair on our chests."

Rita shook her head. "I can't. I'm holding Aaron's bloody tooth."

"I can't argue with that excuse." Peggy examined the object in question. "Gross. I'll drink your cosmo for you."

"You're a saint," Rita mumbled, heading toward Jasper and Aaron. On the way she couldn't help but observe Belmont and Sage. They weren't speaking to each other, but Belmont seemed to be inching closer, little by little, forcing Sage to crane her head back. And then he did something Rita didn't see coming. He dropped his chin onto Sage's head—and just kind of deflated. Their arms remained straight at their sides, but both sets of their lips parted, dragging in oxygen. It was such an intimate moment that Rita had to look away.

She sidled up beside Aaron. "I am the keeper of the lost tooth."

Aaron plucked the tooth from Rita's palm, his laughter lacking any form of humor. "No way I can show up in Iowa missing a tooth. This is fucked."

"Yeah. It is." Since she'd barely spoken to her youngest brother since their roadside shouting match—mostly due to irritation at herself for letting him get under her skin— displaying any kind of sympathy felt unnatural. Oh, who was she kidding? It would have felt unnatural under any circumstances. They might as well be distant cousins.

"I bet you love this, don't you?" Aaron asked, poking the vacant space in his mouth. "Your asshole brother finally gets what's coming to him, right?"

Knowing Jasper could hear every word, Rita spoke in a hushed tone. "You incited Bel—"

"Right." Aaron swiped away the blood beginning to seep from his nose. "Yeah, I incited him. So what, Rita? At least I got a *reaction* out of him. That's the most he's talked to me in twenty years."

A knot tightened in Rita's stomach. She remembered the radical shift in her brothers' relationship when Belmont came home after the incident. Remembered Aaron attempting to resume their usual antics and being closed out, just like they all had. Maybe—similar to the funeral—they'd all coped separately, not taking the time to understand each other's methods. "I didn't realize it was bothering you."

"My brother not talking to me?" He used the hem of his shirt to wipe sweat from his forehead. "Yeah. I can't imagine why I would be bothered by that."

Seeing Aaron through different eyes—despite his always-handy sarcasm—Rita frowned. "Aaron, I—"

"Jasper," Aaron said, cutting her off. "I need a dentist. Someone who can work fast. And I need him yesterday."

"Now that's going to be a problem," Jasper drawled.

For the first time, Rita noticed that Jasper was watching

her with concern. "Why?" she asked. "There has to be someone local."

"Oh, there is." Jasper nodded toward someone over Rita's shoulder. "But he's half shit-faced at the bar."

"Fuck. Me." Aaron dropped his head into waiting hands. "I should never have left California."

Guilt would apparently be the fourth loop on her emotional roller coaster tonight. She'd been the one to press the road-trip idea and everyone was paying the price for her impulsive decision. Her relationship with Aaron was contentious at best, but losing the opportunity in Iowa would be bad for his career. It was her responsibility to fix the situation, even if the word *responsibility* made her gills turn green. "Um, okay. Jasper, we need to store that tooth in a cup of milk. I think that keeps it...fresh, so it can be...reinstalled." She was grateful when Jasper nodded without giving her grief about her lack of dental lingo. "And then we need to sober up that dentist."

Jasper checked his watch. "Might take until the morning." His cheek jerked as if he were trying to subdue a smile. "And then there's the surgery, the recovery..."

Aaron shifted. "What are you getting at?"

"I know what's he's trying to say." Rita couldn't ignore the wings flapping in her chest, especially when Jasper's mouth finally lifted in a grin. "We've got another day in Hurley."

CHAPTER TWENTY

Well, son of a bitch.

If this wasn't a sign, Jasper didn't know what constituted one. Rita had been in the process of kissing him good-bye and divine providence had shown up like a goddamn superhero. Right about now, Aaron and Belmont were third and fourth on his list of favorite people, under Rita and Rosemary. If they weren't coiled tighter than rattlesnakes on either side of Jasper as he walked the Clarksons back to the Hurley Arms, he might have pulled them into a group hug, unmanly or not.

He wasn't even irritated over Rita insisting they didn't need an escort back, because he'd bought himself some time. Or it had been purchased for him, rather, but this was no time to split hairs. He hadn't been about to leave three women to break up a second wave of fighting. Nor was he about to let a chance for more Rita go to waste. What she'd said back in the kitchen—*Don't you want me back?*—

had burrowed under his skin like the gopher from *Caddyshack*. He and Rita were going to clear that up real quick. Assuming he could get her alone. Judging from the sly conspiratorial looks Peggy was sending him, Jasper thought he might have an ally.

When they reached the Arms, Belmont walked off into the parking lot. Aaron stared after his brother a moment before slamming into his room. Peggy looped an arm through Sage's and urged her toward the seemingly endless line of doors. "Come on. Let's have a sleepover in your room."

"W-wait," Rita sputtered. "Have it in *our* room."

"I can't hear you...you're breaking up..." Peggy called back, faking a static noise by using her hand as an imaginary CB radio. "Try again later."

"Unbelievable," Rita muttered, whirling for her own room and shoving the key into the lock. "I'm starting to have that fantasy again where I'm adopted."

Jasper barely managed to catch the door and slip in behind Rita. "The one where a rock star and a supermodel show up one day to claim you as their long-lost child?" He smiled, flipping on a light and viewing the room without the cover of darkness. "I had that one, too. Mick Jagger and Jerry Hall was my personal favorite."

The personal information slipped out without Jasper noticing, because his focus was on Rita's possessions. Her flip-flops stowed in the corner, the giant, noise-canceling headphones on her side table. But the curious, yet guarded, expression on her face had Jasper replaying his words. "I just realized I never asked about your parents," she murmured. "Did your grandparents raise you?"

"They did." He picked up a bottle of lotion, noting the

scent. Winter Forest. "My parents were more than a little young. Tried to make it work for a while after I was born, but went separate directions." That particular hurt had been dealt with a long time ago. Built in to become a part of him. When he spoke about his parents with sympathy—two kids who'd been painted into a corner—he couldn't even remember if he *meant* the sympathy, or if he'd just begun believing his own patented explanation. Like a callus created over time and forgotten until someone pointed it out. "My mother is fine, living in Texas. Not too sure about my father."

He watched as Rita absorbed that information with a line between her eyes, until she kind of shook herself. "We don't talk to our father, either. Lawrence. We called him that, even as kids. Shook his hand and called him Lawrence. Isn't that funny?" She smoothed her palms along her thighs. "He split with Miriam after Peggy was born, but he'd stop by every two weeks, take us to this restaurant called"—she scrunched her brow—"That Pizza Place. He'd give us five dollars each for the arcade and take us home when we ran out. Then one day he stopped coming. And none of us ever talked about it. Or him."

"Why do you suppose that is?"

She lowered herself onto the bed with a shrug. "Maybe because we'd have to decide how to feel."

It took a great effort on Jasper's end not to pounce all over that statement. It sank down into his stomach, making him wonder if wanting to know how Rita felt about him would only ever be a pipe dream. But he didn't say that out loud. Instead, he took a turn around the room, noticing documents beneath the headphones on Rita's side table, a red college logo printed across the top. "May I?" Her hum was wishy-washy, but he was curious enough to pick them up anyway, scanning the contents. "Graphic Communication at Baruch College."

"Just until I decide on something more specific." She glanced at Jasper over her shoulder, then away just as fast. "So, you see, Jasper? Just because we have one more day..."

Yeah, that was his cue to move. He let the school acceptance letter flutter to the nightstand and went to stand in front of Rita. "Yeah, I heard. You're leaving. But I need to straighten something out right *now*." He took hold of her hair, winding it around his fists. The position put her at eye level with his lap, which was exactly where he needed her to be, in a minute. But just then he kept her head tilted back, needing those eyes up. "Don't you need me back? Did you actually *ask* me that, Rita?"

"Hard to tell," she whispered, her lips appearing stiff.

"That right?" Keeping one hand twisted in Rita's hair, Jasper unzipped his jeans with the other. "Would you like a clear answer?"

Her nod was subtle, thanks to his hold, but her parted lips and stained cheeks gave him the answer before she spoke it out loud. "Yes."

His dick was almost embarrassingly engorged as he took it out of the restraining denim. His growl of agony snapped Rita's spine straight on the bed, those big eyes riveted on the swollen, aching wet-tipped flesh he presented. And damn if a little more fluid didn't seep out at her awed reaction. "Still hard to tell if I want to bang you, Rita?"

"No," she breathed.

"No, it ain't," Jasper rasped. "It's pretty obvious I want to strip you naked, fuck you mindless, and leave you whimpering in a pile of sweaty sheets, no idea if you want round two or a week to recover. Isn't it?"

"*Yes.*"

"Good, beautiful. As long we're on the same page."

Pretty sure he would die from the agony of stuffing his turgid cock back into the jeans, Jasper managed the feat, nonetheless. Not without a few pained groans, however. Rita was staring up at him in total shock from her position on the bed's edge, which he half loved, half detested. They'd learned a lot about one another tonight, but he appeared to have overshadowed some of that progress with his naughty presentation. Best to get an agreement out of her before she wondered who the hell she'd let walk into her motel room.

Jasper crouched down with a grimace to plant a kiss on Rita's mouth. "Now, I'm going to see you tomorrow, Rita. Whether you come to me or I show up here, that's your call, beautiful." Another, slower, wetter kiss that made him ponder the merits of standing back up and seeing if Rita would unfasten his jeans again and give that same kiss to his cock. *That's your cue to leave, man.* "It'll be early in the morning when I come looking. Or when you show up." He gripped his erection. "Either way, I'll still have a nasty need to come in Rita's name."

He left Rita swaying on the bed, and prayed like hell he wasn't pressing his luck.

Chapter Twenty-One

So. Wedding planning, huh? That must be...rewarding."

Rita took a long sip of her scalding coffee, not minding the burn one bit. Maybe it would debilitate her tongue enough to prevent any more lame attempts at conversation with Sage. The apple of Belmont's eye didn't seem to mind, however, as they walked along the dusty road, back toward the Hurley Arms.

Turned out, Rita and Sage were both early risers. They'd walked out of their motel rooms at the same time, going through caffeine withdrawals and no longer satisfied by the motel-provided Sanka. Belmont—as if he had some kind of Sage bat signal—had appeared out of nowhere to follow behind them in silence, eyes glued on Sage as they ventured half a mile down the road in search of a buzz. Neither Rita nor Sage had commented on his presence, saying it all by trading a half smile of understanding. Or *non*understanding, as it were, because to know Belmont was to accept that you might never understand him. And that appeared to be fine with both of them.

"Rewarding is a perfect way to describe it," Sage murmured after a time, smiling over at Rita, the rising sun forming a halo on the crown of her head. Some of Rita's nerves over having to walk a half a mile while making small talk faded into the desert grit on either side of them, as if Sage had decreed Rita's relaxation. *Make it so!* "When the couple climbs into their limousine or carriage and everyone is cheering..." Sage closed her eyes and blew onto the surface of her brew. "It makes you believe in fairy tales, you know?"

"Uh...sure," Rita answered, eliciting a clear, clean laugh from Sage.

Rita didn't know what compelled her to look over her shoulder at Belmont, but when she did, he paused in his step—one second, two—before resuming.

"Have you had any strange theme requests? Like—I don't know—a RoboCop or Laser Cats wedding?"

"Not yet," Sage said, after swallowing a sip. "But I've organized seventeen Star Wars weddings, three Cinderella themes, and one Brady Bunch." She looked over. "The couple had been through separate divorces before meeting each other, three children each. That was a fun one. Their maid of honor dressed as Alice."

"No way." Rita shoved her available hand into her pocket, a grin stretching her mouth. "Did they throw footballs at the bride instead of rice?"

"Ohh, my nose," Sage said with a snort, doing her very best Marcia Brady impression before turning a touch self-conscious, shooting a quick glance back at Belmont. "I wish I'd thought of that."

"Ah, there'll be a next time," Rita sighed.

A few beats passed. "There won't be a next time."

"No, probably not."

Up ahead, the motel came into view and Rita squinted, wondering why someone appeared to be pacing in front of her door. As they drew closer, however, the flannel tipped her off to the pacer's identity. Jasper? They'd left to forage for coffee before the clock struck eight. It couldn't be more than a quarter to nine now. *It'll be early in the morning when I come looking.*

Apparently, he hadn't been playing around. And, ironically, he appeared to be holding two paper cups of coffee in his hand, one of them obviously for her. If she'd just waited, she could have avoided coming outside. Life was so unfair sometimes.

There was a window of about thirty seconds where Rita was close enough to make out Jasper's face but he didn't see her approaching. He appeared to be upset. Very upset. One of the flaps of his flannel shirt had come untucked, and his hair stood at odd angles. Concern ticking along her spine, Rita increased her pace toward the motel, only drawing up short when Sage's soft voice called to her.

"Rita?" Sage's shoulders lifted as Belmont came up behind her, stopping about two feet away. "Um. Sometimes fairy tales look different than climbing into carriages. Sometimes."

Not knowing how to respond, Rita gave the wedding planner a graceless nod and continued on, feeling an urge to jog for—*literally*—the first time in her life. Jasper threw both cups of coffee into the garbage can with serious force just when Rita hit the parking lot and almost simultaneously turned to find her closing in. "Rita?"

"Yeah." She slowed to an easier gait, her pulse's rhythm erratic not over the brisk power walk, but because of Jasper's stricken expression. "Uh...you better have a good excuse for wasting earth's most precious resource."

"I thought you were gone. Left." He propped a fist on the motel wall, raking the opposite hand down his face. "No one answered and I don't even have your fucking *phone* number, Rita. And...*Jesus*, you know?"

Two walls on either side of Rita smacked together, flattening her in the middle. One brought a warm, welcoming infusion of—belonging. Here was a man who would miss her presence. She'd actually made a little mark in this big, broad, place, even if it were only with one person. One man. Because that man was so huge himself, wasn't he? There was no avoiding the purity of his strength as she watched him deflate, baked concrete warming the soles of her boots.

The other side of the smacking wall turning Rita into a pancake was hearty rejection of his panic. His distress. Seeing it turned a wrench in her chest, and she was springing forward to connect with him before the mental command fully formed. Although Rita's arms didn't get the memo, because they hung at her sides as she pressed her face into his heated flannel chest, muscles tensing and shifting beneath her mouth. "I just went for coffee."

"I was bringing you some damn coffee, woman."

"I didn't know."

"Well." His arms wrapped around Rita, jerking her close. "Now that you've scared a handful of years off my life, the least you can do is come with me somewhere without giving me any lip."

It was *excitement* that flooded her system, full, flavorful, and a little wild. She regretted a lot of things in her life, but she refused to regret not taking advantage of her time with this man. In this place. "Let's go."

* * *

Jasper figured he must be a marvel of modern science, because his heart had relocated to his throat. It beat there as he drove Rita—where was he taking her, again? The mesa. Right.

Around five miles outside of Hurley, the flat mountain gave a vantage point to the next town and the surrounding desert. When half the nature-made structure had eroded in the late eighties, a local politician had commissioned a roadway be built to the top of the now restored section in the hopes of bringing tourists through the smaller New Mexico towns on their way to somewhere more interesting. So far it was frequented mostly by the Hurley teenagers looking for a place to make out.

Which—and Jasper would take it to his grave—is how he'd gotten the idea to bring Rita. This morning, while purchasing the now deceased coffee, he'd overheard the young clerk flirting with his sweetheart over the phone, asking if they could go to the mesa later. And then Jasper remembered. It had been *the* place to bring girls when *he'd* been in high school—the place for everyone else, that is. He'd never been required to create a romantic, star-blanketed atmosphere to win a girl over. But now? Efforts would be made, and, unfortunately, he didn't have an array of sexy locations at his disposal to bring Rita to. So they were going to the mesa.

And as of now—or back at the motel, rather—Jasper was done holding back.

Good Christ, when he'd thought Rita was gone, he'd been dead set on going after her. *Dead* set. All the times he'd put the brakes on getting physical had flown through his head like winged monkeys, cackling at him. He'd lost his chance. She'd needed him, trusted him to touch, kiss, fuck her body—and he'd said no? Was he goddamn crazy? His mission to be a decent man in Rita's eyes had seemed stupid and insignificant when compared to the seismic pull in her direction. *Why would you pass up the chance to have her any way you could?*

No one like Rita would pass through this place again, and she'd gifted Jasper with her time. She wouldn't be sorry about that. He wouldn't let her be.

Jasper's truck reached the mesa's flat top and he threw the car into park, leaving it running so their air conditioner would remain on. "I won't make you go outside, indoor girl." Having given himself permission to act on his body's needs, his voice sounded rough as he slid an arm around Rita's shoulders. "We can stay in here and look just fine."

Wow. Apparently his smooth talk had been downgraded to high-school level—along with his choice of date spot—because now that he knew sex with Rita was on the horizon, his tongue weighed about eight pounds. Right along with his cock. The damn thing could have reached up and honked the horn if directed.

Rita leaned forward in the seat, releasing a slow breath as she looked through the windshield. "This is amazing. How high are we?"

"Around two thousand feet, if I recall." The way she'd pushed toward the dashboard to look out the window had created a gap at the back of her pants, giving him a nice view of her nude-colored thong. "Rita—"

Rita got out of the truck.

Jasper's surprise kept him in place a moment as he watched her walk to the front bumper, but he finally followed. The wind whipped at her hair, throwing it into chaos around her face, but thankfully the sun was behind clouds that morning, leaving them surrounded by shadows. "I think I need to…get out of the car more often."

His throat—the one scientists would study when he eventually keeled over from lack of Rita—wanted to question that statement. Ask her what it meant. Examine it from seventeen dozen angles. But he'd brought her there with a mission. Urgency the likes of which he'd been battered with at the motel didn't fade easily. So Jasper found himself blocking Rita's view of the scenery, nodding when she correctly interpreted the want in his gaze.

"Oh," she breathed. "Hi."

Jasper curled a finger in Rita's waistband, tugging her up against his body—slow, languid—maintaining eye contact as he walked her backward toward the rear truck bed. The way she stumbled and whispered a curse under her breath, forehead creasing, struck him like a fastball to the sternum. She could have been gone and he'd have missed this chance. No more. No more waiting.

"Jasper…"

He unlatched the tailgate, letting it drop with a bang, then taking her startled gasp as his opportunity to get kissing. God, how long had it been since their mouths had been together? Couldn't have been just last night when he was immediately drowning, fighting against the need for air. His hands wove through her hair, holding tight as he sat back on the lowered tailgate, pulling Rita up onto his lap, her knees thudding on the steel at either side of his hips. Smooth as smoke, they melded together, Jasper taking hold of her ass, urging her to rock against his pained dick, which she did, groaning up at the sky.

"Back of a truck ain't ideal, Rita," he rasped. "I know it. But no matter where you ride it, beautiful, it's going to satisfy you. That's what I do." One-handed, he reached between them and set to work getting his belt unhooked, gritting his teeth over the blinding pressure behind his fly. "I need to do that for you. No idea... you have no idea how bad."

Rita's eyes were at half mast, her chin reddened from his stubble. She couldn't seem to stop kissing him long enough to get her pants off, though, and the longer it took, the more Jasper's pulse slammed in a critical rhythm.

With a gritted oath, he abandoned his own zipper in favor of Rita's, ripping it down, hoarse commands issuing from his mouth without warning. "Need to get you naked from the waist down, need you on my cock." Through the thin material of her T-shirt, his mouth closed around her tits, sucking through the cotton, nipping with his teeth. "What was I thinking, making us wait? I'm sorry. Jesus, I'm—"

"Stop." Rita threw herself forward, whimpering into his neck, taking hold of his busy wrists between them. "Jasper, no. This *isn't* all you do. We... let's... hold on a second."

His brain had a hard time catching up, because every spare pint of blood in his body was visiting elsewhere. "I have condoms. Three of them."

"Good. That's good, but..." Her face was flushed when she straightened. Whatever his expression put across caused her to sag, even as breath raced in and out of her swollen mouth. "Jasper, I got into your truck this morning to be with *you*. I'm here—in the actual outdoors—to be with you. I like *you*." She pressed a kiss to his mouth, then another, those hands sliding through his hair like ocean water. "We'll be together like this. Right now, though..." Unable to completely hide her sexual frustration, Rita winced and sucked in a breath as she shifted off Jasper's lap. "You think we could just talk a while?"

Jasper turned his face away before Rita could see how her question—posed in her typical self-conscious fashion—affected him. Every time he swallowed, someone fed a new golf ball into his mouth, until he finally stopped trying. Had any man in history ever gotten choked up over being turned down for sex? Leave it to him. Make no mistake, his willpower was being brutally tested. If Rita hadn't said the word *no*, he might have spread her legs wide and used his mouth until she turned willing. But damn if lying there under the huge sky, talking to Rita—knowing she wanted conversation with *him*, of all people—didn't take a mighty big bite out of his thwarted arousal.

When Rita lay back, stacking both hands beneath her head, Jasper followed suit. She looked in his direction and every cell in his body went racing.

"So, Jasper Ellis." Seeing Rita comfortable enough to flirt with him—without hesitating or rolling her eyes—made Jasper ache to pull her close. "What is your—"

Jasper stared at his hand, which had reached toward Rita without prompting to brush a stray hair from her lips. "You ruined the sky for me today, Rita," he said gruffly. "It's flat-out mediocre without you up against it. I reckon it always will be now." He took back his hand, using them both to prop up his own head, his booted feet hanging over the tailgate, beside Rita's. "Now what were you going to ask me?"

She appeared dumbstruck for a time, which Jasper decided was a good thing, before answering. "What is your favorite song?" Her breath rushed out. "I thought we were starting slow."

He smiled. "That would be 'Great Balls of Fire' by Jerry Lee Lewis."

Laughter shattered her pensive expression. "That's a good one."

"Isn't it?" He laid his hand down in the truck bed and Rita took it slowly, intertwining their fingers.

I have to make an impression on this woman.

I have to try and give her a reason to stay.

Maybe... I even have a chance to accomplish that.

"Your turn, Rita," Jasper murmured. But in his mind— after the ledge she'd just pulled him back from—he was thinking, *Now it's my turn.*

CHAPTER TWENTY-TWO

Was it self-destructive for Rita to find herself walking along Hurley's main avenue that afternoon, toward the Liquor Hole? Absolutely. She should have been in the waiting room with Peggy, reading *People* magazines from the Bush era while Aaron went through his dental procedure. Or perhaps an even better use of her time would be trying to get the goods from Belmont regarding his obvious infatuation with Sage. These were the people she would be spending the next two thousand miles sharing Suburban air space with. And yet. Here she was. Probably resembling the roadrunner-pursuing coyote, her eyes trained on the establishment ahead.

With the Clarksons Plus One leaving tomorrow—for real this time—she and Jasper were at the end of their plank, leaving very little room to explore the relentless samba in her stomach when she thought of him. But after he'd dropped Rita back at the Hurley Arms—claiming the bar needed his attention—she couldn't have sat still with a boulder on each shoulder.

Pretty much a first for her.

After his attempt this morning to rush them into what surely would have been brain-cell-depleting sex—even if it *was* outdoors—she continued to replay the story Jasper told her last night about what he'd overheard in his own establishment two years ago. *The bride-to-be asked if I was going to be the paid entertainment.* If one thing was clear, as she marched toward the Liquor Hole, it was that she couldn't leave Jasper with that impression of himself. Perhaps she'd made a point this morning on the mesa, but it didn't feel like enough. No amount of time felt like enough.

So she was fixing him for the next girl?

Fuck. That stung like a wasp on steroids. Her step faltered on the dusty sidewalk, and a passerby gave her a concerned smile. Oh, she liked the idea of Jasper being brought out of celibacy by some local chick about as much as she'd enjoyed the view count on her YouTube video this morning. Also known as, not at all.

"Nothing to be done," she murmured under her breath just as she reached the Liquor Hole parking lot. Since the bar didn't open until evening time, she was surprised to see so many cars parked in the lot. Maybe last night's customers had been driven home by a designated driver? At the end of the row, she spotted Jasper's truck and released a pent-up breath. God, even little remembrances such as the capable one-handed way he drove, or the way he'd helped her climb out, as if she were a Fabergé egg— those memories worked her pulse into an insane tempo. Truth was, she didn't *need* a reason to be there at that very moment. Her feet had carried her there because who knew when such a small distance would separate them ever again?

It took Rita a full three minutes—and several irritated curses—to paste a casual expression on her face before testing the front entrance door, even though she suspected she'd have to knock. When it opened with no problem, Rita pursed her lips and stepped inside.

The sight that greeted Rita sent her stumbling back, shaking the wooden door on its hinges. Behind the bar and spilling out onto the dance floor, at least thirty senior-citizen women stared back at her, lips peeled back in bright, welcoming smiles. In front of each of them—on the bar or on folding card tables—little cooking stations had been set up. No stoves or ovens, but an assortment of ingredients, mixing bowls, kitchen utensils. It was like she'd entered a completely different dimension than the bar she'd stood in last night watching her brothers try to off each other.

Rita caught sight of Jasper's grandmother, Rosemary, as she sailed forward through the group of white-haired women. "Rita!"

Her boots felt like cement shoes. "Hi. What…"

Rosemary drew close and encompassed Rita in a big, squeezing hug. "I was so excited when Jasper told me you were staying another day. Why, I got the phone tree lit up right away and moved our get-together to Friday, instead of Saturday. We are raring to be taught a professional recipe, I'll tell you what." She looked Rita up and down. "Black shorts, green shirt. Where is that rascal grandson of mine?"

"I was just about to ask the same thing," Rita said, bolts tightening on either side of her neck. Until Rosemary's explanation, she'd completely forgotten the conversation over lunch about Rita giving a cooking demonstration. Why would she remember something so offhanded when they were supposed to be back on the road by now? It had never really been a possibility in her mind. "Jasper planned this."

It wasn't a question, but all thirty women bobbed their heads with unrepentant enthusiasm, making Rita feel a little dizzy. And at that exact moment Jasper walked out of the kitchen, jingling his car keys, probably on the way to go pick her up at the Arms. Even though Rita had seen him only a matter of hours ago, the sight of his easy ruggedness spiked her blood with longing. When his gaze landed on Rita, she saw the purpose there, knew he'd spent the last few hours working hard to put the demonstration together, but nothing could eclipse the sudden anxiety. It barreled through her like an Amtrak train, releasing black smoke into every region of her insides, covering them in soot.

Jasper was in front of her before she blinked. "Hey there, beautiful," he said for her ears alone, while Rosemary faded back with all the subtlety of a circus clown. "Changed clothes, did you? *Damn*, but those shorts hug your hips. If I didn't have so many hawk eyes on me, I would turn you around and see what they do for your ass."

Why was he talking to her like that? Couldn't he tell she was debating whether or not running and leaping through the plate-glass window was feasible? "Jasper...what did you do? You shouldn't have done this. I'm not..." Her palms started to sting, the sensation traveling up her forearms. "I'm not ready for this."

A shadow passed over his eyes as they reassessed her, a

slow journey over her face. "Sure, you are, Rita." His voice had grown even more hushed. "You were in the kitchen last night and you survived. I thought—"

"You thought wrong." Oh, God, she sounded like someone had hands wrapped around her neck. "I'm sorry, but you were wrong. You shouldn't have done this. I'm going to disappoint them one way or another."

"No. No, you won't." He cupped the sides of her face, eased into her space. And, damn him, it calmed her some. Not enough to ebb the terror, but enough that she could focus on his blue eyes. "This is just a hurdle you need to jump. Let me help you do it."

"I didn't ask for your help."

"No, you didn't. I don't think you'd ask for someone's help if you were on fire." Rita's body tensed at the choice of words and Jasper hung his head with a curse. "Jesus, I'm about as smooth as a pothole."

"Everything okay over there?" Rosemary called, sending Rita's heart into a round of thundering palpitations.

Jasper turned his head slightly. "We'll just be a minute." When he turned back to address Rita, his expression was one of determination. "I didn't ask for your help naming my restaurant or giving my kitchen your seal of approval. Didn't ask for this morning, either. But I'm damned grateful for it. Maybe I just needed to return the favor."

Her head was full to bursting with arguments. Sound ones and immature ones, namely the one echoing the loudest. *I don't need these people. I don't need this. Just turn and walk out.* But then she saw the cookbook lying on Rosemary's workstation. *Miriam Clarkson's Main Dish Cookbook*, to be exact. And there was no doubt in her mind she stood in a room full of people who knew Miriam was her mother. That before she even picked up a spoon, she wouldn't live up to the legacy. "Did you tell Rosemary?"

"No, she figured it out on her own." Jasper sighed. "Every day I wake up wishing I'd never taught her how to use the Internet."

If she walked out of the Liquor Hole now, she wouldn't only be disappointing the women, she would be letting her mother down. Again. They would shake their heads, the way she'd seen so many critics and customers do, lamenting her inability to measure up.

Damn it.

No choice. She'd been given no choice. Resentment at being thrown back into the cauldron so soon making her throat feeling like sandpaper, she shrugged Jasper off and walked to the only available station, observing the ingredients. "I see we're making french toast today."

She picked up an egg and her hand began trembling violently. A ditch dug itself in the very center of her gut, deepening as the silence stretched, everyone watching. Looking for faults, of which there were so many. The egg cracked in her hand and she could only stare. Not really seeing the egg, but all the failed dishes and the fire. Always the fire now.

Jasper walked up behind Rita, reaching around her to collect the broken egg with a clean rag. She didn't turn around to see where he discarded the mess, but his hands were back a few seconds later, lying over the backs of hers and picking up a new egg. Her hands were steadier this time around thanks to the warmth from Jasper's solid touch, his reassuring presence at her back. But the resentment didn't fade, making her acceptance of his help more grudging than anything else.

They cracked the egg together, releasing the yolk into

a bowl as Jasper breathed against the top of her head. *In, out.* Rita finally found the courage to speak after the second egg was cracked into the bowl. "Would you mind bringing out some nutmeg and sugar from the kitchen?" she asked Jasper, craving some breathing room before addressing the ladies. "We'll get the mixture done out here, then I'll bring you to the kitchen in groups to lay your french toast on the griddle."

That was all it took to get her audience chattering, their spoons tapping along the insides of metal bowls, eggs cracking along with jokes between friends. On his way into the kitchen, Jasper turned and glanced back at Rita, but she quickly averted her gaze.

After the time they'd spent together, how could he not have realized being propelled back into the fire would only cause the opposite of progress? And who said she wanted to make any progress *at all* where cooking was concerned? She'd been prepared to move on, happy never to pick up a kitchen utensil again, until being blindsided by this presumptuous surprise party. Jasper's doing.

God, the smells, the sounds of food being prepared were throwing her back to the Wayfare kitchen, flames ripping up the walls, eating up any evidence of her pathetic career. Her live-television flameout. Miriam's quietly patient voice echoing past. Was that smoke filling her nose—or just a hallucination? *Deep breaths.* She would get through this. She *would*.

Hurt was an ugly thing, though, and it wouldn't stop rearing its ugly head, looking for something to swallow. Some*one* to bring down with it. Perhaps Rita had kept the pain at bay too long and it had grown too much to control. There was a voice telling her to calm down before making any rash decisions, but it was drowned out by the ceaseless acknowledgment of bitter disappointment. All her willpower was going into staying put, going through the motions without breaking down, so she didn't listen to the voice.

CHAPTER TWENTY-THREE

You done fucked up now.

Leaving Rita this morning, Jasper had known he needed to do something big. He'd never been a party to the kind of beauty Rita had thrown at him on that mesa. Setting aside her own insecurities to patch up someone else's. *His.* Going a long way in doing it, too, if the new confidence he was experiencing told the tale. Maybe Jasper could fit in a thimble what he knew about a woman's mind, but a man stepped up to the goddamn plate and made an impression when necessary. Of that he was certain.

And Rita was synonymous with the word *necessary*.

Unfortunately—as they entered hour two of Rita refusing to look at him—he'd stepped up to the plate and hit a foul ball. Even worse? A *million* times worse? She looked shaky as hell. Horses-trotting-over-a-rope-bridge shaky. In a way that made Jasper think he might have done serious harm trying to push cooking on Rita. His aim had been to remind her why she loved working in the kitchen. He'd wanted *his* kitchen to make the difference. His presence beside her. She'd made him feel worth a damn, and he'd been compelled to use that gift she'd bestowed.

Yeah, there was even a part of Jasper that had let him believe the impossible. That he could make Rita think twice about getting back on the road. But the distance in her eyes told Jasper he'd been a fool. It also made him want to carry her home, climb into his bathtub with her, and just rock.

If she could just see herself through his eyes in that moment. She moved between groups, giving helpful instructions and smiling patiently, even though it took obvious effort for her to be positive and upbeat. She was good. Really damn good. Her hands were so nimble, the movements of her wrist as she whisked so natural. If he didn't think it would earn him a black eye, he would have told her. *Beautiful, I could watch you move in this kitchen for around a hundred years and never get bored.*

And hell if he wouldn't mean it.

When all was said and done, the demonstration, plus the subsequent cooking and eating of the french toast, took around two and half hours, sending early evening rolling in, about an hour from the staff's arrival. Animated conversations flared between each bite, probably making it last twice as long as necessary, but Rita didn't rush, saying thank you when the women remained behind to help clean, hang utensils and pans back in their rightful spots.

Jasper worried that Rita might make an immediate break for the door once the last senior lady left, but he forced himself not to accost her, knowing it might be too late for patience but trying anyway by waiting in his office. Pacing the floor like a man awaiting sentencing. But when Rita walked into the doorway of his office, locking seductive eyes with him for the first time in hours, Jasper's sentence became clear. And despite the denial his brain shaped on cue, his pulse began to thrum with answering male hunger.

"Rita, please sit down so we can talk."

She sauntered into his office, releasing the bun she'd fashioned before entering the kitchen earlier. It sent glossy black hair spilling over her shoulders, curling at the ends. Curls that would catch around his fingertips, snag in his thigh hair. Jasper expected her to sit in the chair opposite his desk, but she kept coming, strutting right into the space between his outstretched legs, propping both hands on his tense shoulders and leaning down to speak a breath away from his mouth. "I'm done talking."

Jasper knew exactly what Rita was doing. Seduction as a form of revenge. He'd stripped her of a protective layer this afternoon and, hell, he deserved this. Deserved to have his own weakness amplified. But Rita wasn't shaking anymore. At least not in the terrified way. Her poise was back, and he hated the very idea of taking it away from her.

On top of it all, on top of everything in the motherfucking world, he wanted to fuck Rita. He'd wanted to fuck her on the roadside in the hot sun, those black combat boots leaving marks from digging into his ass. Resisting the pull of attraction was wrecking his head, his body. His cock was heavier than an anvil in his jeans, dying to be let out. Dying to ruin that tiny piece-of-shit vibrator for her, for all time. To show her how getting off felt when done *his* way. A shred of determination to talk, to right his wrong, still cycled through his mind, but it thinned every time his dick grew thicker.

Rita's lips were still hovering a hair from his. "God, I

want you, Rita. But not because you're mad or want to teach me a lesson." *Not the first time, not ever.* "Just listen a min—"

"No more excuses," she whispered, licking along the seam of his mouth and frying his ever-loving brain. Her hands slipped down from his shoulders, easing the button of his jeans free.

His deep, prolonged groan widened her eyes a fraction, making Jasper want to grab her shoulders and shake. "*What*, Rita? Goddammit. You don't realize how bad I want this?" Without taking her confused gaze off him, she slid his zipper down, the jagged sound making his stomach hollow out, his hips thrust forward involuntarily. "If you meant nothing to me, I would have rode you on my dick. Night one. Because God knows I'm so attracted to you I can't even see or think or act straight." *Breathe, man.* "But you *mean* something. I'm just trying to mean something to you."

"Stop it, Jasper. Just *stop* it." If he squinted he could probably see the wall she'd built around herself. "I've been respecting your boundaries....I understand them. But you didn't give me the same courtesy. So let's just get to where we're going." *Shit.* Nothing would get through the steel armoring her. Especially not him, since he'd been the one to force her into a hurtful situation. He'd brought this magnetic, irresistible Rita down on his head.

Even worse, he didn't *want* to say no. His willpower had so many puncture holes it was transparent. She was damn gorgeous, a little sad, and, yeah, needy. But no more needy than he was. She wanted a distraction from whatever pain lurked inside her. And there was a sense of responsibility in him—one he'd never experienced before—to boost her into oblivion every single time she required it.

With a barrier a mile wide between them, though, he needed to make an attempt to get them back on even footing, because he would resent anything that came between them when they were finally skin to skin. "I know you're angry at me for this afternoon. I deserve it. So yell at me." Even as he pushed the words out, his thumbs were drawing circles on the insides of her thighs, right below her denim-cradled pussy. *Hypocrite.*

Apparently Rita thought so, too, and he didn't blame her. His brain had no control over his body around her. It craved any form of connection, even as self-preservation tried to apply the faulty brakes. "I'm tired of your mixed signals," she whispered, dropping to her knees with a hollow thud, and Jasper saw curtains come down, signaling the end of the show. "So I'm going to send you a really clear one."

She withdrew Jasper's cock from his jeans, sending his hands flying to the armrests, his teeth gritting so hard they could have shattered. His control thinned and stretched as Rita perused him, base to tip, pleasure—and, yeah, maybe a little awe—infusing her expression. She closed her fist around his thick flesh and jacked him once, twice, making Jasper twist in the chair like a man being tortured for information. "Oh, Christ. I'm in pain here. Real bad. Don't play with me."

His eyes were riveted by the pink, feminine tongue that flicked out against his head, then licked more thoroughly, tilting her head one way, then the other. "Playing is kind of the point, isn't it?"

The armrest creaked beneath Jasper's hands. His rational self was vanishing as if it had never been there. What would come after—after they both relieved themselves of lust? That eventuality was fast being overshadowed by the guarantee of hot, filthy, in-the-moment, unrepentant banging. Needing to be inside her. Needing her mouth, needing to pound the pussy he'd masturbated the night before. It was waiting for him, begging for him. It was his. But not until he claimed it.

Oh shit, that last part did him in. Not his? *Rita was not his yet?*

Moving all on their own, Jasper's hands delved into Rita's hair. "Quit playing," he growled, freedom expanding every molecule in his body. "Get a little purr started in the back of your throat and take me back there to feel it."

Rita's mouth had just sunk down to cover the head of his dick, but she paused at his words, surprise coloring her cheeks.

"Tired of mixed signals, isn't that right?" He massaged her scalp in rough circles, until her eyelids drooped, little gasps puffing past her lips. "I need you hungry for cock. I need you to let me feed mine to you."

Surprise gave way to lust right before his eyes, though, like a cloud passing over the sun. And she obeyed orders, his Rita. Fuck, did she ever obey. That raspy hum in the back of her throat was the sweetest sound he'd ever heard, but the suction from her mouth? A fucking revelation. Jasper's heels dug into the wooden floor, his fingers beginning to ache from being curled so tightly in her hair. If there was a dose of wrongness to having Rita service him from her knees in his place of business, that only served to harden him more at this point. He was gone. Gone for that pouty, torturous little mouth of hers.

"Keep your hands busy," Jasper half shouted straight up at the ceiling. "Jerk me off. I can't stand the fucking *ache* anymore." His thigh muscles were shaking, straining, loosening, tightening, the agony only increasing when Rita fisted his base and stroked in quick, up-and-down motions. "I've wanted that mouth. Wanted to slide inside and feel your tongue along the underside and it's better, so much goddamn better than I thought. If you love it, purr for me, let me feel...*fuck*, Rita."

Jasper's lower back was starting to twist, telegraphing the point of no return. A decision needed to be made soon, or he would bathe that purring throat with his seed. Rita showed no signs of slowing, though, her hair tangling on his thighs as she lowered her mouth, again, again, again.

"Rita, stop. Stop and talk to me." He wound Rita's hair around his fists and drew her away, groaning curses at the loss. And, Jesus, her lust-dazed expression, those puffy, parted lips, almost had him thrusting back into her mouth to finish himself off, but he resisted, beating himself off with tight, slow strokes instead. "Better climb up here now if you want to fuck. Another minute in that mouth and I'll be begging you to swallow for me."

With Jasper's words hanging in the air, Rita rose to her feet, both sets of their hands attacking the zipper of her shorts, knocking into one another. The imminent reality of fucking Rita made him frantic, had him ripping the green shirt over her head, tugging her bra low, then racing back down to assist with her shorts.

"God, Rita. Your tits." He leaned forward to suck one attention-seeking bud into his mouth, pulling back to flick his tongue against it. "You want something done to those pretty babies while I'm giving you this cock, I want to hear about it. Understand? If you want them sucked or smacked or spat on, you speak up." He palmed her breasts, holding the nipples in place so he could rake his tongue from one peak, over to the next. "I'm going to lose my mind when I'm sunk between your legs, but don't let me forget about these."

Slipping into this old skin should have been smoother, but for once, the currents of desire weren't simply below his belt. They were moving in pulsing waves through his chest, through the pounding organ that seemed to be typing Rita's name in Morse code. No, there was nothing smooth about diving off a cliff with only a slim chance of survival, but the fall—*Jesus*, the fall would blow his mind, wouldn't it?

Jasper pushed Rita's shorts down her legs, his mouth racing across her stomach, attacking her hips, inhaling, *inhaling*. Memorizing every whimper, every scrape of his teeth that made her body writhe. He sensed her continually renewed surprise every time he found a new erogenous zone. Deep in her belly button, in the crease between her thigh and pussy. And it stoned him, turned him into a fuck-drunk fiend. Goddamn, how would she react when his dick was finally sliding in and out? Would she expect it to be so good? Or would her lips part in amazement, the way they were doing now? Again and again. Because, hell, if she kept up that innocent shock when they got to the main event, he'd have to close his eyes to prevent coming after one pump.

"I'm getting the feeling"—Jasper jerked Rita's panties down to midthigh before trailing his fingers up the inside of her right leg, toward her pussy—"that you haven't been properly seen to, beautiful. We're going to change that."

"How?" she breathed, sounding anxious.

Jasper stood, bringing their faces close together so he could watch Rita's eyes. Then he pushed his middle finger into her damp pussy, moaning at the way she flexed around him, the way her gaze went blind. "You let me worry about how. You just worry about taking my cock into this tight little sweetheart. How does that sound?"

If he hadn't been so focused on Rita's reactions, her eyes, he might have missed the battle playing out. Being the shot-caller in bed came naturally to him; it wasn't something he had to think about. But with him and Rita on such shaky footing, maybe he should have. Before he could kiss her back onto his side, Rita evaded his mouth, sucking in a gulping breath. She shook her hips, sending the panties gliding down her legs to the floor, before turning around, presenting her upturned backside, and planting both hands on the desk. "I want you like this," she husked over her shoulder.

"Do you." Those currents traveling through Jasper's chest hit a speed bump, lancing him with something akin to pain. Over the last couple days, he'd imagined fucking Rita a multitude of ways, but she'd always been facing him. Their mouths had always been fastened together whether he had her up against the wall or tangled up in the sheets of his bed. This was how she planned to slay him, then.

Keeping it—impersonal.

Unfortunately, being aware of her plan did nothing to lessen the rigidity of his cock or make him any less out-of-his-mind starved for her. Not when her back was arched just enough to give him perfect access to that sweet, pink pussy, from which the dew still slicked his middle finger. Already he was fisting his distended flesh, preparing to smack it against her backside, just a few times, before sinking in up to his aching balls. Lord, she was squirming for it, too. Wanted it down and dirty—and he wanted to satisfy that need. There might have even been a sick part of Jasper that wanted Rita to have a hard time keeping up with his bruising pace, wanted her to wish she'd opted to make love with him in his bed instead of bending over his desk and taking it while his balls slapped the front drawer.

All these thoughts passed in a matter of seconds, but it was long enough for Rita to turn her head and send him a self-conscious—albeit breathless—glance. "Jasper..."

He yanked open the side drawer of his desk, pushing papers aside until he found a condom, rolling it to the root of his dick in seconds. "You keep on saying my name like that while you spread your legs, beautiful." He put a palm flat on Rita's back, pushing her face down on the desk. "Welcome to show-and-tell. You're going to slide those sexy legs apart and *show* me where I'll have the privilege of putting this hungry cock. And I'll *tell* you to spread them wider."

Rita's back started to rise and fall in rapid shudders beneath his hand, but she followed his instructions, feet shuffling wider on the wooden floor. Jasper's own breathing grew erratic, sweat dampening his forehead. He whipped off his T-shirt, resentful of even the split second when his shirt blocked Rita from his view.

"I'm going to finger you. Want to make sure you're a wet girl for me," Jasper rasped, acting out his words with a sharp curse. "Dripping, ain't you? And that's real good, because the next thing you'll feel is my fuck. The only thing you ever need to feel." He smacked his flesh against the underside of her cheeks. "Hang on to the edge."

Rita's hands scrambled for purchase a second before Jasper pushed his dick inside her hot recess, inch by painstaking inch, guiding his girth with a hand. His uneven bellow was unrecognizable, colliding with Rita's muffled scream in the still office. He was forced to rear back and slam forward to stretch her for those final couple inches, lifting Rita's feet off the ground with the force of it. "Oh...holy shit," she cried out. "Oh my God. Oh my fucking—"

"My name isn't hard to remember, Rita. *Use it.*"

"Jasper. *Jasper.* Don't move...okay, move. *Move.*"

As if an apocalypse could convince him to pull out now. She was so tight he could feel the sensation in his throat. Wrong. He'd been wrong. There was nothing down and dirty about this. The act, his words, might tell one tale, but his head and soul heard another. Jasper fell forward and planted a kiss in the center of Rita's spine, trailing his mouth up to her neck for a rough love bite. And then there was nothing but sweaty fucking. He slid his arms beneath Rita's shoulders, curling them around her for leverage. To prevent her from moving, escaping his pounding hips. The desk groaned, protesting the animalistic mating taking place on its surface, but Jasper registered the sound with only dim recognition, because there was only Rita and the perfect, pliant, welcome of her body.

"Fuck, I would love to see myself pumping into you from behind. Love to see you on tiptoes taking it like the devil intended." He released one of Rita's shoulders in favor of fisting her hair. "I'm dripping sweat onto your ass, beautiful. Watching it roll down between those jiggling cheeks. What do you think of that?"

"I like it," she heaved out, pressing her ass up against his belly even higher. "More. I want it."

Jasper jerked her head to the side, sliding bared teeth over her exposed shoulder, up the column of her neck. "How are your tits? Do they need anything from me? I could flip you over and suck them for a while."

"No," she screamed. "Don't...please. Don't stop."

"Who said anything about stopping?" His drives became wild, relentless, the sound of his balls hitting wood and wet flesh, picking up rhythm. "I'd just throw one of these legs over, spin you right around on that cock you're enjoying so much." His teeth snagged her earlobe and pulled. "Flexible as fuck, aren't you? I know what kind of body I've got beneath me. I know what you can take, so don't question me."

His hand twisted the strands of her hair until she agreed. "*Okay.* I won't."

Jasper's eyelids drooped, his lower back muscles going tight. On top of Rita having the wettest, most constricting pussy he could have dreamed up, hearing her submit had pushed him too far. It was only a matter of a minute before his come filled the condom and yeah—*fuck, yeah*—there was a beast raging inside him to lose the latex and ride out his orgasm bareback. An impulse he'd never experienced in his lifetime. It took an actual, concerted effort to check the urge. "Rita, Rita, Rita. You're strangling the fuck out of me." He let go of her hair in favor of throwing one of her knees onto the desk, finding an angle that would drive her over the edge. And then he used the same hand to grip her throat, with only the barest hint of mercy. "Forget the air, Rita. You only need me to breathe."

She splintered apart around him, screaming into the desk surface, her pussy twisting like a vise around his dick. Turning him into a pounding wild man, his hips jerking forward without a single command from his brain. He never released his hold on her throat, knowing instinctively her orgasm would reach another level if he kept up the pressure. *Pressure.* Everything. Zigzagging up and down his spine, filling his balls until he was speaking unintelligible words into the space above her violently shaking body.

"Ahhh, Christ, beautiful. Keep your ass up for me, take my come." He fell forward onto her back, sliding in their mutual perspiration, his hips moving as if detached from his body. Pistoning. Humping in broken patterns, like he'd never been inside a woman before. Like he only knew the pleasure of driving his dick home and couldn't stop indulging. *Indulging.* "Push up on your toes and spread. *Wider.* Wide enough to question your morals later when you look in the mirror." An involuntary snarl left him. "You're going to take all of it. You and this gorgeous cunt."

He watched through hazy vision as her knuckles turned white on the desk's edge, felt her bottom lift against his belly—and lost his grip on reality. The room faded to black around him, or he might have lost consciousness, his body draining of tension, pleasure wrapping around his gut like slowly fading fog. It wasn't the two years of abstaining making his reaction so fierce, so all consuming. Rita. It was Rita. It was so obvious in the way his heart tried to rip through his chest, the way he gathered her up like a greedy man, coveting, holding on to a life raft in a storm.

"Rita, oh God. *Rita.*" They deflated onto the desk, every inch of their bodies molded together in an arch to accommodate the bent-over position. Jasper burrowed his face into the curve of her neck, positive he would never breathe normally again. Or eat or sleep or talk normally. Ever again. An intense urgency still existed inside him, despite his body's utterly sated state. It had something to do with her choppy breathing, his weight pressing her down. Was she comfortable? Had he been too rough? What happened now? She probably *needed* something from him, and he had no experience making a woman feel cared for after sex. They usually just took care of themselves, but he couldn't allow that to be the case with Rita. God, he was *desperate* for the chance to care for her.

Jasper opened his mouth to speak, but stopped when he noticed her knuckles were still white where they gripped the desk. Which led to a whole slew of noticing. Tension crept back into her body beneath him, her breath slowing and eventually stopping altogether. Distance yawned between them, two sides of fertile earth cracking apart with the force of an earthquake. It was like watching his own personal nightmare play out on a movie screen.

"Rita," he tried, hoarsely. "Tell me what's wrong."

Her fingers straightened, flexed, her flattened palms sliding back toward her sides. "What could be wrong?" The sound of her clearing her throat was gentle, guarded. "That was... wow. The best I've ever had."

A hardball hit him square in the stomach. "Good to know."

"Yeah." Rita pushed upward, forcing Jasper to lift off of her, easing from the heat of her body and stepping back to watch her with caution.

She was a goddamn sight, flushed from their rigorous session, the fading sheen of sweat making her fresh and dewy. But all Jasper could see was the way her hand lifted, tucking a stray hair behind her ear. The polite, impersonal, *How-soon-can-I-leave* smile she cast in his direction. And he might have just slipped right into uncharted territory in Pissed-Off Land. The shame, the anger, the denial over acting the available stud—it accumulated, starting in his fingertips, encompassing his entire being in a matter of seconds. Zero to one hundred and fifty.

Best she'd ever had. Nothing about him as a man. Only his skill. Worse, Rita might have initiated the impersonal romp, but instead of correcting the balance between them, he'd followed through and proven himself the good fuck with no strings attached everyone knew him to be. Maybe they'd been right all along.

"Go," he managed to say, pushing the single syllable through stiff lips, replacing his cock inside his jeans with brisk movements.

Rita paused in the act of buttoning her shorts. "What?"

"*Go.*" Self-preservation was a powerful thing, it turned out. More powerful than the voice shouting at him to hold her, to *not* allow her to leave. Because that was exactly what Rita was preparing to do. Fuck him and run. Just like the rest of them, only this time he wouldn't remain standing so easily. He could not—would not—beg and watch her leave anyway. It would kill him. So he would do the opposite. Maybe it would be the difference between folding and staying upright. "Go on. You got what was coming to you. Sorry I made you wait a couple days." Making sure to look her square in the eye so she could see how she'd fucking wrecked him, Jasper strode to the door and threw it open. "Get out."

Rita flinched like she'd been slapped, but somehow Jasper still sensed a lack of surprise over his reaction as she hurried through fixing her askew bra, tugging the shirt over her head. When her arm went through the head hole and she was forced to try again, a sob wrenched from her mouth, fingers tangling in their haste to correct the garment. Without thinking, Jasper lunged toward Rita a giant step, reaching out to assist her, but she was already past him.

"I didn't…this wasn't me. Or-or you," Rita said at the

door, turning slightly, fist pressed to her mouth. "Someday someone will stay afterward. I promise."

Jasper swore he could hear every single footstep she took from his bar to the motel. Counted them off like they were the remaining seconds of a game where his life was at stake. And when the buzzer went off, he'd lost.

Chapter Twenty-Four

Rita was well acquainted with walks of shame. And she didn't consider taking public transportation home from a man's house—in last night's clothes—shameful. No, this half-jog down the dusty main drag through Hurley was the epitome of shame. Passersby slowed in their cars, some even rolling down their windows to inquire if she needed assistance, to which she could only manage a tight head shake. With each step, her feet slid up and back on the soles of her boots, almost as if she'd shrunk with the over-powering self-disgust. Up ahead, the car-repair garage grew larger, and that's where she headed, desperate for the Suburban to be ready so they could get the hell out of Dodge.

I am pond scum.

Jasper's hoarse command for her to leave replayed over and over, making her trip on the sidewalk. *God.* What had she done? Maybe if the cooking demonstration hadn't been so damn long, if she'd just found a way to stop the smoke and memories from crowding out logic, she wouldn't have behaved like such a fantastic tool. But the simple act of cooking again had been too big a reminder of everything she'd left behind. *Everything* had been too big, too encroaching, and eventually the need to sever ties with the whole situation—including Jasper—had taken hold. How dare he foist the past on her when he didn't understand it? No one did. With that sentiment ringing in her mind, she'd used the only weapon she had against him. Sex. Leaving. Treating their assignation in the office like any other depersonalized, no-strings encounter.

Sex with Jasper had been the furthest thing from depersonalized, though, hadn't it? More like life-altering. Jasper talked a big game, and backed it up with something even better. Jasper Ellis was the god of sex. And—*and*—he was way, way fucking more than that. He was everything underneath the sex. An understanding, funny, caring, insightful man who'd only been attempting to break through to her.

Well, she'd saved him the eventual disappointment, hadn't she?

Rita couldn't make anyone happy. Not Miriam, who had failed to impart her genius, despite Rita being the chosen one to follow in her footsteps. Not her siblings, who'd seen no reason to connect or communicate with her post-funeral. Not her staff, her customers, the judges or contestants on the reality show. No one. And it would be no different with Jasper, except she wouldn't have her one-bedroom apartment to hide away in. She'd be in a strange place with unfamiliar people. No way out but failure.

Rita stomped to a halt as a realization occurred like a blast of lightning. Somewhere in the further recesses of her mind, she must have considered the possibility of staying in Hurley. Otherwise, how could she deny the prospect now?

Serving to torture her further, the sound of Jasper's heavy breaths invaded her head, echoing and beautiful. The way he'd gathered her close, like a coveted relic. She'd seen a sliver of light, a tiny chance to correct her mistake before the betrayal took hold. *I can fix this,* she'd thought. *What if I stayed, tried making Jasper happy?* But that same sliver of light had allowed Jasper to see right through her first. When he'd told her to leave, she'd almost been *proud* of him. It was nothing short of what she'd deserved. He'd worked all morning to do something nice for her—she'd repaid the man by treating him like garbage.

Rita looked up to see she'd grown even with the garage. Both corrugated metal doors were shut, no activity on the other side of the Plexiglas windows. In the middle of the day? She jumped with a yelp when Aaron came striding around the corner of the building, an ice pack pressed to his swollen jaw. "We're being fucked with."

Okay, her head was way too wrecked for human interaction, but her usual perfect brother's faulty speech definitely deserved a few minutes of time. "What do you mean?" She pressed two fingers to her forehead, rubbing in a circle. "Shouldn't you be recovering from dental surgery?"

His answer was offhand. "I slept for an hour."

"Probably snored the whole time."

He tore his narrow-eyed gaze off the closed garage. "Excuse me?"

"You didn't snore, as a kid, I don't think. But you do now." She yanked the rubber band off her wrist, pulling her hair back into a ponytail. "No one's ever told you?"

Maybe she should have taken a moment to watch Aaron

closely before now. She'd always thought of him as a cold machine, but thoughts rippled and popped and smoothed under his surface, like a submarine traveling under still water. It was fascinating up close. Normally, looking directly at anyone—especially Aaron—this long would make her skin feel too thin, but she'd gone way past that point this afternoon, and her usual awkwardness receptors were in the shop, alongside the Suburban. "No, I've never been told," her brother said, finally. "Women don't usually stick around to spend the night, thank God."

"Yeah." Wow. None of them were normal. "Yeah, thank God. I guess."

Aaron paced away and came back. "All right, what's with the wounded-puppy act you've got going on?" He adjusted the ice pack. "It's sadder than usual."

"Oh yeah?" She kicked a rock at his shoe, a little surprised by her display of athleticism. "Well…you're being more of a *punk-ass* than usual."

Her brother surprised her by cracking a small smile, but a wince followed right on its heels. "Something to do with Jasper, isn't it?" His attention shifted to the garage. "Jesus. I don't even want to know."

Of course, that anti-permission—and the ingrained sisterly instinct to annoy her brother at all costs—sent the whole damn story tumbling from Rita's mouth. "Well I'm going to tell you, anyway," she heaved out. "He's fucking…wonderful. And I ruined it by having sex with him."

"You must be doing it wrong," Aaron droned, not bothering to look at her.

"I'm doing everything wrong," she shouted. "*Everything.*"

When Aaron removed the ice pack from his jaw and threw it up against the building, Rita gaped. "What did you expect to happen, Rita? Maybe you'd settle down in this population-twenty dust bowl and have little flannel-wearing babies?" His laughter was low. "If that's what you want, I feel sorry for you."

"Don't," she croaked.

It was a visible thing, Aaron shifting his cool veneer back into position. He picked up the ice pack, wiped it on his sleeve, and shoved it back up against his jaw. "Figure out what you want and find a way to achieve it. No one can do it for you. Crying doesn't help, and it's making that black shit on your eyes run."

Oh, man. She *hated* Aaron in that moment for telling her the truth, being so unnecessarily harsh, even if it was exactly what she wanted—needed—after the scene she'd just fled. "I want a new start."

Aaron nodded, a hint of understanding dawning in his expression, before he reared back, kicking the garage door, rattling it on its hinges. "Welcome to the club."

* * *

Rita lay on her side, facing the wall of her motel room. Behind her, Sage and Peggy were sprawled out with vending-machine snacks, watching the episode of *The Golden Girls* where Rose loses her memory. The scratchy comforter was saturated beneath her wet cheek, but she couldn't move to go get a towel, or even adjust herself a few inches to get away from the damp spot.

"I am *worse* than pond scum," Rita said out loud, startling herself. Behind her *The Golden Girls* cut off, but she could still see shadows flashing on the wall, telling her the sound had been muted.

"What was that?" Peggy called. "I couldn't hear you over the sound of this show still being relevant."

There was the unmistakable sound of Peggy and Sage exchanging a high five. Fresh tears welled in Rita's eyes, so she rolled over and stared at the ceiling, willing them to abate. Why couldn't she have chosen a confidante like Sage instead of Aaron? Their angst-fest outside the garage had only plagued her with more questions. She'd told him a fresh start was what she wanted. Meant it, too. Only when she'd attempted to picture herself attending classes in New York, the clear picture she'd left San Diego with had turned murky and undefined. Like a smeared Polaroid. "You're going to run out of *Golden Girls* seasons before we get halfway across the country."

In Rita's periphery, Sage adjusted her glasses. "We've discussed that. And we're planning on moving straight into *The Facts of Life* without breaking."

Peggy scooted to the end of her bed. "Rita, are you crying?"

"No." Just having her condition addressed out loud was unbearable. It made the situation real. She was crying over losing a man. "Maybe." The rings around Peggy's neck clanked against one another, but it took her a moment to speak, as if she were figuring out a way to address Rita without having her head bitten off. Lord, she'd been a crappy sister on top of everything else, hadn't she?

Finally Peggy spoke up. "I can give you advice as one of the Golden Girls. Your pick. Do you want Blanche, Rose, Dorothy, or Sophia?"

"Why can't you talk to me as yourself?"

"Do you want me to?"

Rita covered her face with both hands. "I'll go with Blanche."

Peggy cleared her throat, laughing when Sage started filming with her phone. "Rita Clarkson, there will be time to weep...but not when there's still time to take it deep." Her nod was very wise and an almost perfect impression of Blanche. "Get over to that bar and give him a lasting memory. And make sure to set up the camera on your good side."

"I've already given him a lasting memory—it was just a shitty one," Rita said at the ceiling. "Nice Blanche, by the way."

"Thanks."

A knock on the door had all three women sitting up on the beds. When no one moved to answer, Sage rose and glided across the room, checking through the peephole. "It's Aaron." She pulled open the door to reveal Rita's younger brother, half of his mouth still swollen but minus the ice pack.

"Before you ask, it feels like shit," he grumbled, stomping into the room and dropping unceremoniously onto the dresser. He and Rita exchanged an assessing look, as if to determine where they stood after their earlier conversation, but they broke eye contact without delay. "Just stopped by the garage. They're working on the Suburban now, so we'll be out of here in the morning."

Rita's stomach filled with jagged ice. "Oh. That's... great news."

Aaron gave her a dry look, putting them back on familiar ground. "Yeah, well. Don't go jumping for joy."

Normally, Rita would ask Aaron if he wanted another tooth knocked out, but the reality of leaving Hurley in a matter of hours froze the threat somewhere in her rib cage. Not *only* leaving; leaving while Jasper probably hated her. Maybe even hating *himself* for giving in to her that afternoon.

Rita experienced a sudden burst of restlessness. If she remained in a prone position until they left town, she would just replay the morning over and over again until—what? The outcome changed? That was the actual definition of insanity. She shot up and began to pace. "I need to get out of here. Is there somewhere we can go? Like a movie theater?"

"Or a museum?" Sage interjected. A suggestion that was greeted by an extended silence from the Clarkson siblings. The wedding planner promptly went back to cleaning her glasses with the hem of her dress.

"For once, I'm with Rita." Aaron said, testing his swollen cheek with careful fingers. "This motel is starting to feel like a padded cell."

"Ooh!" Peggy dove off the bed and lunged for her purse, which was hanging on the back of the room's single chair. "Nate gave me a brochure for this nightly drive out into the desert. You make a bonfire and the guide tells ghost stories...."

Sage held up a finger. "Actually, that's not exactly the way Nate described it—"

"Who is Nate?" Rita asked.

"The bartender at the Liquor Hole," her brother answered, his tone dripping with impatience. "Nothing to do in this town except get shit-faced, so we've become well acquainted."

"Yeah, well it worked," Rita shot back. "Your face *does* look like shit."

"*Guys.*" Peggy stepped in between them, waving the

brochure back and forth. "I say we do it. Nothing could be as bad as sitting around bickering."

Another knock at the door. Stupidly, Rita's heart went bonkers, thinking Jasper might be standing on the other side. She must have betrayed her feelings somehow, because the room's three other occupants watched her with interest. "It's probably Bel," she said, taking the few steps toward the door. After a cursory peek through the hole, Rita's heart sank, but she managed to school her features in time to let Belmont into the room. "Hey."

Belmont gave her a brisk nod as he stepped into the cool darkness. His gaze immediately zeroed in on Sage, who tugged the hem of her dress down under his regard, cheeks flaming. "Food?" Belmont asked.

Rita noticed that the brothers refused to look at one another, but, surprisingly, Aaron answered. "I could eat."

Peggy turned in a circle, holding up the desert-excursion brochure like it was Simba from *The Lion King*. "Hot dogs and s'mores are included in the price. Come on, you guys. Adventure awaits."

With a sigh, Aaron plucked the brochure from his sister's hands. "It leaves from the church parking lot in thirty minutes." He laughed under his breath. "No idea where the church is, though. Only the bar."

"It's not far," Sage murmured. "You can see the steeple from the parking lot."

"A bonfire." Crossing his arms, Belmont frowned at Sage. "Is this something you want to do?"

Sage glanced at a frantically nodding Peggy and smiled. "Yes."

"I guess that settles that." Aaron hopped off the dresser, throwing Rita a measuring glance. "Let's go start a fire."

Chapter Twenty-Five

Jasper hadn't been on a bender in two years, but he sorely needed to break that streak. He hadn't moved from his office chair after collapsing into it sometime after Rita had left. No. Not *left*. After she'd been kicked out. By him.

Outside in the bar, bottles of whiskey and beer clinked together, probably Nate filling the ice bins, marrying new liquor with old in preparation for the Friday night crowd. It would have been so easy to tuck one of those bottles—preferably one containing gold liquid—into his waistband and spend the night forgetting what had happened with Rita, but it would be the coward's way out.

So he would sit there and remember every brutally perfect second. Let the touch and feel of Rita drill into his gut, over and over. Or, worse, the way she'd recoiled when he'd blown up. What had she expected? For him to beg and plead for her to stay, like some weak-willed asshole? Much as he'd wanted to, he'd refrained. And wasn't it ironic that the strength of will that had been cemented on the mesa this morning was the very thing that had forced him to send Rita away this afternoon?

Yeah. He reckoned it was. He just couldn't break through the dread of never seeing Rita again to figure out what it meant. Or if she'd imbued him with enough confidence to break it off, maybe he just didn't want to know, because it was too big a kick in the teeth.

Jasper dragged both hands down his face, then gave up the battle to keep from staring at the desk. Seeing Rita as she'd been, body tightening as he slipped a hand around her neck. Trusting. So trusting of a man she'd been in the process of gutting. Or had it all just spun out of their control? He'd spent enough time with Rita to know spitefulness was out of character, so he must have underestimated the loop she'd been thrown for with the cooking demonstration.

The man Jasper had been when Rita arrived in town— the man who'd only been hoping to prove something to himself by spending actual, quality time with a woman— his knee-jerk reaction was to chalk up what happened with Rita as a failure. Proof that he was a good time, nothing more, nothing less. But something must have changed along the line, because new Jasper beat back that belief with a flaming baseball bat of fury. *Fuck that.* He wasn't the town's entertainment anymore. Rita hadn't broken him this afternoon...

...and had she really wanted to? Would she have stayed if he hadn't told her to get lost?

Pain lanced his stomach, doubling him over. No. No, he couldn't do this to himself. Agonizing over a woman whose actions had been so clear earlier. Over. She'd wanted it *over*, whether his gesture had been all kinds of wrong, or she simply needed to move forward in a different place, far from Hurley, and hadn't known another way to cut ties.

Jasper pushed up from his desk, restlessness alive in his blood, wishing for the hundredth time he'd just slammed the door this afternoon and had it out with Rita. Hell, a good old-fashioned argument might have been exactly what they'd needed.

Go on. You got what you had coming. Get out.

Going to find her was a bad idea. Bad. Hell, watching her leave with his temper at full volume had been murder, but a calm, collected *Catch-you-on-the-flip-side* would be so much worse. If he could just *see* her, though—

You should Google me sometime.

"Laptop. Laptop," Jasper muttered, turning in a circle, trying to remember where he'd stowed the damn piece of technology. He used a paper and pen for record keeping. Always had. His home computer seldom got a workout, either, and the office one had barely been used since he'd taken it out of the box. *Please let it be charged.*

Jasper pushed aside a stack of paper on the small file cabinet, finding the flat, silver laptop smirking up at him, still attached to the charging wire.

"Save it. I'm not in the mood." He snatched up the device, opening it on his desk and powering it on. Energy fizzled in his fingertips, knowing he might see Rita soon. Even a digital version of her would be welcome. Anything to replace the shock of being kicked out of his office, her mouth still wet from his kiss. *Please. I'm dying.*

He had Google open in seconds, Rita's name typed in lickety-split. First thing to pop up was a video titled "Rita

Clarkson Knife Attack" and *ho-lee damn*, a lot of people had watched the sucker. His eyebrows lifted as he read the description, mainly because a person usually mentioned when he or she had been on television, but apparently Rita had decided to leave out that vital information, although the title gave him a notion as to why. The idea of so many people putting eyes on Rita made the back of Jasper's neck itch, so his finger hovered over the touch pad a mere breath before punching play on the hit-heavy video brought up by the search engine.

He melted back in his chair when Rita appeared on the screen in a white chef jacket, staring down at an oven with tentative hope in her eyes, while someone screamed in the background—*Two minutes!*—people rushing past in the background, complete chaos all around. A boom mic dipped into the frame, just a touch, but close enough to Rita's face to startle her out of the trance she seemed to be stuck in.

Jasper tugged the laptop closer, as if he could climb inside and calm Rita down. Quiet, stretching-on-the-rug-during-a-rainstorm Rita, caught up in tsunami. What had she been thinking, signing on for this torture? Cooking was a skill Rita had been blessed with, whether she recognized it or not. But this? It was designed to be the furthest thing from the woman he knew. She needed to breathe, and they weren't letting her. She had no room to think or—

One minute! someone shrieked.

Jasper leaned forward in the chair. Rita's hands were shaking as she opened the oven and took out—a soufflé. A *perfect* one. Any layman would be able to see that. Had she won this round of the contest? Lord, she was so pretty, hair pulled back, lips lifting in a small display of pleasure, maybe even surprise—

Someone in a white chef jacket hip bumped her oven.

Jasper leaped to his feet, fist slamming on the desk. "Oh, fuck that. No way."

His heart ached as Rita's shoulders sagged, along with the dish, and he just wanted to shout the whole bar down. Slam the laptop shut. But the video wasn't over yet, so Jasper forced himself to watch as Rita calmly set down the soufflé pan, picked up a kitchen knife, turned, and breezed toward her fellow—bastard—contestant. He expected to see anger or disbelief on Rita's face, but he didn't.

He saw only grief.

The same grief he'd seen on her face this afternoon, when he'd sent her packing. A pattern jumped into focus, so clear he could move it around, rearrange it in the air. The cooking demonstration he'd organized was a reminder of what Rita viewed as a failure, maybe even *failures*. And then she'd thrown Jasper her own version of a knife attack, trying to deflect the pain. Instead of dodging it like he should have done, he'd taken a direct hit and stabbed them both where it hurt.

Jasper didn't bother closing the laptop. Couldn't lift his arm to do much more than grab his keys and fall toward the door. *Have to see her. Can't leave it like this.*

"Boss man," Nate called. "Where you headed?"

He had to clear his throat to speak. "Going to the Arms."

"Hope you aren't aiming to find that Rita," Nate answered, uncapping a bottle of beer. "She's gone on an outing, she has."

Jasper had his bartender by the shirt collar before he

knew his own mind. "Don't…don't you fucking tell me she left town while I was sitting back there."

"Nothing like that." The young man held up both hands, shock radiating from his stiff form. "She's just gone out to the desert, is all. Looking to feel the miracle of trust."

"Christ."

CHAPTER TWENTY-SIX

Desert excursion, my ass.

Rita should have known. Among the four siblings, Peggy was the best liar. Which was ironic, considering that Aaron was the politician. Even knowing her little sister could fudge the truth with the best of them, Rita hadn't even blinked at Peggy's description of their nighttime outing. Hot dogs and a bonfire had sounded foolproof. Now, however, crammed in the back of two Jeeps, bumping along the desert dunes—very likely toward their deaths—it was obvious ghost stories and s'mores were not on the agenda.

Rita's assumption might have something to do with the painted, rainbow-colored signs adorning the doors of both Jeeps: GLEN'S TRUST EXERCISES: GOT TRUTH?

"What the hell did you get us into?" Rita shouted at Peggy, struggling to be heard over the wind funneling through the open-top Jeep. On the opposite side of Peggy, Aaron sat with eyes closed, arms folded, looking as if he were attempting to meditate the anger away. Sage and Belmont were in the second Jeep, probably trying to stare one another to death, a situation that still hadn't been explained to Rita's satisfaction. Hell, at all.

Peggy reached over and patted Rita's leg. "It'll be good for us."

Rita's scoff was lost in the racing wind. "How far out do they need to take us?"

"The idea is to remove yourself from the trappings of everyday life," Glen himself called back from the driver's seat just as they overtook a giant dune, leaving Rita's stomach hovering midair. "To strip down to your most basic layer to get to the truth, with the help of your loved ones."

"Loved ones? That's a stretch," Aaron said. At her brother's words, Peggy slumped down in her seat, twisting a curl around her finger, prompting a sigh from Aaron and a few uncomfortable glances in his younger sister's direction. After a minute of visibly wrestling with himself, he put an arm around Peggy's shoulder. "Crybaby."

Humor trickled into Peggy's dejection. "Shut up."

Pretending she wasn't seeing a rare display of affection between siblings, Rita stared out over the dark, endless expanse of sand, wondering if she'd sold the desert excursion idea short. Maybe her sister was right and any form of forced interaction would be good for them.

Or they'd just die out there in the remote desert, their identifying features pecked away by buzzards, never to be seen or heard from again.

What was Jasper doing right now? Did he think she'd already left?

The unwanted thoughts bombarded Rita just as the Jeeps pulled to a stop alongside a charred cement circle surrounded by three, equal-sized logs. "At least you were telling the truth about the bonfire," Rita murmured.

Ten minutes later they were seated around a crackling fire that whipped side to side in the wind. Rita shared a log with the two guides, Glen and Milap, Sage and Belmont took one for themselves, Peggy and Aaron sat on the other. They were halfway through their hot dogs when Glen stood and circled the group a few times, wrists crossed at the small of his back. "Tonight is going to be a difficult journey, but a rewarding one. I sense a lot of negative energy among this group."

"Yeah. Can I see a business license?"

"*Aaron,*" Peggy admonished, shoving her brother's shoulder before returning her attention to Glen. "That's a very astute observation. Please continue."

Glen inclined his head. "I'd like to begin with—"

The sound of an engine brought everyone up short. Actually, it freaked Rita out. She couldn't see a damn thing outside the lit circle, so heavy machinery barreling in their direction with an unknown occupant was undesirable at best. "Are w-we expecting someone else?"

"We're always prepared to expect the unexpected," Glen hedged, but Rita caught the nervous look he sent the other guide.

Aaron stood up. "All right. I'm really going to need that business license."

Everyone was in a state of suspended animation until the unknown vehicle's engine cut out and a familiar voice broke the silence. "Rita."

It was Jasper. She couldn't see him in the darkness, but it was Jasper. He was *there*. Blood rushed into her limbs, warming them after being frozen solid all day.

"Rita?"

"*Yeah,*" she called.

"Well, don't strive for romance," Aaron commented.

Rita ignored her brother, searching futilely in the darkness for Jasper. When he walked into the circle of light a second later and came to a stop mere inches away, an invisible blanket of relief and comfort draped over her shoulders. God, he was freaking gorgeous in faded jeans and slightly rumpled flannel, hair a total mess. He still hadn't shaved, giving him a rugged appearance, and it was everything Rita could do to refrain from jumping him, holding him, apologizing, but the potential gravity of what she'd done earlier kept her rooted to the spot.

Jasper didn't remove his rapt attention from Rita, even as he addressed Glen. "You were told to shut this operation down. Drive them on back to the motel now."

"Who told you we were here?" Glen all but whined. "Nate again, wasn't it?"

"Knew it," Aaron said, pacing in a circle while Peggy poked him in the ribs. "Never let a hippie drive you into the desert."

"Why did you come?" Rita whispered, hearing the starry-eyed quality to her voice and giving zero fucks. "Just to protect us?"

Jasper stepped closer, obviously prepared to give an answer. "Rita—"

"We are doing this goddamn trust exercise, do you hear me?" Peggy chose that moment to go full tantrum, forcing Rita to look away from him. "We're here and it's happening. And I'm not moving until it's over and everyone stops acting like giant assholes."

Sage moved toward Peggy, laying a hand on her shoulder, which seemed to relax Peggy considerably. Rita recalled the way the wedding planner had calmed Belmont the night before after the bar brawl. Was Sage some kind of voodoo priestess? "We're already here," Sage said, sending Belmont a shy glance. "Might as well give it a shot, right?"

Everyone looked at Belmont, who nodded once, and that appeared to be the final word on the matter. Glen deflated in apparent relief and everyone sat back down, even a quietly outraged Aaron. Which left Rita and Jasper standing, facing one another. Were her own eyes devouring the sight of Jasper the way he appeared to be devouring the sight of her? She could feel the tormented way he looked at her down to her fingertips.

"Can we talk when this is over?" Jasper asked.

After Rita tried not to break her neck nodding, they both sat down on the log, Jasper taking Glen's vacated spot.

"We're going to start with each of us confessing something that's been weighing on our minds. No judgments. No commenting until the person is finished. Just absorb the honesty." Glen scanned the group. "Would anyone like to go first?" As expected, no one made a peep. "No? Fine, I'll start."

Aaron shifted on the log. "This should be interesting."

Glen threw up his hands. "My business license is expired."

"Well isn't that just the confession of the decade? You never had a business license," Jasper corrected, his jaw clenched. "Someone else take a turn, so we can get Rit—everyone back to town. They're leaving soon as the sun's up."

Rita wasn't given a chance to react to Jasper's flatly delivered statement, because Peggy stood in dramatic fashion, drawing everyone's eyes. "I killed my own hamster in fifth grade. It wasn't Gerard."

"Who's Gerard?" Jasper wanted to know.

"Rita's weird ex-boyfriend." Peggy's fingers tangled in her curls, twisting them with near violence. "It was an accident. I s-sat on him and then I hid the evidence."

"The evidence being Fluffy," Aaron clarified, standing as Peggy sat back down. "Well, we've solved the hamster cold case. Seems to me we should end on a high note."

There was only one voice that could shut down the bickering that ensued, and it cut through the arguing voices like a knife through butter. "I've been looking for my father," Belmont stated. That was it. He didn't elaborate. But the revelation had the effect of an icy-cold rainstorm catching them out in the open with no shelter. The siblings traded startled looks, clearly searching their emotionally stunted brains for the appropriate response and coming up empty.

They watched in a state of suspended animation as Sage slid her hand across the log, brushing just her pinky finger against Belmont's, sending a shudder through his body. "Sometimes when I plan a wedding for a truly awful couple, I... secretly hope the marriage doesn't work out," Sage rushed out in a stage whisper, sagging in relief as if she'd just unburdened herself of a murder confession.

Belmont smiled. Actually smiled. Which reminded Rita of the secret he'd imparted. Trying to find his real father? He'd never even mentioned having an interest. And how selfish and blind of them to assume his differing parentage wasn't an issue. Anxiety built in Rita's chest until it felt as though she'd sprinted ten miles. Her throat started to burn with the need to speak, but what would she say?

Abruptly, Aaron stood and took a few steps out of the

lit circle, before returning. "Did you all really think I could take a month off work to come on this ridiculous trip? You just…*believed* me without question." He ran a hand over his mouth. "I got fired. About a week before the restaurant burned down, Senator Boggs dismissed me from his staff." A beat passed while that bombshell sank in among the group. "I fucked up. Did something I shouldn't have done. Iowa isn't about getting ahead, it's about getting some-where. *Anywhere.* Or that's the end for me."

Peggy dropped her face into her lap and started to sob. Giant, shoulder-shaking sobs that made Aaron roll his eyes before he dropped back down onto the log and jerked his sister up against his side.

"It's going to work out," Aaron muttered, as if trying to convince himself more than Peggy. "I won't be a failure."

"You *aren't*," Peggy insisted, tearfully scrutinizing the unconfessed. "Who's up next?"

Rita averted her gaze, staring directly into the flickering fire. It had taken so much courage for the four of them to be honest. She couldn't follow suit, could she? *No.* She didn't have it in her to just—drop the shield. Her confession was so much worse. They would condemn her. Hell, she'd already condemned herself, and that judgment was well de-served. They were on this trip because of a mutual love for their mother and the betrayal would be an arrow, piercing them all in this rare state of exposure.

When Jasper laid a hand on top of hers, Rita realized she'd been holding her breath. But now the oxygen rushed in, as though it were being fed through their physical con-nection. Tears pressed behind her eyes like the cold, blunt end of a hammer. And she just—exploded. "I burned down Wayfare."

CHAPTER TWENTY-SEVEN

Chasing after Rita into the desert had been a big mistake. Monumental.

He should have left things sour. Because now he'd watched her in the flickering firelight. Watched her eyes shine with unshed tears as she listened to her siblings. Heard the note of relief when he'd shown up. His plan simply to make amends for his half of this afternoon's blowup—nothing more, nothing less—seemed like a fool's mission now. Two people didn't burn together—as they'd done—and simply cool off. No. The burn was there between them, brighter and more ravenous than ever.

Those facts occurred to Jasper *before* she confessed to burning down her mother's restaurant. So maybe he was crazy, as everyone used to say, because he toppled over, straight into love with Rita when she said the words, releasing them into the night like tiny torpedoes. With her gripping his hand, the wind blowing her hair in a constantly shifting dark halo around her face, she was the most incredible sight he'd ever beheld. Perhaps because he'd finally gotten to the bottom of her and finally understood. *Oh, yes. I see where the pain comes from. I want it to be my pain, too. Want you to give me half, so we can bear it together.*

"I could have saved it," Rita wheezed, prompting Jasper to tighten his hold. "I had the extinguisher in my hand." She stared into the distance, as if remembering. "It was only in one corner of the kitchen...someone had left one of the burners on and it lit on a greasy apron someone had thrown over the expediting rack. I think...I think? It would only have taken me spraying it down with foam. But I didn't. I just grabbed a whisk and I left. I let Mom's restaurant burn down."

Her fear caused a change in Jasper. Made him want to lift a giant shield to keep her hidden while he defended her actions. And he *would* defend her. Without question. He had zero questions about Rita. Just the love expanding and strengthening and lifting all the parts of his insides that were myths until tonight.

Jasper moved diagonally on the log, bringing his side flush with Rita's. He wrapped an arm around her shoulders, pulled her close, and planted a lingering kiss in her hair. "Everything is going to be okay now," he murmured. "Brave, beautiful Rita."

She turned her face into Jasper's, hiccupping against the side of his jaw. "If I was brave, I would have put out the fire. I wouldn't have been so scared to show up the next day for work that I let it burn to ashes."

Aaron's voice sliced through the silence, making Rita flinch. "Why were you scared to go to work?"

Rita tugged away and heaved a shaky breath up at the sky. "You don't know what it was *like*. Being the one she chose. The one expected to *learn* the talent she was just born with. I couldn't live up. Every day was try, fail, try, fail. After the television show, it got to the point where I couldn't handle failing one more time. I *couldn't*." Jasper was now hanging on to Rita for dear life, the more she revealed about her struggle to live up. Couldn't she see how worthy she was of their pride? Simply by being the kind of person who *did* try that hard? "I'm sorry for what I did. I'm so sorry."

Belmont moved first. He stood, rounding the fire to plant himself behind Rita, laying a hand on her shoulder. Rita went still, those big, golden-brown eyes going wide. She'd expected them to condemn her yet still told them everything? She was twice as brave as Jasper had given her credit for.

One by one, the Clarksons—and the smaller woman who couldn't seem to take her attention off Belmont—clustered around Jasper and Rita. Everyone but Aaron, who watched the scene play out across the bonfire.

"I didn't know," Peggy whispered, giving Rita a kiss on the cheek. "Mom seemed so impressed with you. I-I was even jealous."

Rita laughed tearfully into Jasper's neck. "No, you weren't."

"Sure I was." Peggy gave a dainty shrug, but she was fighting a grin. "For at least a full minute."

Based on the way Rita was trying to crawl inside his body, hiding her face from the light, Jasper reckoned she wasn't comfortable with the shows of affection, even though her relief and shock were palpable things. Emotions he could feel just by holding her—and wasn't that something? Christ, he wanted to take her home. Wanted to reward her for the courage she'd shown, wanted to apologize until his face turned blue over the way he'd overreacted that afternoon. But it was clear the siblings were waiting for Aaron to join them. Belmont, for his part, looked about ready to start a second bonfire with the glare leveled in his brother's direction.

Finally, Aaron found his feet, joining his family to ruffle Rita's hair. "*All right*, already. It was a good soufflé, Rita." He adjusted the collar of his shirt. "You didn't have to burn down the fucking restaurant just to make me admit it."

Rita shook with laughter and was joined almost immediately by Peggy and Sage, Belmont's rumble rounding out the sound. When the laughter died down, Rita lifted her face to Jasper's, and he could read her expression. It said, *Holy shit, that just happened...but please get me out of here*, plain and simple. Whether or not she would like his methods? Now *that* remained to be seen.

"I haven't given my confession yet," Jasper said, drawing several pairs of eyes to himself. He cleared his throat and braced for the fallout. "The Suburban has been fixed since Wednesday. You could have left two days ago."

Rita's mouth fell open. "Wait. What?"

Aaron's good nature was gone in a flash. He released a blue streak of curses that had Sage covering her ears and Peggy giggling. And Jasper wouldn't swear to it in a courtroom, but he thought Belmont might have started growling. "I couldn't let Rita up and leave me so fast. You understand." In a move that felt perfectly natural, Jasper pulled a still-agape Rita onto his lap. "I'm not sorry about bribing the mechanic," he murmured against her temple, not caring whether the rest of the group was still listening or not. "Hell no, I'm not sorry. But, God, I'll be sorry to watch you go."

"Jasper—" Rita started, but he cut her off.

"I'll just ask for one favor from you Clarksons, if you don't mind." He pushed Rita's hair back behind her ear, memorizing the texture against his finger pads. "Hearing the way Rita—and you all—talk about Miriam, I know going to New York is important. Rita wants to learn a new trade and there's no better place to do that." God, he was still hanging on. Still pushing for more. Maybe he wasn't capable of giving up. "But I need one more day. I need Rita there when I open Buried Treasure tomorrow night."

As expected, Aaron was the first to protest. "You've got nerve. I'll give you that." He started to turn away, but his gaze snagged on Rita. Whatever he saw in his sister's expression made him do a double take and sigh up at the desert sky. "Ah, fuck it. One extra day, right?"

Peggy jumped up with a series of fluttering hand-claps. "All of us can help out. If the Clarksons know one thing, it's the restaurant business."

"She's right," Rita husked, a smile playing around her mouth. "We all had summer jobs at Wayfare, even before I went to culinary school. They'll be a big help if they don't annoy you to death first."

"I'm sold." Damn, Jasper was so glad that haunted look was gone from her eyes that he was considering going to church on Sunday to give thanks. There was nothing holy about what he wanted from Rita tonight, though. Not a single thing. He leaned in to whisper against her ear. "Come sleep in my bed, Rita."

She was nodding before he finished speaking.

Everyone had stood to leave, all appearing slightly shell-shocked in their own way, when Glen's voice brought them up short. "Hell's bells. The exercise worked." He whooped loud enough to flicker the fire. "Do y'all mind leaving a Yelp review?"

CHAPTER TWENTY-EIGHT

Showing his house to a woman was a first for Jasper. Rosemary had been over a few times to fuss, way back when he'd purchased the property. But having Rita walk the old floorboards, her eyes roaming over his couch, his bread box, his wall of old maps—that was something different altogether. Her voice made his living room softer, somehow. Made the lights glow like lanterns. Made his furniture seem more inviting. Oh, mother of God, he loved having her there. She accepted a glass of wine from him in the kitchen and something began to sing in the back of his mind. A comforting hum with an underlying note of steel that insisted handing Rita wine in his kitchen was an activity meant to be performed as a routine.

Stop. Stop thinking like that. You have Rita here now. Don't waste time wishing for the impossible or being greedy. Just savor the moment.

"I can't believe they didn't yell or...God, they didn't

even seem mad," Rita breathed over the rim of her glass, referring to her siblings. She smiled to herself a moment, then appeared to shake herself. "How much did you pay the mechanic to lie about the Suburban?"

"Well." Grinning, Jasper braced himself on the kitchen island. "He had a bar tab at the Liquor Hole as long as my arm. Let's just say we called it even."

"Very crafty." Her eyes sparkled. "If Belmont hadn't busted Aaron's tooth, would you have made a second bribe?"

"My firstborn. Without hesitation."

She laughed and Jasper about buckled over the way the sound slid down the walls of his home, filling it with life. "Thank you." The words from her own mouth seemed to startle her, but, maybe in the spirit of the evening so far, she kept going. "For bribing someone to keep me around. For wanting me around so badly."

Jasper's feet carried him around the island until he was in his favorite place: within reaching distance of Rita. He tunneled his fingers through her hair, drawing her the remaining foot toward him. Promises dug like tiny tractors in his gut, excavating vital components of what impulse directed him to say, leaving messes behind. Allowing anything to go unsaid when so much had been admitted already tonight, when they were barefoot in his kitchen, seemed like a damn travesty. *I would make a new bribe every day for the rest of my life if I thought staying here would make you happy.*

He couldn't say those words out loud, lest she balk at the pressure. But he could sure as hell show Rita how they made him feel. How *she* made him feel. "Thanking me for wanting you around is like…water thanking a man for taking a drink...on the hottest day of the year." When Jasper pressed their mouths together, she went a little breathless, making his head buzz. "I'm sorry about this afternoon, Rita. I've been tied in a goddamn knot."

"No. *No.*" Without looking, she set her glass of wine down on the island behind him, before crossing her wrists behind his neck, elevating onto her toes. "I can't believe I haven't apologized yet. Maybe I was hoping you'd forgotten."

"Forgotten?" Jasper reversed their positions in the space of a second, pushing her backside up against the island. Using the hair around his fingers for leverage to tug her head back. It allowed him to look down at her, because, yeah, she liked that. Liked when the dominant part of him came out to play. "You think I'll ever forget the way you lifted your ass at the end and tightened your pussy muscles?" He growled deep in his throat. "A man doesn't forget coming so hard he forgets his own name. A man doesn't forget a woman like you gasping when she sees his cock."

"Did I?" she whispered. "Don't answer that. I know I did."

Jasper expected Rita to rip his shirt off or climb his hips. Something. Her expression spoke of all sorts of filthy intentions. So when she slipped out from beneath his pressing body and paced toward the rear of the house, Jasper saw his own puzzled features reflected back in the glass door. "Rita?"

She unlocked the sliding glass door leading out back. "There's enough moonlight to show me around outside." Why did she look flustered all of a sudden? "Show me your favorite spot in the backyard."

He followed Rita out the door, but needed a few moments to start breathing again upon spotting her beneath his piñon tree. In comparison to the giant white moon she looked so small—the opposite of his heart's reaction, which sounded like the bass from an industrial stereo system crashing against the walls of his chest cavity. She stood with one hand on the swing, which had hung from the tree since he'd bought the place. He'd never used it. Never even considered it, really. But there wasn't a doubt in his mind it would never look the same now that she'd touched it.

Distracted by the tension in her shoulders, Jasper joined her at the swing, planting a kiss on her bare shoulder. "Why did you run away from me like that?" His mouth traveled up to her ear, tasting, breathing. "Lord, I'm in a fucking state over you. Pushing me away when I need you this bad is cruel."

"That's just it," Rita shuddered out. "I don't want you to think I came here just so you'll take me to bed. Not after today."

Lord above, he was going to be a medical phenomenon by morning. The first man to die from his heart tearing straight out of his chest. "Rita, I know—"

"No, you don't." Rita actually stomped her foot. "You don't know how much I like spending time with you. *Anyone* would." Her fingers twisted in the hem of her shorts. "Maybe it wasn't intentional, but keeping my family in town these two days...you might have started something you'll never fully realize. You've got so *much*. Someday some—"

Jasper lunged into her space, framing her jaw with both hands. "Don't say it. You say the words *someone else* and it won't be pretty, Rita." Enough was enough. He appreciated Rita wanting to reassure him that red-hot fucking wasn't her sole reason for coming home with him tonight, but he'd

already known that. It had been right there in her eyes on
the mesa that morning. Then again when he walked into the
glow of the campfire. *Thank God.* Thank God he'd gone out
into the desert tonight instead of licking his wounds, staring
at the clock next to a half-empty whiskey bottle, waiting for
her to leave town. "If I did something for you, your family, I'm damned glad. But I've got one night with you and I
don't intend to waste it. I went two years without sex, Rita,
and that lack barely registered most days." He unsnapped
her shorts, pushing them down her hips, allowing them to
fall to the ground. "But one full day without being inside
you? And it feels like I've gone a fucking millennium without coming."

CHAPTER TWENTY-NINE

Rita was going to disgrace herself any moment by panting like a golden retriever. Big, erotically focused, and dangerous in the moonlight, she'd never seen anything or anyone hotter than the man touching her. Jasper's flat, calloused palm smoothed back and forth between her legs, wearing a path in the silk of her panties. *God*, she could have come just from the friction, but when he hooked a finger in the material and continued to run it from the beginning of her feminine lips to the underside of her ass, she stopped breathing altogether, her body jerking at the skin-on-skin contact.

"Sensitive girl. I make you that way this afternoon?" His knuckle teased her clit, up and down, in a circle. "I was rough, wasn't I, beautiful? Going to make it up to you." The groan that left his mouth blew a shiver up her spine. "And then I'm going to fuck you up all over again."

"*Yes.*"

No sooner did the plea leave her mouth than the panties were snatched clean off her body, her backside landing on the smooth wooden swing with a *slap*. "Spread your thighs wide for me, beautiful. I need a look at my fantasy pussy." He waited until Rita obeyed, breathless anticipation in the provocative movement, before he unzipped his jeans and drew out his heavy-looking flesh, holding it inches from her exposed center. Already, his teeth were gritted, sweat dotting his forehead. "This is what's going to pass for conversation tonight. Small talk is going to be my tongue flicking against your clit until you cry out my name like a swear word. My headboard slapping the wall is going to be our heart-to-heart. And that gorgeous body riding my dick is going to be our nighttime prayers. You with me, Rita?"

Uncle. She almost shouted the surrender. Because who in the world even spoke like that? It was magnificent and filthy and she couldn't match that kind of sensual mastery. Could she? The way Jasper ran his thumb over the head of his erection and licked his lips, the way he'd praised her for that afternoon, forced Rita to consider that she was more than just a match for Jasper's lethal skill. Maybe she was even the perfect counterpoint for it.

"Whatever you're thinking about, beautiful, scoot to the end of the swing and think about it harder." He dropped to his knees in front of her open legs, sliding his palms along her inner thighs. "It's making you all wet and shiny. Should I be jealous?"

"No," Rita whispered, holding on to the swing for balance, because, yeah, Jasper was definitely blowing warm air along her dampening flesh. Oh, Christ, who knew that could feel so good? It was as if he traced her with a single fingertip. "I'm thinking about how you talk to me. Wishing I c-could get away with saying things like that."

Jasper smiled against the inside of her knee before trailing his tongue higher, toward the core on which his eyes were so intently focused. "Ah, beautiful. You're welcome to say whatever comes into that head of yours. But I reckon there will be consequences."

So close. He's so close. A little farther. "What kind of consequences?"

Rita grappled to hang on to the ropes when Jasper threw both of her legs over his shoulders, grabbing her backside and yanking her to the swing's edge. "Why don't we find out?" Locking blue eyes on her, Jasper delivered a long, stiff-tongued lick, starting off an electric buzz between her ears. "Let's hear what you have to say while I'm going to work"—another devastating slide of his tongue—"on this delicious pussy you're showing off for me."

Concentration was not a viable option with Jasper's hands squeezing and releasing the globes of her backside, with his determined tongue wreaking havoc on her every sense. Her every nerve ending. The ropes creaked inside her hands, her heels finding purchase in the flexing muscles of his back. "Oh, please. Oh...can you...?"

"Can I what?" Jasper paused midlick to growl. "Ask me, goddammit. I'm on my knees giving you head, beautiful. That means my mouth is at your service."

Rita struggled to inhale. "I just...I love your fingers and—"

"Ahh, Jesus." He dropped a kiss on top of her clit. "This pretty thing remembers me from before, doesn't she? Misses being filled up, poor girl."

"Yes," Rita gasped, then louder, "*Yes,*" when Jasper

pumped his middle finger into her, flicking his tongue against her tingling bud, attention on her all the while. His eyes were glazed over, his sounds of masculine pleasure rippling over her flesh. Did she taste as good as Jasper made it seem? Because wow. *Wow.* Had he just snarled against the slight entrance to her body? Jasper was just as desperate for her as she was for him, and that assurance imbued her with breathtaking confidence she'd never experienced before. It toppled her barriers and let words overrun the ruins. "You were so big in my mouth this morning. I wanted you to keep going...wanted to taste you."

Rita's confession ended in a scream when Jasper bent his finger inside her, attacking a spot she'd always sworn was a mythical location. "Consequences, Rita," Jasper breathed against her, his cheekbones more prominent from what appeared to be rampant desire. Brought forth by her words? Yes...

"When y-you asked me if I wanted you to touch my breasts..."

His tongue slipped inside her, causing her to trail off with a moan, but Jasper slapped her outer thigh with a resounding smack, putting her back on track, even as he drove his tongue in and out with an efficiency that made her dizzy.

"I wanted to ask i-if you would..." He sucked on her clit, drawing hard, forcing the rest of her confession out on a rushed exhale. "If you would put yourself between them. My breasts."

Jasper's guttural exhale, coupled with the pull of his mouth on her most sensitized flesh, pushed Rita past the point of return. The thighs slung over Jasper's shoulders shook, totally out of her control. His crooked finger was joined by a second, those skillful digits combining forces to exploit Rita's G-spot, while he quite simply feasted on her. Jasper's tongue licked around the bases of his fingers and over her clit, never stopping, never easing up. Making a meal out of her.

Just when Rita thought she couldn't take another single second of the perfect torture, Jasper shoved to his feet, wrapping an arm around the back of Rita's hips. Their lips went wild against each other, tongues thrashing inside Rita's mouth, then Jasper's. When he finally pulled away and allowed her to take in a hefty drag of oxygen, ripping Rita's shirt over her head, the sex in his eyes sucked that air right back out. "You wanted me to fuck your tits, is that right?" He plowed his available hand through her hair before bringing his open mouth down on hers for a kiss so carnal her thighs widened without a command from her brain. "Slip my cock up and down in your sweat. Right in front of your gorgeous face. *Fuck.* You know how hot that would make me? Watching you watch me thrust, up close like that?" As if picturing the scene, Jasper bent down and sucked at the swell of her right breast, cheeks hollowing. "That would have ended with me dripping off your nipples."

Rita released one of the ropes to grip Jasper's tight backside, pulling him closer, his body heat, his touch now a necessity. "I would have loved that."

There was no way to prepare for Jasper's entering her body. One moment, they were french-kissing like the two most sexually charged people on the planet, Jasper covering himself with thin latex ... the next—*ahhh*—she was filled to stretching with his arousal. "Consequences," he grated right into her ear, seating himself more firmly, curling Rita's toes with the zap of sensation. "Christ, beautiful. You didn't start slow with the dirty talk, did you? Telling me you wanted me to flood that sexy mouth. Telling me new places you'd like to feel me."

"I want to feel you right where you are," she husked. "Oh my God, it's so thick. I can feel it beating."

"*Rita.*" Jasper nudged her forehead with his own, a frustrated action that ended in them sliding into another erotic kiss. "You knock that shit off right now. I'm trying to savor you, not jackhammer your brains out."

"Do it," she moaned, propping her bent legs higher on his hips, using them as leverage to lift off the swing. "I *need* you. Hard like before."

"Hard like before, yes. But this time you'll look me in the eye while I'm ringing your bell. You understand me?" Jasper pressed her back down into the swing, bearing down with his lower body, grinding her into the wood until she whimpered. "And at some point tonight, I'm going to make love to you. The kind of sex that takes an hour of slow rocking and pumping. The kind where we wrap our fingers together, then twine them around the headboard. And I whisper things in your ear I can't say in the light. Promise me."

"I promise," Rita responded, her thighs already starting to tremble from the way he pressed down on her oversensitive flesh. But there was more now. Her heart was in the game, squeezing and lifting and twisting at the beautiful words coming out of Jasper's mouth. She couldn't allow them to sink in too deep, though. Couldn't dwell on them or hurt would follow—and she didn't want to hurt tonight. Tonight and some of tomorrow was all she had, which meant she needed a distraction from the reality that she only had one full night to spend with this man. "P-please, Jasper. Move inside me."

The tension inside him snapped and the world started spinning again. He burrowed his face into her neck with a groan, his hips beginning a slow rhythm of knocking back the swing on which Rita was perched, before letting the wooden seat carry her back down onto his erection. A back-and-forth arc that resulted in Rita bouncing off of Jasper's lap with the sound of smacked flesh, swinging back, then gliding forward again on the air.

"Jesus. Jesus, Rita. Why did you have to be such a sweet little fit?" His pumping deviated from the pattern he'd set, starting new, erratic drives that were as uneven as his breathing where it warmed her neck. And each one of those thrusts jolted Rita on the swing, the momentum slamming her back down, rattling her teeth. "I can't...I can't pump as hard as you need it," Jasper groaned. "Need you held down and *still*."

Rita opened her mouth to tell Jasper that he could do whatever he thought best, although in *far* less articulate terms, when he yanked her off the swing and batted the hanging object out of the way. She couldn't see where he was walking them after that because his mouth distracted her, moving over hers like a dirty promise, low growls emanating from his throat, clashing with her out-of-control whimpers. They dipped after a moment and then Rita's back met the soft grass she'd spied upon exiting the house. After that, nothing existed to her but the man driving himself like a bull between her legs. The sky turned into a blurry vortex above his advancing and retreating shoulders.

His hands shoved Rita's knees open as far as they would go, down into the grass, his body roiling like a storming ocean. Peaking and breaking, dropping back down, before coming back twice as hard. "This is what you wanted. This is what you love." Her wrists were pinioned above her head, forcing her back to arch on a cry of his name. "You can't walk away from how good I fuck you, Rita. You could go anywhere and never feel this again. I need you to acknowledge that. God knows I'm acknowledging the reverse."

"*Yes.*" Her arms strained, fingers flexing underneath his uncompromising grip. "I know, I know, I know. Don't stop. It feels so good. *Hurts.* Feels good."

"I know all about it, beautiful," he grated, head tilting back so she could see the sweat pouring down the sides of his face. "I know all about the hurt. I know all about the good. You give me both, too." The muscles in his neck and shoulders bunched, shifted. "This pussy is all fucking good, though. Every scarce inch. Every sweet stroke of it."

Rita's climax almost stripped her vocal cords of their function. They locked down, only allowing a strangled scream to emerge as she arched off the ground in what would have been a full backbend if Jasper's weight wasn't crushing her down, forcing her to sail straight into the eye of the orgasm, experiencing its possession of her entire body. Her legs were jerked up to his shoulders, his hips never ceasing their drives, masculine groans branding her shoulder, her throat.

"Oh fuck, *fuck*, I'm giving it to you right *now*. All of it." Jasper went rigid, his arm muscles tightening beneath Rita's raised legs, teeth bared in the near darkness.

Jasper having an orgasm might have been the single most remarkable event Rita had ever witnessed in her entire life. He choked on the intensity of it, but still attempted to repeat her name again and again, the word coming out sounding like an expletive rubbed raw. His every muscle stood out beneath sunbaked skin, glistening with perspiration. And his eyes—God, his eyes—they were twin anchors keeping Rita stationary on the ground as she watched this incredible man take his pleasure. Let it wrack his body. The sight was so amazing and arousing that it only took Rita reaching down and sliding a finger over her clit to get her off again.

When Rita regained consciousness, her arms were limp, thrown out in the grass as if she'd passed out in the process of making a snow angel. Jasper still moved on top of her, sliding their slick bodies together, murmuring things into her hair that ranged from filthy to adoring. "So beautiful lying there all rosy and dewed up. I could turn you over and bang you again just for looking so damn delicious. Would you take it for me, Rita? Yeah, you would. You'd rest your cheek on the grass and let me beat that pussy."

Whoosh. There went what little breath she'd managed to catch. "I think you still have me beat in the sexy-talk department," she managed through parched lips, followed by a sigh. "Always a bridesmaid."

On top of Rita, Jasper's big body shook with laughter and she sucked in the moment, because nothing had ever felt better in her life. Being laughed on by someone who knew how to make her laugh back. "I'll let you borrow my gold medal, long as I can lie here a few more minutes." He reached down and used a fist to drag himself from her body with a throaty groan, removing the condom and setting it aside. Then he granted Rita another long slide of their bodies, his muscled, hair-covered thighs making her feel even more light-headed. "There. I can feel all of you now."

Rita ran the arches of her feet up and down his calves, massaging his lower back with kneading thumbs. "Are you planning on doing this until you're ready to go again?"

"Should only be another minute or so." His teeth flashed in a smile, but it faded in degrees. "I've never done this after part. I've never wanted to."

Rita's hands stilled on his back before resuming their exploration of his muscles. "I've never done it, either."

"Good. So you can't tell if I'm doing it wrong."

When his lips skated up Rita's throat, she gasped, pinpricks traveling up her spine. "If what you're doing is wrong…"

His head lifted when she didn't continue. "You don't want to be right?"

"Yes, sorry. I drifted off."

Jasper's body vibrated on top of hers again and Rita didn't think, she simply threw her arms out once again—and made a snow angel. In the grass. With a sexual dynamo pressing her into the earth. And she laughed.

CHAPTER THIRTY

Jasper leaned back against his kitchen counter, listening to the sounds of Rita taking a shower in his bathroom. Using his soap, his water, his towels. If he didn't think she needed a second alone, he might have asked to watch. Although that scenario would have led to them remaining upstairs for the remainder of the night, and he wasn't ready to turn out the light just yet. There would be plenty of time for sleeping when she left.

I'm in love with you, Rita. Would she hear him in the shower if he yelled it at the top of his lungs? With the head of steam he had built up? Damn straight. Probably best to keep the words ringing in his head instead.

What the hell kind of cruel fate was in play here? He finds the woman of a lifetime on the side of the road, gets just enough time with her to hand over his soul—and then she gets snatched away.

No, that wasn't entirely true, was it? She was leaving of

her own accord. Not being snatched away by some evil, unseen force. Before bringing Rita into his home, he'd been determined to be unselfish. Determined to understand that Rita needed to walk along the path of her own choosing. Yeah, he was still clear-headed enough to believe that. In his mind. The life-giving organ in his chest, however, had landed on another conclusion. If Rita was intent on leaving, hell, he would make it as hard as possible for her. Didn't he have that right? When a man loves a woman, didn't he fight tooth and nail to keep her?

Christ, yes. *Yes.* She'd crossed the threshold of his home and now everything would be laid at her feet like an offering, whether she liked it or not. He couldn't live with the stark prospect of never having her there again. Waking up in two days' time without the possibility of finding Rita beside him, downstairs, or in the backyard? Jasper would fight against fate to keep from having to live that nightmare.

And it was just possible he might be worthy of the dream, instead. The dream being Rita. Rita being the one who'd convinced him his presence meant something. It mattered. She was here *now*, wasn't she? In his house, being with him—happy with him—even though they'd gotten physical, even though he'd fucked up, made her angry. Still here. But not for long? *Can't let it happen.*

Hearing Rita exit the bathroom, Jasper reached into the cabinet and added a belt of whiskey to his coffee. He had less than twenty-four hours to convince a woman he'd known for three days to cancel every plan she'd made for her future—and stay in Hurley. For him. A man who'd never been on a second date. Not even with Rita yet. So he needed all the help he could get.

Rita walked into the kitchen wearing one of his flannel

shirts; his coffee mug froze in midair. The sleeves went so far past her hands that she'd rolled them up in giant bunches at her elbows, the hem dangling somewhere below her knees. Jesus. How could anyone ask him to withstand the sight of watching her drive away after she'd worn his clothes?

"Find everything okay?" Shit, it sounded as if he'd eaten a porcupine.

She nodded, twirling her damp hair into a bun at the top of her head, keeping it there with a rubber band. "You have a lot of flannel."

Jasper poured her a cup of coffee, hoping the task would lower his pulse so he could concentrate. "I'll have to pick a different get-up now. You look a damn sight better in it than me."

"That T-shirt-and-jeans look is working pretty well. Might want to go with that."

The husky tone of her voice, the golden-brown eyes checking him out, made Jasper's tongue feel thick. Among other things. He gave his worn-in, gray T-shirt a cursory glance before handing Rita her coffee. "Keep looking me over like that, beautiful, and you're going to see what's underneath real fast."

Her cheeks turned a pink hue, eyes lighting up. "You mean that, don't you? I'm making you hot."

Jasper watched her over the rim of his coffee cup as he sipped, then set the mug down on the marble island with a resounding *clack*. "Come over here."

Rita took her time sauntering around the island to stand in front of Jasper. But he let her stall, enjoying the sound of her bare feet on his floor, the way she teased him without the visible reservations from before. She leaned back against the island and quirked an eyebrow. "Can I help you?"

She's cute on top of everything. God help me. Jasper framed her face in his hands, careful not to let their bodies make contact. The plan was to spend at least some part of the evening *not* fucking the stuffing out of her, and Jasper was determined to see it through. "If you made me any hotter, Rita, you'd singe off my damn eyebrows. I'd have to draw them on with a Sharpie or something. Not even Rosemary would be seen with me in public."

Her warm chuckle made his chest ache. "No, I wouldn't blame her."

"So you just keep those eyes above my neck until I tell you otherwise." He pressed his thumb against her full bottom lip. "I don't know who led you to believe you aren't white-goddamn-hot, but I'd like to have a conversation with them."

"A conversation?"

"I'd like to break their nose." He nodded. "Twice for good measure."

"Better." She shook her head, her fingers toying with the buttons of the flannel shirt. "It was no single person. So much of my time was spent in the kitchen, everything outside of it felt awkward. Unnatural. I just…" A frown worked its way between her eyebrows. "I just didn't think there was any point in trying. Wouldn't I let them down eventually?"

"No." Rita jumped at his tone, so he grabbed her arms to steady her, squeezing them in apology. "No, you wouldn't have. But I'm a selfish man, so I'm glad you didn't date someone smart enough to make an effort. They would have tried to hold on to you at all costs." Realizing he was revealing too much, Jasper cleared his throat. "And then I'd have to break more than their noses."

A heavy moment passed as she studied him, her lips spreading into a smile. "I want to cook something."

"Right now?"

"Yes." She sounded surprised, her gaze darting around his kitchen. "Now."

Oh, God, there was no chance of getting his pulse to simmer down now. Had something he'd done brought on this sudden urge to face her fear? Damn, he prayed that was the case. Prayed like hell. "I don't have too much here, but..." He dropped a kiss onto Rita's forehead and turned to open the fridge. "Eggs, milk, butter, cheese...I think Rosemary stuffed some spices into the back of the pantry."

"A cheese soufflé," Rita murmured, opening his cabinets to remove bowls, utensils from the drawer. "You have everything to make my least favorite dish."

"Sounds like a good time waiting to happen."

She took the carton of eggs he handed her. "The eating part will be the good time." There was a slight hesitation in her movements now. "If I don't screw it up."

Jasper was still new at comforting a woman. *Anyone*, really, since his only close female family member was perpetually positive and happy. The two times he'd tried to reach into Rita's head and repair things, he'd gone and fucked up good. So he was betting the inclination to bearhug her into being brave wasn't the soundest course of action. Although touching her did have incredible appeal. Still, he needed to do better this time.

"You might screw it up," Jasper started, rubbing the back of his neck, because his words sounded all wrong. *Resist the bear hug.* "I might screw up tomorrow at the restaurant opening, too. It could be a total disaster. Everyone in town—they all want me to go back to being the Jasper they could laugh about. I don't reckon they want me to succeed at all. Until you gave the place a name, I wasn't even sure I'd ever open the doors." He couldn't gauge her thoughts, but he barreled on through his own. "You gave me that...lift. You're going to help me through tomorrow, so let me help you through the soufflé. That way, if it turns out like shit, it's on both of our heads."

Okay, that might have come out sounding ridiculous, but what he'd meant was *Trust me, take my help, let me be your other half. Please.* He'd just said it in a way that wouldn't put the fear of God into her.

Rita pursed her lips. "Does this mean if the opening doesn't go well, you're going to put half the blame on my shoulders?"

"Sound fair?"

"I'm in either way." Seeming to battle a smile, she flipped open the egg carton. "Let's get this party started."

When Jasper came up behind Rita, laying his hands on hers, he realized what a brave face she'd been putting on, because she was shaking. A protective streak about a mile wide mowed down everything in its path, hardening into a bridge he silently begged her to walk over. The air around them buzzed a little, as if it were anticipating something. "When I said let me help you, I meant it. I want to feel where your hands go," Jasper said, kissing the top of her head and smelling his shampoo. "I want you to talk me through it. If I'm going to be culpable in this soufflé's potential demise, my guilt needs to be authentic."

Her shoulders lowered slowly as she released a breath. "I know this is silly. It's just a bunch of ingredients being thrown into a bowl, right?"

"Is that how you feel about it?"

"No," she whispered. "No, it's more important than that. A pinch too much flour or paprika could throw the whole thing off. And then there's the way you stir it. The tempo and direction. It's patience. How you place it on the pan. I'm always just guessing, though. It never comes natural like it did for her."

"Your mother." Jasper pressed his face against the side of Rita's neck, trying to warm her cool skin. "Some people have to work at things, right? Some people have to open a dive bar named for cunnilingus before they get their shit together."

Her soft hum of appreciation made his eyes drift shut, but they opened again when she moved their stacked hands to the carton, took out an egg, and cracked it into the bowl. She halted her progress just as suddenly, though. "Wait...I forgot to preheat the oven." When Jasper remained wrapped around her from behind on their way to the oven, each of their hands lifting to set the temperature, Rita broke out into laughter. And somewhere along the way back to their workstation, she stopped shaking. "You're taking this very seriously."

"Woman, I don't fuck around with soufflés."

"Oh, me, either. I almost stabbed someone over a soufflé once." Jasper studied her reflection in the kitchen window, saw her expression go from humorous to surprised. "That's the first time I've laughed about it."

Jasper watched as she cracked another egg into the bowl, then whisked the eggs with a large fork. "How did it feel?"

"Good," she murmured, transferring their attention to the large saucepan she'd set on the stove, melting a generous amount of butter inside, adding flour when the mixture began to foam. They moved into a side-by-side position, their hips rubbing together as Jasper followed Rita's quiet but efficient instructions. "Can you grate this cheese?" She watched him perform the task a second before guiding him in an easier way with her own hand. "There," she breathed, her gaze dipping to his mouth before skating away.

Jasper tried not to stare at her, but, Jesus, it was hard. She was actually transforming right there in his kitchen. The further they got into the process, the more she glowed, the smoother her actions became, until she was this tiny fairy winging around the space in some complicated ballet Jasper could only marvel over. Where had this brilliant goddamn woman been hiding his entire life?

Stay with me, stay with me, stay with me.

He noticed Rita fanning her face, obviously hot from working over the stove. "You want to change into something lighter?" Jasper asked, not surprised at all to find his voice sounding like it was scooping rock-hard ice cream. "A T-shirt of mine, or—"

"No, I think..." Rita's attention snagged on the outline of his erection, that fleeting glance making him swell even bigger. But she damn near had Jasper reaching into his jeans to beat off when she pulled her next move. With nimble fingers, she pushed each button of the flannel shirt through its respective hole before letting the garment fall to the floor, leaving her in nothing but a purple-and-white polka-dot thong. "I think I'll be fine working just like this."

And then she went back to adding salt to the mixing bowl. As if she hadn't just aroused him straight into another time zone. "*Damn*, beautiful. Just...*damn*." He took two handfuls of his hair and pulled, just to feel pain somewhere besides his aching groin. Feeling a gravitational pull toward Rita, he moved—or stumbled, really—toward the mesmerizing sight of her slick little body, the smooth globes of her ass. "How much longer until we put the soufflé in the oven?"

"Not long," she said breezily.

Jasper licked his lips. "Going to need specifics."

Rita turned, giving Jasper a front-row seat to watch her nipples pout. When her hand drifted over his cock, Jasper cursed under his breath, and he cursed again when Rita smiled. "You look hot, too, Jasper." A squeezing of his flesh began. Rough and rhythmic. But her gaze was glued to his covered chest. "I could be persuaded to hurry if you got a little more comfortable."

Jasper had whipped off his T-shirt before Rita finished making the not-so-subtle request. "Look your fill, Rita." She removed her touch from his dick and he growled in reproof, reaching out to tug a fistful of dark hair. "You're very brave teasing me like this. Especially when you've felt what you've got coming in your hand."

Her nipples visibly straining at Jasper's words, Rita's eyes went liquid with an added depth. "I think you make me brave."

Christ. His palms were sweating, his cock filling up in the thigh of his jeans. But his heart, now that demanded his attention more than anything. *I made her brave? Hallelujah, I finally did something right.* In that moment, he knew a lifetime of bad decisions was worth that new sparkle in Rita's gaze as it traced down his stomach, roving over his belt buckle. "Starting now, Rita, for each minute it takes to put that thing in the oven, I'm going to give your incredible ass a slap. You understand me?"

"Yes," she breathed, turning after a beat passed to add the batter she'd mixed into a baking dish. It gave Jasper an opportunity to appreciate the flexing of her naked thighs, the contours of her perky butt. Sure as shooting, that thong wasn't leaving this house, because he'd be using it to stroke off for the next forty-odd years. The time he'd been allotted to check out his woman also gave Jasper time to get impatient, unfortunately.

Closing in on Rita, he pressed his lap to her tush, his right hand sliding around to grip her pussy. "You wouldn't be going slow on purpose, now, would you, Rita?"

A feminine whimper, a dip of her knees, was his answer.

"Get it done," he rasped into her hair. "So I can get you done."

"Oh my God, oh my God," she chanted, her movements far less graceful now that he was rocking his cock against her bottom, groaning with the need to fuck. Her hips bumped against the counter with the motion of his body. When he decided a minute had passed, he stepped to the side and delivered a spanking that echoed off the walls of his kitchen. Arrested by Rita's profile, Jasper watched her go through so many reactions at once he couldn't name them all and settle on delighted outrage.

"Clock's ticking, beautiful," he husked, conforming his lap to her bottom once again, getting back into that dirty, rolling rhythm. Squeezing her compact pussy in a way that might be distracting to her but turned him inside out. Had him growling into the back of her neck. "Such a hot fucking piece."

"I—I can't think."

"Don't think, then." He looked over her shoulder to find her holding the bowl over the baking dish, getting ready to pour. *Almost there.* "Just do."

After only a slight hesitation, Rita let the batter fold over itself—again and again—into the dish. Slowly, like ribbons falling from steady hands. Not even faltering when his palm glanced off her backside twice more. Knowing the moment was more important than his rampant need, Jasper released Rita, allowing her to insert the dish into the oven and carefully close the door.

Rita's radiant smile when she faced him again almost knocked him over. "Get over here," he said instead of letting gravity take him.

The command emerged despite his throat being strangled, thankfully bringing Rita running the three steps separating them. She leaped into his arms, legs sliding around his hips like a wet dream. There was no way to hold back now. Jasper set to devouring Rita's mouth, tongue-fucking it, blissing out over the greediness of her fingers in his hair. "You did it," he murmured, pulling away just enough to deliver the praise she deserved. "You did it, Rit—"

Apparently, Rita only wanted praise of the physical variety, and that was just goddamn fine with Jasper. He reversed their positions, ramming Rita's tight body up against the refrigerator. Giving her lewd thrusts right through his jeans, her thong. Her head fell back against the hard surface, giving him the arch of her neck to feast on.

"I know when my woman needs a fuck." Jasper yanked aside Rita's thong, then set about unzipping his jeans. "I know all about it, don't I?"

"Was it the naked cooking that tipped you off—"

Jasper cut off her sarcasm with a nip of her earlobe. "Knew you were a smart-ass when I spotted you on the side of the road."

Her laughter was pure, free exhilaration. "A smarter man would've kept driving."

"*No*," he snapped. Then softer, "No. If you were stranded on that road every day, from now until eternity, I would stop, every single time. I would replay the last few days over and over again, trying to change the outcome."

"The outcome?"

"Yeah." Maybe it was the clear quality of her gaze, the impending sense of finality, but honesty poured forth like the soufflé batter, twisting and spreading. "There might have been something I could have done differently along the way. Something to make it impossible for you to leave. I'd do it over until I got it right."

And the flash of genuine sympathy in her eyes was not welcome. Not welcome to a man who was hours from having his heart dragged away like cans on the back of a rented limousine. It pissed him off good. His common sense sent a memo to his male pride and was staunchly rejected. "Jasper…"

"Let's use that mouth for kissing, instead of saying things you don't mean," he said, retrieving a condom from his pocket, ripping the wrapper open with his teeth. He tasted the trepidation in Rita's kiss when their lips tangled again, but licked her tongue until it melted away. Turned into breathy sounds and writhing hips. Jasper used his body to brace Rita against the refrigerator and reached between them to roll on the condom. "Round two, Rita."

He pushed himself home, already halfway to a climax from hearing Rita's shocked intake of breath. "*Oh.*"

"Yeah." He sucked her lower and upper lips in turn, scraping his teeth over the curve of her neck, harder than necessary. "Feels real good after you've been acting the cock tease, doesn't it?"

There was anger in his voice, punishment in his harsh

movements, but nothing could curtail it. Rita didn't want him to, either. It was easy to tell by the way she absorbed his first thrust with almost a relieved cry, thighs tightening around his hips. Maybe she even wanted to be punished on some level for leaving him. Jasper hated the idea of that, but his body didn't pay the logistics any mind. It wanted sustenance, and Rita was a royal feast.

"God, Rita. I can feel that little lace edge of your thong rubbing up and down my cock." He gave her a full minute of nonstop bucking, stopping only when her pussy locked up, a telltale sign she was near the edge. She wailed and dug her nails into his shoulders when he paused, but she settled when he started a slow bump and grind. "Yeah, beautiful. Fucking is that much sweeter when you've driven a man to the point where he wants to jack off in his own kitchen, isn't it?" He dropped his forehead onto her shoulder and groaned. "I'm not finishing you down here. You're going to leave your scent in my bed, you understand me?"

"*Yes,*" she moaned, curling around Jasper as he advanced toward the stairs, still impaled on his dick. There was a mirror at the top of his staircase, and something about the way he could see her dangling feet vibrate every time he took a step made him hot beyond words. Almost hot enough to drop down onto the top step and fuck, fuck, fuck until they were both shaking and screaming. "Please, hurry," she said near his ear. "I'm dying. I'm not going to make it."

"You will," Jasper returned through clenched teeth. As soon as they cleared the door frame to his bedroom, Rita was flat on her back on the bed, Jasper covering as much of her body as he could. Arms wrapped beneath her shoulders, stomachs flush. Not able to get close enough. With a powerful need to feel the orgasm move through her body,

Jasper fastened their mouths together and worked himself into Rita, again and again, groaning over the feel of her heels buried in his lower back, digging his own heels into the bed so he could fuck her as hard as humanly possible. "Go on, Rita. Give me that come. Give it to me in my bed. Mess up my sheets like you've messed me up."

Dammit, the anger in his voice had no place between them. There was room for nothing between them. *Nothing.* But he couldn't rein it in, couldn't stop the overflow. Tears were rolling down her temples, from regret or arousal, but her body urged him on. Begged his body to use hers. Her fingernails broke the skin of his ass as he pumped, her pussy starting to quake, and Jasper kissed her through the storm, guiding her safely to the other side, asking for her to do the same.

"Rita. My *God*, Rita." He tucked his sweating forehead into her neck and rocked himself into her perfection one final time, letting go with a muffled roar. It should have been enough to clear him from the downpour, but all the same obstacles remained on the other side, urging Jasper to gather her body close and hope they disappeared. "I guess...I guess we'll make love on the next try, huh?"

His attempt at humor didn't ease the tension in Rita's shoulders any, nor in his. But she didn't leave. She didn't leave. She allowed Jasper to tuck her into the safety of his body, falling asleep shortly after. Jasper was the only one left awake to hear the timer go off on the oven downstairs.

Done.

CHAPTER THIRTY-ONE

Rita was unsettled. *Everything* was unsettled. Her stomach housed an army of nerves so rowdy they were leaving little footprints wherever they trampled. Looking back at the last twenty-four hours, the revelations from her siblings and herself, the all-night, mind-blowing sexual awakening, she should have been exhilarated. Relieved. Definitely not stressed, being that she'd lost count of her orgasms somewhere around eight. But the man she'd gone to sleep beside, the man who'd acted as her second set of hands while making a soufflé? That was not the stiff, quiet man who'd just dropped her off outside the motel on his way to the Liquor Hole.

Of course, when Rita walked into the room, Peggy greeted her like a college roommate does after a kegger. Big, speculative eyes and a knowing grin. Although, to be fair, that was the expression Peggy usually wore. Whatever she saw in Rita's face caused some of her enthusiasm to slip, however. "Sage is trying to read and I was distracting her, so I'm heading Aaron's way to check on his tooth. You want to walk with me?"

Until yesterday, Rita would have avoided Aaron like the Black Death, but things were different now. They'd both admitted to being fuckups, putting them on even footing for the first time in—forever. And, honestly, she didn't feel like avoiding much of *anything*, anymore. "Okay, sure."

Rita tossed her purse onto the bed and followed her sister out of the room. "Why does Aaron need his tooth checked? Isn't that something he can do himself?"

Peggy combed slim fingers through her curls. "He's refusing to take the unmanly painkillers, so I've been crushing them up and hiding them in his food. Like a good sister." She wrinkled her nose at Rita while locking the motel-room door. "You're not behaving like a woman who spent the night getting the bejeezus boned out of her."

"Where do you come up with this stuff?" Rita hedged, following Peggy down the path. Having no desire whatsoever to describe the blurred line that had formed overnight between her and Jasper, she intended to leave the conversation there. Until she remembered Peggy's attempts to talk—*actually* talk—to her on their first night in Hurley. How Rita had basically blown her off. How hard could it be to make a small effort, especially when Peggy had helped unburden all of them by forcing the trust exercise? "How does one usually behave when they've had the bejeezus boned out of them?"

"Hmm." Peggy visibly tried to hide her grin, but white blasted across her face when her lips surrendered the fight. "There's usually some gloating. I could really go for some gloating."

"Gloating." Rita drummed her index finger against her lips. "I think towards the end, I bypassed Jesus and actually glimpsed the three wise men."

"Oh, no fair." The words traveled out of Peggy's mouth on a giggle. "I've only had three-wise-men sex once."

"Well, it is the trickiest kind of sex, due to the wise men being very barn-animal adjacent. You don't want to go quite that far."

Holy shit. Who knew it would feel so awesome to make her little sister laugh? Watching Peggy bend at the waist and let loose the musical sound, she could see Peggy at age nine, laughing exactly the same way on her towel at the community pool.

I think I might leave Jasper worse off than when I arrived. She wanted to say the words out loud, to see if Peggy's reaction mirrored her own horror at the thought. But saying it out loud might make the possibility real. So she simply allowed the words to continue ricocheting around her head. *I should have stayed away from him when he told me his issue with women leaving. I was selfish and when I drive away he won't be reachable to anyone else. Maybe ever.*

"I'm thinking of staying in New York," Peggy said suddenly. "When we get there. I'm thinking I could spend some time applying to the major department stores. What personal shopper wouldn't want to work in Saks or Bloomingdale's or Barneys—am I right?"

Peggy was rambling, meaning she was nervous. More nervous than the news warranted, although it was still a big bombshell. "Okay. That's a pretty huge move. When did you—"

"I was thinking we could do it together. You know?"

Peggy shadowboxed the air. "Two sisters, making it in the big city. Laverne and Shirley with better hair. And hopefully some hotter neighbors."

Shock struck Rita in the belly, robbing her of speech. Now more than ever, Rita was convinced her mother had had an ulterior motive when she'd made the final wish. The four of them had already begun to drift apart when Miriam got sick, and although their mother made a practice of staying out of her children's business, it wouldn't have escaped her notice when they stopped having even the obligatory holiday brunch at Wayfare. Less than a week out of San Diego and her siblings had become less of a mystery. But they were still complicated riddles she hadn't begun to decipher. Miriam might have forced them into this situation, but she'd done it for a reason.

So why was Rita hesitating? An image of their imaginary apartment rolled to the front of her mind. Half pink, frilly pandemonium. Half dark and eclectic. Loud pop music that Rita would be forced to drown out with Black Sabbath. It would be a nightmare. It would be—the chance of a lifetime to get closer to the sister she barely knew. To find out why Peggy—the type of woman any man would want to nail down—was carrying a torch for one who apparently didn't want her in return.

The longer she went without answering, the more Peggy withdrew, growing quiet and staring out into the parking lot without her signature smile. "I guess that's a no."

"It's *not* a no," Rita rushed to say. "You've just had more time to think about it than me. Like…a whole three days…"

"Well, *there's* a roundabout way of saying I'm impulsive."

Rita stopped outside Aaron and Belmont's door, tugging

her sister to a stop before she could knock. "It's a great fucking idea, Peggy, just let me think." The inside of her throat felt itchy. "I'm just... I'm having a hard time thinking past tonight. Once we get back on the road, things will be different."

Peggy's gaze was suddenly wiser than Rita had ever seen it. "You really believe that, don't you?"

Behind Peggy, the door swung open to reveal Aaron. The swelling in his cheek had gone down, along with a hint of his outward ego, it seemed, after last night. He gave Rita a brisk nod before ruffling Peggy's hair. "What are you two squawking about out here?"

"Nothing," Peggy chirped. "Just getting back on the road."

Aaron stepped aside, signaling they should enter his room. "Yeah. I guess we've all been thinking about it."

Rita stepped across the threshold, aware that it was her first time in Aaron and Belmont's room, while Peggy had probably been in there countless times. Both sides of the space were meticulously clean, although Belmont's was tidy to the point of not even looking slept in. Maybe the divide between the two brothers was invisible, but it was there in the air, hanging down, like jungle vines. Just another reminder to Rita how much she had left to find out about her family. What had Belmont and Aaron been avoiding speaking about for so long?

"Do you have a game plan for Iowa?" Rita asked, sitting down on the corner of Belmont's bed. "Besides show up and be charming?"

Aaron smirked while uncapping a bottle of water. "That's been enough to work for me in the past." He gulped a sip. "But, yeah. Not anymore. Not after San Diego."

Peggy flopped down beside Rita. "You going to tell us what happened?"

"Nope. Although you'll find out once we hit Iowa. Shit tends to follow you around in politics." He shifted in his loafers. "I'll be glad to have you both there. Climbing my way back into the fold isn't going to be easy."

Rita felt Peggy glance over at her but didn't look back. Instead, she focused on her brother, the unnatural tension in his shoulders, the set of his jaw. "You sure that fold is somewhere you want to be, Aaron?"

"Of course it is." His sharp gaze lifted. "I don't fit anywhere else."

"Maybe we were never meant to fit in," Rita murmured up at the ceiling. "Maybe it's a good thing."

Rita thought of the way Jasper's kitchen had embraced her. Thought of the sense of coming home when she'd walked into Buried Treasure. When she'd stood on the mesa's edge, looking out at the desert. Lying in the grass of Jasper's backyard. So many times since crossing Hurley's county line, she'd faced an odd sense of adjustment. Almost uncomfortable. But, just as often, she'd experienced the sensation of sinking into a warm bath. There was no way to judge the effect of three days *anywhere*, though. Doing so would be silly. Giving up everything for a fling, knowing damn well there was a major possibility she could disappoint Jasper, would be shortsighted. This trip with her siblings, this promise to her mother—it was where she needed to be. She owed it to Miriam. Owed it to them. Owed it to herself.

Why did her body—including her heart—fill with lead at the prospect of climbing back into the Suburban?

CHAPTER THIRTY-TWO

Jasper usually left the bar's busywork to Nate, but cutting limes and replacing cash-register tape was helping keep his mind occupied, even if the silence acted as needles beneath his skin. In just under an hour, the Clarksons—including Rita—would arrive to help him and the chef prep the kitchen for Buried Treasure's first ever dinner service. The specials menu lay on the bar in front of him, but it resembled more of a eulogy to Jasper.

If that were true, dropping Rita off this morning had been a wake. Their impending separation had filled the truck's cab so thoroughly he hadn't even been surprised when Rita simply climbed out with a sad smile over her shoulder, setting off bone-deep agony so thick he hadn't been able to swim through it. Hadn't been able to call her back and say a proper good-bye, the way two people did after slaking each other's lust for damn near ten hours.

She'd said his name in her sleep. When he'd returned to the room after removing the perfect soufflé from the oven, he'd slipped in beside her, rain beginning to pelt the roof, feeling more contentment than was wise in their situation, but unable to help himself. He'd lain awake, watching the reflection of raindrops play on Rita's back, refusing to believe at first that she was breathing his name. But she was. She'd done it exactly three times, all in different ways. Insistent, sweet, and longingly. That last time had prompted Jasper to roll her over, slide down between her thighs, and wake her up with his hungry mouth. He could still taste her. Probably would for the rest of his life.

By the end of the day he would know if he'd get to refresh that taste every day, the way he craved the chance to do.

When the front door of the Liquor Hole opened, shedding light on the dim bar, Jasper squinted into the sunlight. The prospect of seeing Rita an hour earlier than expected sent his pulse haywire, but when the door closed again, Jasper saw it was only Belmont who had arrived. *Interesting.*

Jasper sent Rita's older brother a nod and stood, going behind the bar to toss a coaster in front of him. "Get you a drink?"

The stool creaked under Belmont's size. "No."

"Okay." Silence stretched. "You stop by for a reason?"

"Yes."

When it became apparent that Belmont was going to take his sweet damn time revealing his reason for stopping by early, Jasper set about icing down beers, cleaning the empty liquor bottles, and making a fresh pot of coffee. He might still be sticking to his sober guns, but he had no self-imposed rules against being caffeinated. Damn, he hoped Belmont had stopped by to talk about Rita. It would be nice to talk about her with *someone*. And Belmont's interest in his sister's relationship would mean it hadn't been some elaborate daydream.

Belmont cleared his throat, bringing Jasper's head up. "Do you have intentions?"

"Intentions for what?" Jasper asked, wanting to have the words said out loud. Wanting the last three days to be real.

"My sister."

Jasper picked up a bar rag and started cleaning. "I do. But you might have noticed she has intentions of her own."

He swore another five minutes passed before Belmont spoke again. "You could try and change her intentions to match yours."

Jasper's laughter hurt on the way out. "Thank you for the advice." He threw down the rag in his hand. "You know, I'm a little out of my fucking depth here. I couldn't have made it any clearer how I feel about her. Now, I'm going to be selfish and I'm going to fight, but it's like trying to race a clock and I only had three days to compete."

"That true?"

"Which part?"

Belmont ran his thumb along the crease of his chin. "You made it clear how you feel about her?"

Jasper started to say *Yesgoddammit*, but realized it wasn't true. Not yet. Still, a man didn't expose the most vital parts of himself—as he'd done with Rita—without wanting that woman to hold them in her hands, accept them, did he? He'd showed her his restaurant, introduced her to

Rosemary, held her in his bed. He'd all but screamed, *Take everything of mine. Please take it.* Hadn't he? "I made it clear," he hedged.

"How did it go?" Belmont asked after a minute. "When you told her?"

If Jasper had blinked, he would have missed the way Belmont shifted, tension creeping into his lumberjack shoulders. As if maybe he'd come to the Liquor Hole to get advice, just as much as needing to give it. "Why do you ask?" Jasper propped an elbow on the bar, a few feet from Belmont. "Something to do with your fifth traveler, maybe?"

Blue eyes frosted over. "She's not your concern."

"No, I reckon she isn't," Jasper said, burying his amusement. "Pretty obvious she's your concern, though."

Belmont's hands balled into fists on the bar and once again silence filled the room, making Jasper wish he'd had the presence of mind to put on some music. "Love is kind of a selfish business, isn't it?"

"I don't know," Belmont muttered. "What if it's really the opposite?"

Jasper's throat constricted. "What do you mean?"

At once, Rita's older brother just seemed irritated by the whole conversation. "If you love something, let it go. Seems to me that sentiment hasn't gone out of style just because it got older."

"No, I don't suspect it has," Jasper said slowly. "So what's a man supposed to do? Take his happiness or watch it from a distance?"

A muscle ticked in Belmont's cheek. "What if the answer is there is no answer?"

Jasper grabbed two shot glasses and slid them onto the

glossy bar. "I think that means we should have ourselves a drink."

Belmont's eyes were steady on the glass as Jasper poured. "When Rita was younger—a kid—she didn't like to watch movies. Even on rainy days when there was nothing else going. She would hide off somewhere while we watched *Home Alone* or *Gremlins*. *The NeverEnding Story*." Belmont rolled the drink between his palms, unaware that Jasper held his breath, dying for something, *anything*, about Rita he could think about and replay a million times. "Miriam finally asked her why. Why she refused to watch movies. And she said, 'Once you watch it, you know how it ends. I want to not know a little longer.' "

More than anything in that moment, Jasper wanted to rewind to that morning and keep Rita in bed an hour longer. Bury his face in her neck and beg her to talk. Talk about any goddamn thing, as long as he could listen. "She had a point."

The other man brought the glass to his mouth as if he would take a drink, but stopped and set it down, with a barely perceptible air of regret. "I found her in the middle of the night about a year later, watching them all back to back. Crying into a pillow." He pushed the glass of whiskey away. "She does things in her own time, my sister. You have to let her."

"I don't have a year." Jasper poured his own whiskey into the closest plastic-lined garbage pail. "But thank you for telling me, all the same."

Neither of them moved when the entrance opened to reveal three Clarksons and their unrelated traveling companion. The one who wore her connection to Belmont like a cloak. Rita was the last to walk in, and Jasper barely prevented himself from vaulting over the bar to sweep her up, hold her close.

When the door blocked out the sun and their eyes met, Rita's throat worked in an up-and-down movement. "Everyone ready to open this restaurant?"

CHAPTER THIRTY-THREE

Jasper moved through the dining area of Buried Treasure straightening chairs, looking at the room from different angles. He wanted to be in the kitchen with Rita, but she was going over preparations and talking about the menu with the chef. The chef who would take over once the Clarksons left tonight. Her husky voice climbed up the walls and drifted down, making itself at home, leaving its mark. Only about one more minute remained on Jasper's internal countdown clock before he busted into the kitchen and carried the woman out over his shoulder.

Belmont watched him from the front entrance, so still he could pass for a marble column in a museum, but Jasper could hear Rita's older brother loud and clear. Unfortunately, the same man had confused the shit out of him in the bar with what Jasper supposed was meant to be a pep talk. Pep talk, his ass. Turned out there wasn't a man around who knew what was to be done about women. So Jasper interpreted Belmont's dark observance as *Hurry the fuck up and pick your option. Be selfish or let go of the woman you love...and let me know how it works out.*

That was just dandy, wasn't it? Being the guinea pig when his happiness was at stake? "I'm getting there," Jasper grumbled at Belmont, picking up a water glass and thunking it back down. "By the way, you're acting as the bouncer tonight. Not the house therapist."

Belmont crossed his arms and leaned back against the door frame. Jasper thought he might have seen the guy crack a smile, but when Sage—he'd finally learned her name—floated into the dining room to lay out silverware, Belmont went back to being a statue. Jasper snorted and checked his watch for the hundredth time in under an hour. The restaurant was set to open at five o'clock and they'd just turned the corner on four. Already the parking lot was full, customers peering in through the windows, talking animatedly amongst themselves in groups. Children were perched on car trunks, teenagers tossed footballs back and forth.

True to their word, the Clarksons had slipped right into various positions, ready to train the skeleton staff of Buried Treasure in the way they'd been taught as they were brought up in the world of fine dining. Belmont would act as a bouncer, keeping out anyone who'd had a little too much to drink next door at the Liquor Hole. Aaron and Jasper were handling the money, Sage and Peggy were training the hostess and waitstaff, while Rita worked in the kitchen. Jasper was damned glad to have them there, although they filled up the small space with their big presence in a way that would make it seem empty when they left.

Jasper swallowed hard as Rita's voice reached him from the kitchen. A soft, encouraging laugh that reminded him of last night, the way she'd painted his house with a glow. The memory fresh in his head, Jasper crossed the dining room toward the kitchen, well aware that he appeared to be a man on a mission. Goddammit, he was. It was obvious that Rita caught the drift, too, because when Jasper entered the kitchen she dropped her pen, bent down to retrieve it, and bumped her head on the waist-high refrigerator.

When she rose again, rubbing the sore spot, Jasper was already by her side, taking over the task for her. "Ah, beautiful. You okay?"

"I'm fine."

"*Really*, okay?" His concern must have reached her, because understanding passed between them, as real as anything he knew.

She nodded slowly. "Everything—even the kitchen—feels a little easier after last night."

"Good." Pressure pushed against his jugular, but he was too aware of the chef regarding their exchange, so he lightened the mood. Temporarily. "Can I talk to you for a few minutes before you knock yourself into a coma?"

A smile smoothed across her mouth. "Funny."

Just like that the silent tension of the morning faded, leaving them searching one another's eyes for what came next. The hand he used to soothe Rita's head drifted down to hold her face. "Talk to me about the specials."

Pink highlighted her cheekbones, obviously pleasure that he'd remembered that talking over the specials menu calmed her. Made her less anxious. Except Jasper was pretty sure it would benefit them both right about now, considering he was about to lay everything on the line. He gestured for Rita to precede him into the office, closing the door behind them. He leaned back against it, watching like a starving man as Rita perched herself on the edge of his desk, a piece of paper pinched between her fingers.

"Okay, well." She tucked a few strands of stray dark hair behind her ear. "I looked over the menu your chef planned on using and offered a few suggestions. I hope that's okay."

"Don't use that professional tone with me, Rita Clarkson."

Her flush deepened. "I don't mean to." She used the paper to fan herself. "You were so different this morning. I wasn't sure I should still come."

Lord, she might as well have fired a round of bullets into his stomach. Had she misinterpreted his silence for checking out early? "I can't even imagine you not being here." He advanced toward her. "Read me the specials."

She traded glances between his approaching body and the menu, as if unsure whether she should proceed. "Um." Her voice wobbled. "There were some great items. I just added some spice, I guess you could say. The strip steak is already on the main menu, but I thought as a special, we could encrust it with blue cheese. Serve it with baby spinach and..."

Jasper rested his hands on either side of her hips, tracing the curve of her neck with greedy lips. "Keep going."

"Keep...?" Her head fell to the right and Jasper pressed his advantage, raking the sensitive skin with his teeth. "Going?"

"Yes, keep going," he breathed, punctuating his words with a soft bite.

It took a few moments for Rita to continue, her breasts

puffing up and down beneath her white tank top. "Fried Kobe meatballs...served with spicy mayonnaise. Th-they—we—glazed them with teriyaki sauce."

"You're making me hungry, beautiful."

"Maybe I should stop."

"*Don't.*"

"Oh, God. Okay." Her exhale washed over him. "The chef had a shrimp cocktail on the specials menu, but I-I think that should be on the regular appetizer list. A buffalo-shrimp po' boy for the specials menu, though. Ohhhh, what are you doing now?"

Jasper smiled against her neck. "Just unhooking your bra for a little while." The snap made them both moan a little. "That okay with you?" She nodded without hesitation, giving Jasper the green light to slide his hands around front and palm the two sweetest tits he'd ever held. "Anything else you want to tell me about the menu, Rita?"

God, her panting breaths were sexy as all get out. "I-I did a little research and found a fish market not too far from here. They're willing to deliver, but I just took a drive and picked up some bluepoint oysters—"

"What?" Cement bags piled on top of Jasper's shoulders. "You drove somewhere?"

Golden-brown eyes, still a little lust-fogged lifted to his. "Just a few towns over," she murmured. "The Suburban is fixed now."

The room tilted around Jasper. "I knew that. I knew." Fuck, he had no control over his mouth or his pulse. The latter sped up so fast his head felt like it might float off. If he reacted this way to Rita leaving and coming back, how the hell would he cope with her never returning? Not good. Really fucking bad. Catastrophically. "*Stay*, Rita."

She stared at his mouth, as if the words were painted there. "What?"

"Stay in Hurley, Rita. Don't leave me." His hands skated down from her breasts to enfold her waist, shaking her body on the desk. "Sit here every day and read me the specials menu. This place—Buried Treasure—it became half yours when you walked inside, and we both knew it."

"Jasper," she whispered, sounding out of breath. "I don't—"

"Please, just don't act surprised. I won't be able to stand it." His mouth fell to hers, kissing, kissing, like a man mouthing a furious prayer. "You can't be surprised when the last few days have given me *life*. Act upset or happy or storm out. But I can't handle surprised, like maybe you didn't even consider me for a second."

"I've considered you," she sobbed. "Of course I have. Just stop talking like that, stop stealing my breath when I'm trying to catch it."

"No." He pressed their foreheads together. "I don't want you to catch it. I want it to stay lost and I want to be the man who steals it. All day, every day. Forever. Stay with me right here."

"I want to say yes," Rita said with her eyes closed. "It's crazy after only three days to—to toss everything aside and start a new life. And I still want to say yes. But somewhere over time, I lost my family and I'm just starting to get them back. They...I think they need me. I think we need each other. I don't know if I can just say good-bye when we're on this road I never expected."

Jasper found her so achingly gorgeous in that moment with honesty pushing at all her seams and tears falling down her cheeks. How could something so beautiful rip his soul out and stomp on it, even if it wasn't on purpose?

"I lost myself in the kitchen." She shook her head. "What if I lost myself in this one, too?"

"I wouldn't let you."

"Jasper—"

"You don't have to work the kitchen," he rushed to say, even though it stung. "You don't have to work here at all."

Rita only looked saddened by his words. "Then I'd be denying this place. This place you already adore, whether you know it or not." She glanced down. "How can I set them on this journey and desert them? How can I burn down my mother's life's work and disregard her final wish? I'd be a terrible person. I wouldn't be the person you—"

"Say it." He gathered her hair in two fists and spoke right against her forehead. "Say it. You know how I feel about you. Say the words."

Rita shook her head, lips clamped together. "Let me think. Give me a secon—"

"No," Jasper growled, ripping the white tank top over her head. For a breathless beat of time, they ran eyes over one another. Confused, aching, heartsick eyes. And then Rita surged off the desk, pushing Jasper back into the armless office chair facing his desk. While Rita made quick work of her pants and slinky little underwear, Jasper unfastened his jeans, taking out his cock. "Come on, then. You won't say the words, do the deed. Use that body that makes me fucking crazy and show me what we already know."

Hurt clouded her expression, but their need was too thick in the air, the pull too strong, and they both had to feel it. Rita straddled Jasper's lap, taking his hand and pressing it over her mouth. A safety measure against the scream that ripped past her lips as she sank down onto his ready cock. "*Oh my God,*" came the muffled words, branding his palm. "*Jasper. Oh, God.*"

Maybe someone should have covered his mouth, too, because hell if he didn't almost curse the walls down. How many times had they abused one another's bodies last night and still—*still*—he might as well have been living like a monk for ten years, the way his cock hurt. "If this is going to be good-bye, Rita, you better make it count." He gave her tight bottom a slap. "But remember, I'm already going to be desperate for you the second this ends. I'll spend my whole life this way. Desperate and dying for Rita. In my bed, in my house, riding my dick. All of it. All of you."

"Stop, please, stop," Rita demanded, wrapping her arms around his head, giving his mouth perfect access to her tits, which he sucked out of pure necessity. Her hips were a thing of magic, bucking and rolling, knowing when he needed easy to rein in his impending release, knowing when he wanted a few rough bounces. "So *good,*" she breathed, already beginning to shudder, her teeth chattering.

Jasper's mouth moved over every inch of Rita's skin, tasting, trying to memorize the feel of life pulsing beneath her flesh, tucking her scent into his memory bank and locking it away. "It's so good because I love you, Rita," Jasper confessed through stiff lips. "It's good because you love me back. Fuck the amount of time it took. When it's right, it's right. We're above time."

Her face fell into his neck with a sob, but she didn't respond.

The helplessness wrought by Rita's silence forced Jasper to regain power and self-respect some other way. He lunged to his feet, taking her with him. When her back hit the wall,

Jasper kept pumping, trying to imprint himself on her body, inside and out. Giving up a little more of his soul with every rough movement. "Remember how good it was. Remember who would *always* give it to you like this, even if it meant giving up his final breath. You hear me?"

"Yes," she clenched around him, her sweet mouth falling open in a silent rendition of his name, her pussy milking him down below, so tight, so eager, there was no choice but to take his own climax, groaning into her shoulder as it drained him. They stayed that way for an unknown length of time, Jasper trying to will her into repeating back the three words he'd let fly free of his heart. But when her legs slipped down his sides and her back straightened, she still hadn't said them.

CHAPTER THIRTY-FOUR

Rita walked on shaking legs back to the kitchen. Nothing compared to the quaking behind her ribs, though. The pounding in her head. Jasper had crucified her against that door and she hadn't given him what he needed—to be crucified in return. Or maybe she had, only in a different way. A way that felt like betrayal, no matter from which angle she looked at it.

Jasper *loved* her. Wanted her to stay in Hurley and share his life. His livelihood. Her own life's recipe hadn't called for him as an ingredient when she'd left San Diego. Now she was mired in that state of uncertainty, caught between the menu she'd chosen and a new one that called to something unfamiliar and wild inside her. But the last time she'd gone for the unknown and reached outside her capabilities, she'd fucked up bad enough to burn down a restaurant.

Staying in Hurley would mean dropping the family she'd

only begun to win back, nixing the mission she'd laid out for herself, and beginning new in a strange place.

As a chef, no less. She'd fallen into a familiar rhythm immediately upon walking into Buried Treasure, inspecting the kitchen, devising plans. Simply beefing up the specials menu sent her right back to the holding pattern she'd fled in San Diego. Now she had a chance to start over in New York, free of the failures she'd courted by being a chef, but the kitchen seemed determined to pull her back in. Because she loved it, loved the man who'd given her the fresh slate? Or because she didn't know anything else yet?

Rita entered the kitchen to find Aaron and Peggy tossing a lime back and forth. The chef clearly wanted to be irritated but couldn't quite pull it off in the face of Peggy's giggling. Sage danced into the kitchen behind Rita, catching the lime in midair and giving the two siblings a stern look before making it a three-way game of catch.

"I'm done going through the books," Aaron said to Rita without looking at her. "Your boyfriend knows what he's doing. Low overhead. Great cost efficiency. He doesn't need me so I'm here to offer my cooking expertise."

"You can't fry an egg," Rita pointed out.

Aaron rolled the green fruit along his shoulders, making Peggy and Sage laugh. "I was thinking more along the lines of official taste tester."

A minute earlier Rita had sworn she might never smile again, but having them all in the same kitchen reminded Rita of days when Miriam would cook and they'd all congregate around the stove, trying to steal bites of food. And something mended itself inside her chest. The only one missing was Bel—

"Am I the only one working here?" Her older brother grumbled from behind her.

Aaron tossed Sage the lime, but she missed the catch because her wide gaze had fastened itself on Belmont. The fruit thudded on the ground.

Rita decided to take pity on Sage. "Hey, what song was it Mom used to sing when trying out a new menu? I can't remember. ..."

"'Raspberry Beret,'" Aaron said. "By Prince."

"That's right." Peggy hopped up on a waist-high refrigerator, ignoring the chef, who tried to shoo her off. "Except she would change the words to 'Raspberry Sorbet.'"

It was well known that nary a Clarkson could carry a tune, so they all raised eyebrows at one another, waiting for someone to start. Rita went to the pantry and began pulling out ingredients, wondering if she was a lunatic for putting her dignity on the line. But a distraction from the ache in her stomach whenever she thought of Jasper was necessary, so she took a deep breath and started to sing.

Peggy joined in halfway through the first verse, her voice a much higher pitch than Rita's. Aaron's baritone was low and almost inaudible, but there nonetheless. And when Sage chimed in, Rita thought Belmont might throw himself down at the girl's feet, but no one expected her older brother to sing. And he didn't.

Ingredients were diced, sauces mixed, meat prepped around the big white cutting station, each of the Clarksons—and Sage—focused on their work. The singing eventually faded away, leaving the sound of slicing knives and murmuring voices as they compared notes and talked over ideas to leave Jasper for menu changeups.

The more time passed, the more Rita began to experi-

ence a winded feeling. An impending sense of loss. Movements that were usually natural felt stiff. Scenes with Jasper
filtered through her mind like sunshine through lace. Being
picked up on the side of the road on his motorcycle. Dancing in Rosemary's kitchen. Kissing in the motel parking lot.
Seeing Buried Treasure for the first time, seeing all he'd
worked for without anyone the wiser. Lying side by side
in his truck bed, watching clouds shift, talking about anything that entered their minds. While she and her siblings
were healing one deep-seated scar, another one was forming, making itself permanent.

And when she turned around to see Jasper watching
her from the doorway, where she stood huddling with her
laughing siblings, that scar deepened and gushed fresh
blood. Because without saying a word, in that moment,
she'd given him her answer.

* * *

The dining room of Buried Treasure was full. With a line
out the door. Several customers had already made reservations for the following night. Sage had started some sort of
Instagram account—although God knew how he'd keep that
straight when he was on his own—and pictures were post-
ing steadily. Pictures of food. Food Jasper could look at and
see Rita's touch. See the subtle changes she'd made to give
it the right flair. Even without seeing the dishes she sent out
from the kitchen, he would have known they'd have little
quirks, just like Buried Treasure.

A parmesan crisp in the shape of a heart stuck in the
center of mashed potatoes. Little sticks of hardened sugar
bundled together to resemble firewood. She sent out little

pieces of her heart on the plate, and every time one passed, another piece of his own chipped away.

His conversation with Belmont that afternoon had come into stark focus when he'd walked into the kitchen. As he'd stood there, watching Rita exchange tentative looks with Aaron, noticing the way she watched Peggy thoughtfully, as if dying to get inside her little sister's head and rearrange things. Seeing the way everyone, especially Sage, stopped on a dime whenever Belmont spoke, staring at him as if it could be the final time he ever communicated in the open. So many intricacies. So much at stake. And it was all happening right before his eyes.

Jasper had one distinct thought, directed squarely at himself:

What a selfish son of a bitch you turned out to be.

He stood in the bustling dining room, witnessing the magic wielded by the Clarksons, and still he wanted to break that chain. Take his precious link—Rita—and stow her away in the kitchen. A place from which she'd only just broken free. So what if he would be standing there, right beside her. A teammate. A lover. Yeah, maybe if he got really fucking lucky, she would wear his ring one day. So what, though, when their three-day love affair couldn't compete with the family she was fighting to get back. With the new life—far from the restaurant business—she so desperately wanted.

He loved Rita. So he had to let her go.

Dinner service wound down gradually, customers filing out the front door with surprised smiles in his direction. Waving, telling him they'd be back tomorrow. Nearly every table in the place was empty, save the one tucked in the corner. Jasper did a double take when Rosemary stepped out of the hidden nook—her hand tucked into the crook of his grandfather's arm. A tinny ring began in his ears, the sides of his throat feeling tight, as his grandfather approached, eyes that Jasper shared scanning the room with something akin to approval. But that couldn't be right.

Finally, the older man's gaze landed on him. "Jasper," he said, holding out his hand to shake his grandson's. "Well done."

For so long this moment had been what drove Jasper. Repaying the man he'd let down. Now that he'd reached that moment in time, there was definite relief. A rushing landslide of it down his back. There was appreciation, too, for having gained back the respect he'd lost. But when he searched that same landslide for happiness, it eluded him. Just then, he was positive it always would.

"Thank you," Jasper said to his grandfather, leaning over to kiss Rosemary's cheek. "For everything."

After watching the people who'd raised him walk out the door—the final remaining customers—Jasper turned to find Rita watching him from the waitress station, one hip propped against the counter. Sadness lurked in her eyes, but there was pride there as well. In him. In Buried Treasure. The apron she wore was covered in splashes of sauce, a dash having made it up to her cheek, flipping his insides around like a pancake. Without thinking, he went to Rita, used his thumb to wipe away the sauce.

"Congratulations," she whispered, watching his hand move away. "We had nothing sent back to the kitchen except for compliments. Sage said you're booked solid for the next three weeks." She reached out as if to lay a hand on his arm but let it drop, her tongue wetting her lips in what looked like a nervous gesture. "I'm so glad you created this place. It's going to be a town landmark, and it's due to your hard work."

Lord, Jasper wanted to shake her. Her words were genuine, but they weren't coming at the right time. They were unwelcome when good-bye was so close on the horizon. "I appreciate that. Everything your family did tonight." A cannonball materialized in his stomach, dragging him down, down. He didn't want anyone there to witness when he hit bottom. Especially her. "But this is where I let you go, Rita. I need you to go. I can't look at you anymore without making a fool out of myself."

Rita closed her eyes, opening them to reveal twin pools of tears. "I'm so sorry." Her hands trembled as she peeled off the soiled apron and laid it on the waitress station. "I never expected you. Or them. Or any of this." She swiped beneath her eyes. "Leaving at night feels wrong, doesn't it? But I don't think I'll be able to resist one more day if we wait until the sun comes up."

It was like releasing a gorgeous, majestic creature back into the wild. Except she was a woman he damn well believed was born to be his second half. And she wouldn't go. The longer she stood there, the more hurt she heaped on him. So he leaned in close, careful not to let their bodies make contact, and he kissed her forehead. "Hey. Maybe I'll wake up tomorrow and find you on the side of the road again. My own version of *Groundhog Day*. Maybe I'll get a second chance to do it all over again."

Her breath puffed out against his neck. "Good-bye, Jasper."

The last sound he remembered hearing was the screen door smacking, signaling that she'd gone. That was when the thunder began to roll in his ears, muting the world around him as he stumbled across the restaurant. He pulled out the chair Rita had sat in the first night he'd shown her Buried Treasure. The night she'd named the place. He sat, buried his face in his arms on the table. And he didn't move.

CHAPTER THIRTY-FIVE

It took only twenty minutes for everyone to clear their belongings out of the motel and climb into the Suburban. Something about that felt very wrong to Rita. Surely twenty minutes was insufficient for erasing any evidence of their stay in Hurley. Wasn't it? On impulse, she'd left a T-shirt in one of the motel-room closets, closing the door on it while a tiny intruder played Whac-A-Mole in her stomach. Now they all sat in silence in the Hurley Arms parking lot waiting for Belmont, who had disappeared without telling anyone where he was going. Although, since that was typical behavior for their older brother, no one commented, even if Sage appeared anxious, her head on a swivel as she waited for his return. Aaron scanned e-mails in his cell phone—humming "Raspberry Beret"—while Peggy clinked together the engagement rings around her neck.

All so normal. *Fuck.* Why was everyone acting so normal? Air was being siphoned from Rita's lungs, her skin itching, the interior of the car growing smaller and smaller. With a curse, she pushed open the back door, allowing the warm desert wind to roll into the Suburban. It slithered in under the sleeves of her shirt, climbed up her neck and held, held so tight. As if Jasper had taken the form of invisible wind, deciding to reach out for her one final time. His face, his words, the failure evident in both clawed at her consciousness. *No, not a failure. You won me. I just have to leave anyway.*

The reasons were all around her, taking up the seats, joining her on this insane journey, but something besides Jasper was missing. Realizing what it was, Rita reached into her slouchy canvas bag and removed Miriam's journal, flipping to an entry toward the front, placing it in her lap and pushing two handfuls of hair back over her shoulders as she began to read.

My family isn't one for noisy emotion. My children were meant to—

Belmont opened the driver's-side door, starting up the Suburban without a word regarding where he'd been. While they released a collective sigh of relief, Belmont reversed the Suburban from its parking spot, the rumble feeling like an earthquake beneath Rita's feet. A seismic shift. As they pulled out onto the main road, a rope that had been tied around her chest without permission began to pull and pull. As if it were tied to the motel and the farther away they drove, the more it threatened to slice her in half. The urge to turn around to glimpse the Liquor Hole—no, Buried Treasure—was vast and unrelenting, but some irrational voice said everything would turn to dust if she followed through, like Sodom and Gomorrah. Or maybe it would just be her? She would turn to dust and float away, just a tiny speck that couldn't possibly fit all the feelings.

Jasper. Jasper. What was he doing? Had he left Buried Treasure yet? Would he go home and sit down on the swing where they'd made love? Or maybe have a cup of coffee while leaning up against the kitchen island, casually looking over that night's numbers? It took precious little concentration to envision herself perched on the island beside him, wearing his flannel shirt, stealing a sip of his coffee.

Oh, Christ. *Ouch.* Pain speared through her rib cage, hot bread rolls pressing behind her eyelids. Remembering the distraction in her lap, Rita ducked her head to begin reading once again, trying with all her might not to look out the window and watch the town repair garage pass. The place Jasper had appeared the second morning on his motorcycle, hoping she'd consent to lunch with Rosemary. Feigning surprise over the Suburban's lack of function when he'd damn well *been* the reason. God. *God*, who did something so sneaky just to get one more day with a woman? Jasper did. Her Jasper.

Swiping at the moisture on her cheeks, Rita focused on the open page flapping in the breeze provided by the open window. Focused on the concise nature of her mother's handwriting, attempting to find solace.

My children were meant to take different paths. They diverged early and intersect rarely, but when they do, they make beautiful music. Even if they don't always hear it. I hope they know I heard it for them. Beats and bad notes alike. Some families reunite every year at scheduled events—and I admire that. I really do.

*But spontaneity just happens to suit the Clarksons.
Those rare moments when my children's paths take
unexpected detours and they crash together, coming
away different without realizing. Refusing to believe
they can be influenced by someone with so little in
common, but having it happen all the same.*

*Be brave! I wish I would have said that more
often without throwing my own bravery in their faces.
Be brave, crash together and fall apart. It's okay.
It's okay to diverge, knowing sometime in the future,
you'll collide again. As long as those rare times are
remembered, their meanings retained.*

*Listen to me. I sound like such a mother. Here's
one more mom-ism for good measure... You kids stop
bickering, or I'll turn this car around right now—*

"Stop," Rita croaked. "Turn the car around."

She looked up from the journal to find that the Suburban
was already pulled over on the side of the road, its occupants staring at her from all corners. Tears plopped down
on her hands, wetting the pages of Miriam's journal until
Aaron tugged it away, and stowed it in his briefcase. Belmont watched her steadily in the rearview mirror, and
Peggy gave her shoulders awkward, but enthusiastic, pats
from the backseat.

And with those knowing eyes on her, she could suddenly
see. See all the things she'd been blind to for so long.
Being in the kitchen earlier that night—she'd *enjoyed* herself. Maybe for the first time ever in a kitchen. Because
those dishes had been made for her. For Jasper. No one else.
She'd finally figured out how to cook without fear. And it
was due in part to the man she was leaving behind. The man

who'd spent days breaking her free of that prison, maybe without even being conscious of the difference he made, moment by moment.

Could she—stay? Stay and love a man without the terror of disappointing him? Disappointing *herself*? Yes. *Yes*. Last night, a seed had been planted in Jasper's kitchen. The seed of enjoyment, love. Things cooking had made her feel *before*. Before they got lost in the attempt to be someone other than Rita. She'd proven tonight it wasn't the cooking that had broken her. She'd broken herself. But, dammit, she'd also fixed the damage. With Jasper. Oh, *God*, Jasper. The only way she could disappoint him would be by leaving.

"I'm sorry." She spoke to Belmont because it was easiest and he'd never had the ability to pass judgment with his face. "I'm sorry...I know this was my idea. But I think I might have found a home with that man. The one I'm meant for." Rita doubled over, tucking her face between her knees. "Oh, God, I feel like I'm dying. I *hate* it."

Silence reigned for long moments before Aaron broke through. "It was Mom's idea, Rita. That's why we're here." He shifted, looking out the window. "You don't have to take responsibility for it. We would have found our way here somehow, all right?" He reached over and nudged her shoulder. "And...if you finding a home is all that comes from this trip, it was worth it. I think maybe there's more for us four on the road, but the road ends for you here. You and your flannel-wearing babies."

With a watery laugh, Rita unbuckled her seat belt and lunged across the seat, throwing her arms around Aaron's neck. "I'm sorry we were such assholes to each other."

"Me too." He planted a kiss on her forehead. "Although I maintain I was right most of the time."

A jagged sound left Rita as she pulled back, turning to Peggy. "God, Peggy. About the apartment—"

"Don't worry about it." Peggy's eyelashes were clumped together with dampness, beautiful despite her red nose and distressed expression. Her hands fluttered a moment, and in what looked like an effort to anchor them, she nodded toward the front passenger seat. "I'll just have to convince Sage to move with me."

A low growl from the driver's seat raised everyone's eyebrows, but Rita took the focus off her older brother by climbing out of the Suburban. After a moment of searching for her suitcase in the rear and coming up empty, Belmont's shoulder brushed against hers, making her look up in confusion. "Where's my suitcase?"

He glanced back toward Hurley. "I left it in the kitchen at Buried Treasure."

Rita's throat tugged with so much gravity she had to circle it with two hands. "What if I hadn't figured it out?"

Her brother's sigh joined forces with the desert wind to ruffle her hair. "Then we would've had to come back. Or Jasper would have brought it to you. And maybe by then you'd have figured it out."

"Thank you," Rita breathed, certain she couldn't carry the weight of so much feeling. Loving her family, missing Jasper. Something had to give. Pressure was pushing her from the insides, expanding by the second. On impulse, she reached out and laid a hand on Belmont's cheek. "You're a great man, Belmont. A *great* one."

Rita let her hand drop and stepped back, finding her siblings gathered around her. Sage, too. There they stood, on the side of the quiet road, draped in moonlight. And somehow it was the worst moment of her life, while doubling as the most important. The *best*. Surrounded by her past while the future lay a quarter mile away, a beacon glowing softly with subdued light. Rita hugged Peggy hard, still wishing like hell she'd gotten to the bottom of her sister's heartache, but knowing Peggy had the inner strength to face it. Something she hadn't been sure of before the trip started.

Rita embraced Sage, whispering in her ear, "Take care of my brother," and then she stepped back, away from the group. Toward Hurley. "I'll be on the beach New Year's Day. One way or another, I'll be there. That's a promise."

Sage gestured to the Suburban, still looking a little flustered from Rita's show of affection. "Don't you want us to drive you back to town?"

"No," Rita started jogging backwards, taking one last look at her family. "I have to do this myself."

"Rita, you failed gym class three times," Aaron called. "You can't run for shit."

Her laughter rang out in the night as she turned and ran.

Toward Jasper. Toward her life.

* * *

Jasper would never know what made him stop outside Buried Treasure, halfway to his car. Maybe he was listening for the sound of the Suburban pulling out of town. Maybe he didn't want to go home to an empty house just yet. Whatever the reason, Jasper paused at the edge of the parking lot, keys in hand, listening for something. When nothing presented itself but silence and the whispering of sand being carried from the desert to the asphalt, circling his feet, Jasper took another few steps toward the truck.

Those few steps gave him a view of the main road. Having grown up in Hurley, he knew every bump and lump of the town. So when something in the distance appeared to be getting larger, moving under streetlights and vanishing before reappearing again, his curiosity forced him toward it, needing to get a better look, an erratic pump beginning in his chest. His fingers loosened, his keys dropped to the ground, but taking his gaze off the approaching figure was impossible, so he kept walking. Walking down the center of the main road, like some kind of sleepwalking maniac. Sand crunched underneath his boots, less and less time passing in between the sounds. Was he running now? Yeah—yeah, he was running.

Rita. It was Rita. His heart had known it back in the parking lot, but his eyes had refused to accept the gift. He'd truly thought the woman couldn't get any more beautiful to him, but watching her sprint toward him in the partially illuminated darkness, hair streaming out behind her, face broken into a smile—yeah, he changed his mind. She *could* get more beautiful. So beautiful he stumbled in the road and fell to his knees, opening his arms just in time for Rita to dive into them, knocking them both backwards.

"I love you, too. I love you, too." The words were rambled sweetly into his neck as he stared up at the sky, a man thanking God for his fortune. "I want to stay right here with you. I don't want to leave." Her sobs jabbed his heart with sharp little swords. "I'm sorry I even tried."

"Okay, beautiful. It's okay." Jasper stroked shaking hands down Rita's hair and back, reassuring himself she wasn't a hallucination. With the goal of sitting up and gathering her in his lap, Jasper attempted to move but found his legs were paralyzed, clinging to the road like melted plastic.

"No, it's not okay, actually. You damn near killed me. I'm not recovered yet."

She smoothed hands up and down his chest, as if trying to warm his heart into jump-starting. "Keep saying things like that. I deserve them."

That got his blood flowing, mostly out of protest. Jasper moved into a sitting position, releasing a heavy sigh when Rita wrapped her limbs around him and clung. "No. I don't want you feeling guilty. I don't want you to feel anything but glad you came back to me. Not now, not ever."

Her lips moved over his jaw, his cheeks, leaving kisses. "I never really left. My heart stayed here the whole time."

"It must have crossed paths with mine. It left town when you did." He pushed open her lips with his own, groaning at the perfection he'd thought never to feel again. His Rita. "You brought it back. You're...staying?"

"Yes."

Don't flatten back onto the road again. Hold fast, man. Make sure this is the best thing for Rita before you let the relief completely take over. "Your family—"

"My family." She seemed deep in thought a moment. "They know I need to be here. And I know they all need to be someplace else. I'm not sure where yet." Her sweet breath was a thing of dreams coasting over his face. "They'll find it. The way I found you. Hopefully it won't take them driving away to realize they can't live without it."

A dam burst inside Jasper, finally allowing relief to rush in and fill all the cracks her leaving had caused. "I'm not making presumptions, Rita, but you're moving in with me." Another fierce trading of kisses. "All right, I'm making presumptions. I need you walking my floors. Need your touch on everything I owned before, the things we'll own together after today. Need your touch all over me, too. I need so many things and they all begin and end with you."

God, he loved the way his words visibly affected her, made her eyes go soft. Loved knowing that the constant ache behind them was worth every second. "After thinking I might never see you again, I've never been more sure I can't go a day without you," Rita breathed. "Take me home."

Jasper stood, taking Rita with him. "I'll take you to our home." He kissed her on the silent street beneath the lamplight. "I'll read you the specials until you fall asleep." Another kiss. "I'll tell you I love you between each one."

"I love you, too," she whispered. "Did I mention that?"

He slung her up into his arms, heading for Buried Treasure. "Did you?" His throat constricted. "I'm feeling a bit of amnesia coming on. Might need to hear it again…"

She chanted it against his neck the whole way home.

Their home.

EPILOGUE

Aaron watched through the giant back window of the Suburban until Rita became a speck, growing smaller and smaller beneath the streetlights of Hurley. *Goddamn.* He really hadn't thought his sister had it in her. Kind of made him wonder whom else he'd underestimated or discounted recently. When Aaron accidentally made eye contact with Belmont in the rearview mirror, he feigned great interest in the contents of his briefcase. Although, yeah, not really feigning, right? He'd read the initial entry from Miriam—the one that had taken them on this heinous ride through hell—but hadn't gone beyond it. Mostly due to the journal being in Rita's possession since—

Liar. Quit being such a fucking liar.

No one wanted to go through their parents' final thoughts on this earth and have confirmed what had been so obvious all along. He was the only one in the family who had been born without a heart. Their mother had never been able to hide her discomfort with Aaron's ability to lie, to cajole, to win at all costs. The ease with which he moved from one girl to the next, no discernable shame concerning relationship overlaps. What would Miriam think if she knew why he'd been fired from his job working beneath the senator?

Her lack of surprise would have been the stuff of legends.

Which is why he wasn't opening the journal. Not today. Not in twenty years. Being a great liar gave him the ability to pad the reality of how soulless he was against the backdrop of his siblings. Peggy was the bleeding heart who had such a hard time saying no that she'd yes'd four proposals so no one's feelings would get hurt. Belmont's still waters ran deep—deep enough to keep everyone the hell out. Even if it hadn't always been that way between Aaron and his brother. They'd even been friends. Or maybe he'd just imagined the whole thing—it sure seemed that way now.

Aaron cleared the discomfort from his throat. At one time he'd thought Rita and he were most similar among the Clarksons, but he'd never experienced the kind of emotion it took to sprint a quarter mile toward anyone. Shit, he'd never gone past a second date. So here he sat, minus a sister and still an asshole. What the hell was he thinking, crashing the campaign trail in Iowa? He could very well be crucified.

Or. *Or* he could rise again. No. He *would*.

The Suburban passed a blue-and-white-painted sign that read NOW LEAVING HURLEY and Belmont tapped the horn twice. Aaron swallowed the smile he felt trying to form when he thought of Rita buying a pair of cowboy boots and started to return his attention to the Internet research documents in his briefcase. But a flash of white alongside the road caught his eye. A dog?

"Hold up." Aaron jabbed the back of Belmont's seat. "Hit the brakes."

Belmont grunted, stormy gaze lifting to the rearview again, but he finally pulled over, the Suburban groaning with the sudden stop. Aaron felt ridiculous the minute he stepped onto the gravel, the utter silence of the desert like a void around him. Peggy and Sage were watching him with curiosity through the back window, the glow of *The Golden Girls* playing on the laptop illuminating their faces. Belmont's scrutiny burned a hole in his back. *What?* Everyone else got to act crazy in this family but he pulls over to get a closer look at a dog and suddenly *he's* the candidate for a straitjacket?

Aaron put two fingers in his mouth and whistled. "Come on. Don't leave me standing here like a dick," he muttered. Peggy and Sage came up on either side of Aaron after a minute passed, watching him instead of the black nothing before them. Just as Aaron poised himself to give up, a white blot of fur trotted into the light provided by the Suburban brake lights. "Took you long enough," Aaron said, unsure what to do now that he'd confirmed what his eyes had seen.

Peggy almost swallowed half the desert with her gasp. "Puppy, puppy, puppy."

Sage breathed a tremulous laugh, covering her mouth with both hands.

"That's not a puppy," Aaron said, hunkering down. "That's an old man."

The dog stopped trotting abruptly, as if insulted, sending

both girls into a fit of laughter. Which cut off as soon as Belmont's boots crunched up behind them. Aaron ignored his older brother and whistled again. Why? He had no idea. They'd never had pets growing up. He wasn't even sure if he *liked* dogs. But leaving some poor mutt in the dark desert seemed like a shitty thing to do.

"Come on, old man." Aaron clapped once, his lips twitching when the dog only tilted his head. As if to say, *You talkin' to me?* Good *God*, this was stupid. Standing on the side of the road in between towns trying to attract a stray animal. Maybe Aaron was just bored, his brain having gone so long without a challenge. Maybe he needed a distraction from the journal that had unexpectedly landed in his lap. Whatever the reason, he wanted the damn dog in the damn Suburban.

"Could be a lost dog," Belmont rumbled. "Someone might want him back."

"I can see from here he has no tags," Aaron returned.

Peggy hummed in her throat. "Can you see from here that it's a he? Could be a girl. A little baby puppy girl."

"It's a he. And *he* is ancient." Aaron stood, swiping an impatient hand through his hair and striding toward the dog, bringing him to the edge of the light. His intention was to crouch down and pet the dog enough to make it affable, then carry it back to the Suburban. But the closer Aaron got to the animal, the more it cowered, which slowed him to a stop. "Hey," Aaron murmured, checking over his shoulder to make sure none of the others could hear him. "It's all right. We're...peaceful people. Toward animals, anyway. Not so much to each other."

Right. So he was talking to a dog now. But—was he insane or did the dog's brown eyes calm with total understanding? Yeah, the dog's paw even slid a little bit in Aaron's direction, causing a mild disturbance somewhere in Aaron's gut.

"Huh. Well, my sister just bailed and there's an empty seat. There's food—" The dog stood, ears perked. "Ahh, now I'm talking your language, right? We literally have restaurant doggy bags in the car. It's like we knew..."

Aaron trailed off when the dog coasted past him, heading for the Suburban. After three unsuccessful tries, the streak of white fur vanished into the backseat, leaving the four passengers staring at one another. Peggy was first to react, cramming her knuckles against her lips to muffle a squeal, while Belmont watched Sage for her reaction, giving Aaron the overwhelming urge to roll his eyes. The sexual tension between those two was enough to turn Sunday mass into an orgy.

"What are you going to call him?" Sage breathed, addressing Aaron but staring at the Suburban. "You saved him. It's up to you."

"We'll call him Rita," Aaron deadpanned, earning him a slug in the shoulder from Peggy. "All right, we'll call him Old Man. Just until I can come up with something better." Reluctantly, he looked over at Belmont. "You have a problem with the dog?"

Belmont watched Aaron for a moment without responding, a muscle ticking in his jaw, before turning and heading back for the vehicle. When Peggy patted Aaron's shoulder, necklace jangling, he shrugged it off. Where the hell had she gotten the impression he needed comfort? He was well used to being disregarded. By anyone other than voters, his constituents, the press. Which was why Iowa better look out.

Aaron Clarkson is gunning for you.
And nobody could stand in his way.

* * *

Rita's legs were beginning to shake when Jasper guided her hands to the wrought iron of his headboard, wrapping their entwined fingers around one of the thin, curved poles. Since they'd retrieved her luggage from Buried Treasure and sped home in the truck, Jasper had spent the last hour taking her to the edge of heaven. Only to guide her in a floating gulfstream back down to earth and start the process all over again.

"I told you, didn't I?" His voice was rough and smooth, all at once, in her ear. "Told you I'd make love to you, just like this. With our fingers wrapped nice and tight around the headboard." A leisurely grind of his hips turned biting at the end, eliciting a slap where their flesh connected. "What else did I say?"

"You..." Rita wet her lips, enjoying the strain of her arm muscles on the pillow, the sweaty glide of their bodies as Jasper rolled up and back. "You w-were going to say things in my ear. Things you can't say in the light."

Rita shifted her hips so the base of Jasper's erection would make contact, both of them groaning when their sensitive spots rubbed, glided, rubbed. "That's what I said," Jasper panted, dropping his mouth to her breasts, laving her right nipple with a skilled tongue. "And I'm a man of my word."

"I know," Rita whispered, wishing her arms were free so she could run greedy hands down his back, yank him deeper. Hold him. "I know you are."

Jasper plowed slowly into her, receding, driving forward again. "When I saw you on the side of the road, Rita"—his perspiration-soaked head fell into the crook of her neck, but he lifted it to say the next words in her ear—"I saw my wife. I knew."

A sound she couldn't describe—maybe an overjoyed whimper—left her mouth. She turned her head to kiss Jasper, falling into some deep, dark rabbit hole of passion when he made love to her with masculine lips, an eager tongue. All the while, his lower body pumped, robbing her of reason. Except for one circular thought that spun in revolutions inside her head. "The way you looked at me, like no one else was there. No one has ever looked at me like that." Her fingers tightened on the headboard, a quickening beginning in her middle. "If you had kept on driving your bike, right out of Hurley...just kept going. I would have held on tight and let you take me."

"Rita." Hard kisses rained down the side of her face. "*Rita.*"

His movements hastened, the headboard beginning to bump the wall each time he demanded entrance into her body. She started to spiral higher, her thighs lifting to take Jasper deeper, back bowing, sobs breaking past her lips. "*Jasper.*" Her eyes widened when one of Jasper's hands left the headboard, drifting down to surround her throat. That familiar thrill only he had ever brought to the forefront blazed bright, her release so close, so close. "Please."

Jasper's eyes were glassy, filled with lust as his grip tightened. Just enough to propel Rita into oblivion. "Feel that, Rita? That's the grip I've felt around my heart since you got here. Don't ever let go. *Please.*"

"Never. I never will." Managing to get her arms free,

she threw them around Jasper, holding him as his body imploded on top of hers, loud, male growls bathing her ears. His body undulating, working his need free in stilted, feverish thrusts. The headboard gave a few final slams against the wall.

A short time later, sweat drying on their bodies, hearts beating full with contentment, Rita turned on her side to face Jasper. "Is that what the kids are calling 'reading the specials' these days?"

Jasper rolled her into a bear hug, his husky laugher already as familiar as a favorite song. "You want specials, beautiful?" The house settled with comforting creaks around them, as if it had been waiting, hoping—and now it was satisfied. "I was thinking for Sunday brunch, we could serve belgian waffles—"

"With blueberry compote, drizzled butter-cream sauce... and bacon. Always bacon..."

"Always." She felt Jasper grin into her hair, prompting her to do the same against his neck, enjoying its vibration. "We can test it out in the morning."

"In the morning," Rita sighed out. "Every morning."

Legs twined together, arms holding one another close, they agreed without words to drift off together. After all, come tomorrow, they had a restaurant to run.

They woke up with the dawn. Smiling.

Aspiring politico Aaron Clarkson
needs to get his career back on track,
and a pit-stop in Iowa is his big break.
But a green-eyed vixen in leather
pants is about to show Aaron that
politics don't stand a chance in hell
against the laws of attraction...

Please see the next page for a preview
of *Too Wild to Tame*.

CHAPTER ONE

Welcome to hell," Aaron muttered, maneuvering the Suburban to avoid a patch of ice on the narrow road. In the passenger seat, Old Man lifted his white, furry head—and if dogs could grimace, Aaron's new, unexpected pet was nailing it. Their eyes met across the console, one fuzzy eyebrow twitching as if to say *This is where you bring me, human?*

Aaron sighed and went back to scanning the street for the campsite. The term *man's best friend* was apparently up for interpretation. He'd barely achieved grudging respect with Old Man between New Mexico and Iowa. Still, the bare minimum of mutual appreciation was more than he could garner from the other occupants of the Suburban, wasn't it? When it came to his siblings, he took what he could get. Although now only three Clarksons remained, as opposed to the four they'd started the journey with. A cross-country journey with no discernable purpose.

Unless you counted fulfilling your mother's dying wish as a purpose. In Aaron's opinion, they were simply indulging a whim that might have been different had their mother been in a different mood or written the fateful journal entry—which had put them on the road to New York City—on a different day.

Rita, his oldest sister, had shaken them in New Mexico, making for greener pastures—or rumpled bedsheets, depending on whether you were a realist or a romantic. Aaron still considered himself the former, even if he'd definitely felt a minor blip of something gooey over the whole inconvenient business. With Rita shacked up in the desert with her boyfriend, only Aaron, Belmont, and Peggy Clarkson remained. Sage, too, although the wedding planner wasn't related by blood. *Some people are just naturally lucky.*

Aaron caught sight of the campsite turnoff up ahead and gave a loud cough—his way of waking up the other travelers—before easing the rust bucket that passed for transportation to a stop outside a small redwood building marked TALL TIMBERS RENTAL OFFICE. Okay, it wasn't the Ritz-Carlton, but with a series of pre-election events set to begin the following morning, every fleabag motel from there to Des Moines had been booked out. Fortunately, they were only a short drive from some of the event sites, where his fellow politicians would begin holding rallies for the hometown hero and rising-star senator, starting bright and early tomorrow morning.

Or they had been his fellow politicians at one time—his equals—before he'd gone and fucked his rapidly growing career to hell. Now he'd come to Iowa to fight his way back in, by fair means or foul. For the first time in his life, Aaron was desperate. Desperate enough to share a cabin with his brother in the backwoods of Iowa in a place with a half-lit vacancy sign.

Jesus Christ, don't let this downswing last forever.

"Are we there yet?" Peggy asked on a yawn, her stretching arms visible in the rearview mirror. "I'm starving. Is there a bathroom?"

"Yes. What's new? And probably," Aaron answered, pushing open the driver's-side door to climb out of the Suburban, followed closely by Old Man, who trotted off, presumably to take a leak and maybe chase a squirrel or two. This was how their arrangement worked. Aaron chauffeured the dog around, fed him, and didn't meddle in his business. Old Man would show back up when he was good and ready.

Aaron stopped short when he saw that Belmont had somehow already beaten him out of the vehicle, all without making a sound. His brother stood still as a monument, hands tucked into his jean pockets, running cool eyes over the wooded campsite. "Good enough for you?" Aaron asked, moving past his brother at a crisp pace, eager to drop off his luggage and hit the bricks. If he wanted to find a way into the first function tomorrow morning, his work began now. *Would* have started last week if Rita's boyfriend hadn't sabotaged their only ride out of New Mexico.

As expected, Belmont didn't answer him, but Aaron hardened himself against giving a shit. Ever since Belmont had knocked his tooth out and cost him four hours of dental surgery, their relationship had gone from dwindling to nonexistent. In a barely conscious gesture, Aaron prodded the sore tooth with his tongue, watching as Belmont turned and helped Sage from the Suburban, in the same fashion a reality-television baker might transport a wedding cake. Even Aaron found it impossible not to watch his brother and Sage orbit each other, like two slow-motion planets. They were simultaneously a frustration and a fascination. Frustrating because they refused to just admit the attraction and bang—at least that Aaron knew about—and fascinating because Sage seemed to be the only person capable of getting reactions out of Belmont. Hell, Aaron had busted his brother's nose and barely gotten an acknowledgment.

Moving on.

"Right." Aaron tugged at the starched collar of his shirt. "These cabins are shit cheap, but after the extra nights in the motel back in Hurley, not to mention the car part, I think we should limit it to two rentals. Sage and Peggy in one. Me and Bel in the other." He traded an uneasy look with his brother. "I don't plan to be here much, so you can brood in the dark and write sonnets—or whatever it is you do—until the cows come home. Just don't use my good aftershave."

Being the plan man felt good. This was his role in the Clarkson clan. The asshole with the directions. The one whose lack of a functioning heart gave him the ability to make hard decisions on everyone's behalf. Aaron was more than fine with that job description. History didn't remember the nice guys; it remembered the sons of bitches that got things done.

"Do you need help?" Peggy asked a little breathlessly, setting down her oversized suitcase. "You can bring me along to charm people. I'm very charming."

Beside Peggy, Sage nodded. "She can't help it."

Aaron wondered if Sage realized she was a stunner herself—albeit on a far less flashier scale—but mentioning it would result in getting another tooth knocked out, courtesy of Belmont. He didn't have time for that. "I'll let you know if I need help," Aaron said, knowing he wouldn't. "For now, let's stick to the plan. Once I've secured a position with the senator, you three can keep driving to New York. I'll meet you there for New Year's." He picked up his leather duffel. "For now, let's go rent some cabins. As if the last time we camped together in California wasn't disaster enough."

As he'd known she would, Peggy laughed, following in his wake toward the office. His younger sister was desperate to bond them all on this trip and, while it would never happen, sometimes Aaron had a hard time turning off his greatest talent: telling people what they wanted to hear.

"Aaron sprained his ankle in a gopher hole carrying me back to camp after I was stung by a jellyfish," Peggy explained to Sage. "Mom was too busy perfecting her s'mores technique to keep track of us. Rita staged a protest of the outdoors and wouldn't come out of the tent. Belmont, where were you?"

Refusing to look curious, Aaron nonetheless paused with his hand on the wooden handle of the office's front entrance. Belmont might have no qualms about ignoring everything that came out of Aaron's mouth, but when it came to their baby sister, feigning deafness wasn't an option. "I fell asleep on the beach." His voice sounded like a creaking boat hull lifting on the water. "When I woke up, you'd gone to the hospital."

Silence passed. "I don't remember that," Peggy said, a wrinkle appearing between her eyebrows. "How did you get hom—"

Belmont moved past them, pushing open the office door

and ducking inside. Aaron stared after his brother a moment, weighing the impulse to tackle his hulking ass from behind and maybe divest him of a tooth this time around, but he managed to hold back. Instead, he nudged Peggy with his elbow. "Hey, it's your fault for surpassing your one-question-per-day maximum."

This time his sister's laughter was forced. "Silly me," she breathed, moving past him to join Belmont inside.

Aaron turned his head to find Sage looking like a deer caught in a pair of high beams. "What about you, *Ms.* Alexander. Are you the outdoorsy type?"

"I've planned some outdoor weddings," she answered softly, still not giving Aaron her full attention. Pretty unusual, considering she was a woman with a pulse, but he'd had eighteen hundred miles to stop taking it personally. Aaron started to ask if she was planning on standing there motionless all day, but she hit him with a look. "He doesn't mean it."

Aaron braced a hand on the doorjamb. "Who doesn't mean what?" Aaron asked, even though he already knew the answer.

"Belmont. He doesn't mean to cause everyone frustration. This trip...being away from his boat...he's trying. Really, he is." From the way her breath caught, Aaron knew she'd locked eyes with the man in question over Aaron's shoulder and through the glass windowpane. "While we're alone, I just wanted to say thank you." She spoke in a rush now, which probably had something to do with the footsteps that grew louder, pounding toward the exit. "For complimenting my dress yesterday. It was really nice. But if you do it again—or flirt with me to make Belmont angry anymore—I'll break your nose."

Sage delivered the final word of her promise just as the door swung open, Belmont's shadow appearing on the staircase where Aaron stood with Sage, with what felt like a bemused expression. *Fair enough.*

"Come inside," Belmont rumbled. "Please."

With a final nod in Aaron's direction, Sage pushed a handful of hair over her shoulder and sailed past, somehow managing to keep a thin sliver of daylight between herself and Belmont as she moved through the doorway, joining him and Peggy inside the rental office.

Aaron dropped his head back, imploring the bright blue Iowa sky for patience, consoling himself with the fact that as soon as he got away from his family there would be peace. Maybe not in the classic sense, but at least he would definitely be in a situation he could decipher and handle.

A prickle at the back of his neck had Aaron pausing once again, one foot inside the door as he looked toward the woods, but he shrugged it off and continued into the office, holding up his credit card in a signal for his party to make way, allowing the plan man through.

* * *

What brought Aaron to the edge of the forest in the middle of the night? No idea. His excuse for pulling on rumpled dress pants and crunching through the woods was to look for Old Man, but when dog found him first, their party of two had kept on going. Now, the mutt walked alongside him, throwing him an occasional *What the fuck?* glance.

"You're free to go back, you know. I don't remember issuing an invitation."

Sniff. Sniff sniff.

"What is that? Morse code?"

Okay, Aaron had *some* idea of what had sent him on Nature Quest. He just had zero notion of what he hoped to achieve by walking to the site of tomorrow morning's Breakfast and Politics, a nationally televised, invite-only event for which he was most definitely *not* on the list. Oh no, he was on only one list, and the word *NAUGHTY* was in permanent ink at the top. Presidential hopeful and Iowa senator Glen Pendleton, however, would be in attendance, and Aaron needed to get the man's ear. Before Aaron had flushed his career down the toilet back in California with one bad decision, his boss had confided that Aaron was on the short list for adviser with Pendleton himself. A big-ass deal when the man already had one foot in the White House. What he'd needed was the youth vote—and that was where Aaron would have come in, if he hadn't neatly erased his chances.

Tomorrow, he needed face time with Pendleton. The question was how.

As Aaron and Old Man reached the perimeter of the forest, a series of connected buildings came into view. The local high school, which would serve as the site of Pancakes and Politics come morning. Already news vans were parked outside. Police vehicles. What the hell was his goal here? To get arrested for trespassing?

Old Man seemed to be asking the same question with a silent look, so Aaron moved in the opposite direction of the congregated vans, prepared to head back toward the cabin and get some much-needed sleep. The kind that would allow him to bring his A-game in the morning. As if he ever brought anything else.

Just as he turned, Old Man stopped, ears pricked, nose twitching. A noise behind them. Aaron heard it, too. A long slide, followed by a soft, feminine hum. Better than the sound of a gun being cocked, but definitely not what he expected to hear in the pitch-black woods at midnight. Aaron stepped back behind a tree, giving himself a good view of the school's closest building. He watched as a leg dropped over the southernmost windowsill and dangled a moment before a head ducked under the frame. The figure jumped to the leaf-padded ground without a single crunch, the hum never ceasing or losing its melodic rhythm.

Girl. There was no question. In the dappled moonlight, he could make out curves beneath tight-fitting clothing. Slight ones, but *nice* ones. And even if his attention hadn't been magnetized by the tight jut of her ass—*fuck*, he'd been a while without having a woman's cheeks in his hands—the hair would have tipped him off. It was *everywhere*. Even the muted darkness couldn't hide the wild, colorful nature of it. The mass of it fell to midback, interrupted every inch or so with a corkscrew curl or a braid or a ribbon. Her hair was schizophrenic. Looked like it hadn't been brushed in a while, but maybe the lack of diligence had been on purpose.

Old Man chose that moment to make a *sloff* sound, which jolted the girl, sending her careening back against the building. She slid to the ground into the shadows before Aaron could get a good look at her face, and for some reason the delay made him anxious. What kind of a face went with hair like that?

"Hello?" She called, just above a whisper. "Please don't be a bear. Again."

That wish sparked so many questions—again?—Aaron

didn't grab Old Man's collar in time and the furry bastard slinked toward the girl, totally ignoring Aaron's sharp command to retreat. He lay down a few feet from the shadows where the girl was hiding, laying his face on two paws. *Showing her he isn't a threat?*

Just when you think you know a dog.

The girl entered the moonlight again, this time on her knees, hands reaching out—palms up—to Old Man. And so the first time Aaron saw her face, it was washed over with pleasure. "Hi," she breathed. "Hi, pretty...boy? Boy, I think. Thank you for not being a bear. Again."

Aaron felt a twinge in his fingers and realized he'd been gripping the bark of the tree too hard. *This is why I came into the woods. She's why.*

"That's ridiculous," he muttered, raking the sore hand down the side of his trousers. He was prowling around in the middle of the night on some misguided mission to get the lay of the land for tomorrow. Not to accidentally run into a girl with freak-show hair and an unrealistic fear of bears.

"Are you alone?" she asked Old Man, under her breath.

Aaron made a sound of disgust as the pooch turned his head, tongue lolling to the side like a drooling fool. He had no choice but to step out from behind the tree, but felt the need to put his hands up. So she would know he wasn't a bear, for the love of God. "It's just a human. You're safe."

The girl shot to her feet, her back coming up hard against the stucco building. Her eyes were as turbulent as her mane of braids and curls, but they seemed to calm when he halted his progress. "Humans are most dangerous of all," she finally said. "Why aren't you wearing a jacket?"

O-kay. He had to be back in his cabin dreaming, right? "Excuse me?"

"It's freezing and you're wearing a T-shirt."

Aaron looked down, as if he wasn't fully aware of his attire. Come to think of it, he was pretty goddamn cold, but he'd been too distracted to notice. "I'm from California."

She nodded gravely. "Are there bears in California?"

"We have one on our state flag." He chanced a couple steps closer, but Old Man actually growled at him, cutting off his progress. *Really?*

"Your dog doesn't seem to like you very much," the girl remarked.

"Yeah, thanks for noticing. The feeling is mutual." Aaron tilted his head, irrationally vexed that her face was half shaded by shadows again. "Hey, do you mind coming out here into the light?"

A beat passed. "Yes, I think I mind."

Not what he'd been expecting, at all. Had he completely lost his touch with women? "Why do you mind?"

"Because you saw me climbing out of the window." He could hear her swallow across the distance separating them. "I didn't do anything *wrong*—not really—but if someone were to disagree and claim I *did* do something wrong, you could identify me."

Aaron snorted. "I could pick your hair out of a thousand-person lineup."

"Thank you," she murmured, her hand reaching out of the darkness to scratch behind Old Man's ears. "Yours is nice, too."

"Are you talking to me or the dog?"

She laughed, the sound more solemn than he would have expected from someone with five hairstyles thrown into one. Maybe even a little sad. His desperation to catalogue her features shot up into the stratosphere. They would provide some type of answer to the riddle of her—and, honestly, why was he even confused? Even his confusion was confusing.

"What were you doing inside the school?" The question came out harsher than intended and he watched as her hand stilled on Old Man's head. A movement that increased his suspicion, even though he kind of wanted to go on ignoring the elephant in the forest.

"What do you *think* I was doing?"

Her throaty answer caught him below the belt, thickening the flesh inside his briefs. Ten seconds earlier, they were just two people crossing paths in the woods, but with the issuance of those two questions, they were challengers. It didn't help that the girl was still on her knees while Aaron stood at full height. The symbolic positions caused awareness to descend where it hadn't been before. "You're not a student inside that school, are you?" he asked because it seemed relevant, now that his cock had exhibited a hearty appreciation for her voice, her presence. "You're not a high school student."

"No, I went to private school." A pause. "And I graduated."

Aaron cleared the relief from his throat. "In my experience, students sneak into their own high school at night to set up pranks or make out. So if you're not a student, we can rule that out." He held up his fingers and began ticking them off. "Are you a journalist? Maybe setting up a hidden microphone to catch a politician off guard at tomorrow's event?"

"Yes. That's what I was doing."

"Ah," Aaron said, shaking his head. "See, your agreement was too quick."

A long sigh came from the shadows. "Are you a lawyer?"

Aaron reached for the knot of his tie to adjust it before remembering he wore only a T-shirt. "I went to law school—"

"Politician?"

"Of a sort," Aaron hedged. "But you're changing the subject."

"You must know all about that."

Old Man growled at Aaron again, but the girl reached over and placed a hand on the dog's head, quieting him. Aaron curled his lip at his pet, wondering when the hell his famous canine loyalty was supposed to kick in. "Listen, I really don't want to report you."

"But you will?"

Would he? The high school gymnasium would be filled with politicians, voters, and media tomorrow. Despite his gut feeling to the contrary, she could very well have an agenda that included setting the place on fire. Stranger things had happened than someone using a political event to make a statement for their cause. Still, he couldn't connect that particular dot to this girl. Even without having gotten a decent look at her face. "I don't know."

She was silent for long moments. "Really?" Her tone was laced with surprise. "When was the last time you said those words?"

"I don't know?" He searched his brain. "I don't know."

Her laughter almost pulled him headfirst into the darkness. It hadn't sounded sad or solemn that time. And he liked it better the second way. "I can..." Now she sounded almost shy. How often were they going to switch gears here? "I can owe you a favor. If you just pretend we didn't meet."

Fuck that. The words very nearly left his mouth on a shout. He couldn't find a way for his unspoken denial to make sense, but he really didn't feel like pretending this encounter hadn't happened. Another hour or so in the forest and he would have the frostbite to prove it. Maybe he'd already succumbed to the initial stages of delirium, because he was placing way too much importance on this interaction. He needed to get out of there and gear up for tomorrow. Tomorrow was what mattered. "Look, forget it." He signaled to Old Man, as if that was going to work. "There's nothing you can offer that would help me. Just..." Discomfort invaded his throat. "This never happened."

Walking away felt distinctly shitty, but what else could he do? Stand in the freezing-cold woods in a T-shirt with a spiteful dog and a probable anarchist for another hour?

"*Wait.*"

Aaron turned at the sound of footsteps jogging up behind him. And then he just stared. Her face fully exposed now in the moonlight, the girl blinked up at him with vivid green eyes, that wild hair blowing around her shoulders. His stomach dipped like a ladle into a boiling pot of soup and hung there, the forest feeling stiller than death around him. Anything would feel still, so close to so much—life. *Go back to the cabin. Or wake up from this bizarre dream. Just do something before you go completely insane.* "What am I waiting for?"

"Me," she whispered, before squeezing her eyes shut and shaking her head. "I mean, I asked you to wait. I can help you."

"How do you know I need help?"

She looked almost perplexed by his question. "We all need help."

Why couldn't he get his stomach to stop twisting and diving? "Not me."

"No?" She broke his stare to gaze out at their surroundings. "You were out here for a reason, too. What was it?"

"I don't know anymore," he murmured.

"That's the fourth time you've said it now." Her smile revealed her teeth, the two overlapping ones up top, dead center. "Isn't it wonderful?"

Jesus, he almost said *I don't know* a fifth time. "I need to get into that pancake event tomorrow morning. I doubt you can help me with that, so—"

"I *can*, actually," she said, arching a cocky eyebrow.

"Really." He doused the flicker of hope. "Through a window, I assume?"

When she shook her head, braids and curls and ribbons rioted everywhere. "I'll walk you right past security through the back door."

"Not the front one?"

Another flash of those imperfect teeth. "Beggars can't be choosers."

That husky tone of voice was back, and it flexed his abdomen muscles, compelling him forward a step, where he could look down into her uniquely pretty face. "My name is Aaron. And I never beg."

"My name is Grace." A deep breath, a step back. Away from him. "And I know better than to ever say never."

Aaron stood at the edge of the woods, watching as Grace slipped around the building outcropping and into the darkness, still convinced he was dreaming. Until he felt a warm, liquid sensation on his right foot, and found Old Man pissing on his favorite pair of loafers.

"Really?" He removed his foot from the line of fire and shook it. "We're literally surrounded by trees."

He cast one final glance in the direction Grace had disappeared, dismissing with some effort the urge to follow, and went back to the cabin, somehow knowing that tomorrow wouldn't be any less confusing than tonight.

New York Times bestselling author **Tessa Bailey** can solve all problems except for her own, so she focuses those efforts on stubborn, fictional blue-collar men and loyal, lovable heroines. She lives on Long Island avoiding the sun and social interactions, then wonders why no one has called. Dubbed the "Michelangelo of dirty talk" by *Entertainment Weekly*, Tessa writes with spice, spirit, swoon, and a guaranteed happily ever after. Catch her on TikTok at @authortessabailey or check out tessabailey.com for a complete list of books.

You can learn more at:
  TessaBailey.com
  Facebook.com/TessaBaileyAuthor
  Instagram @TessaBaileyIsanAuthor
  TikTok @AuthorTessaBailey